In The Shadow Of The Hill

Helen Forbes

TP

ThunderPoint Publishing Limited

First Published in Great Britain in 2014 by
ThunderPoint Publishing Limited
Summit House
4-5 Mitchell Street
Edinburgh
Scotland EH6 7BD

This book is a work of fiction.
Names, places, characters and locations are used
fictitiously and any resemblance to actual persons,
living or dead, is purely coincidental and a product of
the authors creativity.

ISBN: 978-0-9929768-0-4

www.thunderpoint.co.uk

Cover Image: © Sue Campbell

For Ammie and Ella,
bringers of love,
light and hope.

<u>Acknowledgments</u>

The prologue of *In The Shadow Of The Hill* began as a short story entitled *Dead Scorched Birds*. Thank you to the Kirkcaldy writers for their encouragement and enthusiasm when the story was read out with trepidation in the back-room of Betty Nicols;to the Edinburgh Writers' Club and the suggestion that there might be a novel in the story; and to HISSAC, Northwords Now and Global Shorts Anthology for commending and publishing Dead Scorched Birds.

Grateful thanks too to the former Hi-Arts Work in Progress scheme for a very helpful critique of the manuscript; to the Highland Literary Salon and Moniack Mhor for providing writing retreats in a wonderful setting; and to the staff at ThunderPoint for all their help in publishing the novel.

But above all, sincere and profound thanks to my daughter, my family and my friends. It has always amazed me that so many people seem to believe in me.

Prologue

Forked lightning is shooting from the end of the girl's arm. There is no hand, just jagged gold, crackling and jumping, balls of sparks bouncing off the ring of pink fur that trims her sleeve. Nothing but the lightning moves. Not her arm. Not her face. Not even her eyes. Someone speaks. Her mother. She has shining chestnut hair and sparkling white teeth. Lightning in both hands, she swirls her arms, making golden streaks in the night, dazzling circles and great swooping trails. She's writing something, the girl's name, perhaps.

"Look!"

The girl doesn't look. Her eyes are still fixed on her own fire, her arm still rigid. At the end of the garden, three Catherine Wheels are spinning on the newly-painted fence. Faster and faster, showers of coloured sparks dance in frenzied spirals. In the child's hand, the lightning is fading. Frowning, she watches it die, then she drops the burned-out sparkler and runs.

Her brother stands in front of her, his arms outstretched. "Not too close, silly," he says. She laughs as he lifts her and swings her round, then he carries her to where their mother stands. As she takes her mother's hand, the scarf slips from her little oval mouth. Fragments of breath escape through the gap in her front teeth, float from her and disappear into the freezing night. On the fence, the Catherine Wheels splutter and die.

"This one, Dad?" The brother lifts a rocket from the metal box and hands it to his father. They set the rocket in a small bucket of sand.

"Stand back, son."

The night's stars dim and disappear as the sky explodes. Beyond the fence, the solid bulk of the hill is illuminated in showers of cascading colours. Again and again, the hill lights up, the sky sprinkled with stars of gold and purple and red. The fireworks whistle and crack and bang. The sounds bounce off the hill, slam against the windows, echo across the sand.

In the house next door, thumping feet on the stairs and the watching boy drops down on his bed. The door's shoved open and he shrinks from his mother's whisky breath. "Like a bloody war zone out there!" Her voice is harsh. "Shut those curtains and get to sleep."

But . . . the word stops before it reaches his throat. He swallows it and tugs at the curtains. They don't meet. Sometimes he watches the moon through the gap. Sometimes it's a pale sliver of gold, sometimes just a shadow behind bruised clouds. Sometimes he stays awake all night waiting for the first signs of daylight to trickle from the sky.

He pulls the cover up around his ears, but it can't shut out the chattering voices carried on the still night air. A sudden barrage of bangs shakes the whole island. He has to get up; he has to see. Slowly, slowly, so the bed won't squeak.

The moon is a huge orange ball and, around it, white rockets of light are flashing and skittering randomly. They whistle, then they die, falling from the sky like the feathers of dead scorched birds.

It's silent now, the moon shining down on the garden next door, on the giant heap of rotting wood that was once Old Alasdair's shed. The father is crouching, fire in his hand. He touches it to the base of the heap.

"It's not going to work," the boy says. "It's not, Dad."

The man laughs, pokes some more among the wood and the fire catches.

The boy in his bedroom watches as the fire takes hold.

He watches the father stand behind his son, drape his arms over the boy's shoulders, pull him close against him and smile down on him as if he is the most precious thing in the whole world.

The watching boy shivers. There's a memory in him, in his shoulders. A memory of being held close like that, warm breath on his head and his neck. A man with kind grey eyes and broad shoulders, presents in his pockets, and laughter that rang out and made a small boy giggle. A man . . . It's gone, evaporating into the night until it was never even there.

The burning wood is roaring and crackling. The mother crouches beside the girl, holding her tight. The girl's little mouth curves into a huge smile and then it's distorted by a yawn. She sinks against her mother.

When the flames are almost done, the father tells them it's time to go in.

"Come on, sleepy head," the brother says, taking his sister's hand. As they approach the back door, their faces have turned blue in the moonlight. The girl looks up. The watching boy hesitates, swallows, and waves, but she's gone.

The father takes his time tidying the garden, lifting the spent fireworks, dousing the bonfire until not a spark is left, locking the shed and checking the back gate. A window creaks open. A lisping baby voice: "Night night, Daddy."

"Night night, sweetheart." He grins up at her. As the window creaks shut, he blows her a kiss.

The boy's face is in the pillow, tears soaking into the lumpy stuffing. He wishes it was a war zone. He wishes a giant missile would land on their damp house. On his mother and her hidden half-bottles and gaunt wasters of boyfriends. On the village boys and the fat headmaster with his prize ram and his bad breath. On the neighbours with their perfect garden, their perfect children. The girl blown to fluffy pink smithereens, strewn across the moor; her brother and his shining Raleigh BMX jet-propelled into outer space and annihilated. The whole island smashed to

3

bits and scattered across the sea.

But it's not a war zone. It is nowhere; just a tiny scrap of land crouching on the shores of the ocean. And now the sky is dark, the moon and stars shamed into hiding. The hill squats, black and unyielding.

Chapter 1

Job. A wee word, but such a big deal. His pals thought he was nuts. Half five in the morning? What sort of time was that to start work? Didn't bother him; he'd always been an early riser. And he was finished at one o'clock. Could do whatever he liked then. Could even go back to sleep. Not that he would; not on a day like this. Mountain bike in the back of the van, and he'd head across the bridge, try the black trail at Learnie. His mother's frown would follow him all the way, and her muttering. That biking nonsense would be the death of him. Look at Chrissie Martin's brother's wife's cousin. Broke his neck falling off a bike. Time he was giving that nonsense up, now that he had a job and a uniform.

A job. A uniform. The pride on his mother's face. A massive fry-up this morning and a gallon of sweet tea. How come she didn't know that he didn't take sugar in his tea? Didn't even like tea that much, and he could still taste the bacon grease coating his tongue. Ach, she'd not be getting up every morning before five o'clock; that was a certainty. But she'd be waiting for him at one o'clock today; waiting at the window with that smile, and more tea.

Maybe he wouldn't tell her what round he'd been given. He'd never hear the end of it. Her wee boy delivering mail down the Ferry? What about Chrissie Martin's son's girlfriend's neighbour? Mugged in broad daylight. And he wasn't even properly down the Ferry; he was three streets away. Talking to his mother on his fancy new mobile telephone when two of those neddy boys came and took it off him. Best to stay away from that side of the town.

Aye, Mum. He'd tell her he'd got one of those new schemes that kept appearing on the outskirts of the City of Inverness. City? Whenever his mother read that, usually on every front page of every local paper, it made her laugh. They could build as many new housing schemes as they liked, she would say, but Inverness would never be more than a big village.

Ach, it was fine down the Ferry. Not that different from anywhere else, really. Just people getting on with their lives; three mothers pushing pushchairs, a boy and his staffie, an old lady with shopping bags, and a mobile mechanic bashing a car wheel with a hammer. Must be too early for riots and muggings.

These stairs were tiring, though. Three blocks of flats; twenty-four flats in each block; one block down, two to go. A row of birds were singing on the roof of the derelict building opposite the middle block. Their melody made him smile as he pushed the door open, and turned.

No. This couldn't be. No way. Backing towards the door, shaking his head as the hot sweet tea, the greasy bacon, the half-cooked sausages, the soft fried eggs rushed back up his gullet and splattered across the floor.

***

The postie wasn't the only one who couldn't believe it. Detective Sergeant Joe Galbraith was sceptical when he got the call. Murder? Who murders pensioners on a common stair at half-ten in the morning, even down the Ferry? But, unless she'd managed to bash herself over the head with a hammer, and thrown herself down the stairs, it looked like murder, right enough.

Joe leaned closer to the window, his hands on either side of his eyes. The crumpled body lay at the bottom of the stairs, head resting in a halo of congealed blood. A foot or so away lay the blood-stained hammer, and between that and the door was the postie's colourful and fragrant pool of vomit. The victim's dark hair was newly set, smooth curls glinting in the flickering rays of sunshine that sparkled through the glass. Her clothes looked expensive, the purple skirt knee length, her top black with a trim of gold at the neck. Her shoes were high, too high. There was no sign of a coat or a bag. Strange. Despite the sun, it was a cold April day, and she just didn't look as if she belonged here. From inside the flats, the sound of a howling dog echoed through the stairwell. It made the hairs on the back of Joe's neck rise.

A movement to the side caught Joe's eye. Two boys at the door, one of them with a key. "Hey!" Joe shouted. "You're not going in there!"

The older boy smirked. About thirteen, all spiky gelled hair, acne and attitude. He reached for the lock.

"You deaf?" Joe said. "I told you not to go in."

"He's not deaf, mister," the younger boy said, with a slight childish lisp. He was cute, about eight years old, with blond curls and a grubby face. "Mum says he's just a bit stupid."

His scowling brother shoved him. "You're so dead, Liam."

Unperturbed, Liam smiled at Joe. "Why can't we go in? We live at number nine. Mum's waiting for us and Ryan's already in deep shit for coming home late."

"That's total crap." Ryan kicked the wall, knocking a shower of stone chips to the ground.

"How did you get past those officers?" Joe gestured to where DC Roberts was standing at the small parking area in front of the flats with two uniformed policemen and a group of disgruntled men.

"Came through the wee garden," Liam said. "Sneaked round behind the policemen when Baldie Parker and Geordie were arguing."

His brother was less polite. "Call themselves policemen? They're a shower of dozy gits. Wouldn't notice a passing herd of hip-hopping elephants."

Ryan might have a point, but Joe wasn't going to let him off with that. "You fancy a night in the cells?"

"Whatever." He shrugged, but Joe saw a hint of uncertainty in his eyes. It didn't stop his cheek. "What is that you're wearing? New uniform for pig . . . I mean policemen?"

The white paper suit crinkled as Joe tapped the side of his nose with a gloved hand. "None of your business."

"Well, Officer, much as I'd love to stay here and chat, we're hungry. Our social worker says we have to be fed at proper times. We've got rights, human rights."

"Aye?" Amazing how much the great unwashed and their offspring knew about their human rights these days. And having a social worker was no longer shameful. It had become a badge of honour, along with an ASBO and an electronic tag – no self-respecting yob would be seen dead without them. "You're hungry now? Think what you'll be like after a night in the nick. Bread and water, that's all you'll get, if you're lucky."

There were tears in Liam's eyes. Ryan glared at Joe.

"You'll get in as soon as possible," Joe told them. "What's your surname?

"MacRae," Liam said, his voice wobbling.

"Grass," his brother said.

"Right, Liam MacRae and Ryan Grass, I want you to walk along that path." Joe pointed to the line of square metal treads laid down by the uniformed officers to protect the crime scene. "Go back to the policemen, and then do as you're told. I don't want you to step off the path. Just walk straight over there. Can you do that?"

Liam nodded, his face serious. "I can do that. I can."

"Duh," Ryan said, his voice slow. "That's really difficult. Not."

It would be so satisfying to give him a smack. Just a wee one. Not enough to do any permanent damage.

"You got a gun?" Liam asked.

"Aye, semi-automatic." Joe moved his hand towards his back pocket. Liam ran, the sound of his feet echoing on the metal treads.

"Saddo," Ryan muttered, then he walked.

Joe took one more look in the window. He was glad the woman was face down. He would have to look into her eyes soon enough.

The sun was gone. Under a cloudy sky, DC Roberts agreed that he should have been more vigilant, but a fight had almost broken out between two tenants desperate to get into their flats. The one they called Baldie Parker was angry at missing Jeremy Kyle. The other, Geordie, called him a –

"Nigel," Joe interrupted, "it's just not good enough."

Roberts' childish face coloured. Only his mother, and the older, more sadistic, officers called him by his hated first name. "Sorry, Sarge; it'll not happen again. Just got a bit overwhelmed. My first major crime scene." He looked around. "Bloody crime having anyone living in this dump. Think she lived in there, Sarge?"

"Could have, but I'm not convinced. No disrespect to the fine people of the Ferry, but she doesn't look as if she belongs here."

The Ferry's official name was South Kessock, but no one called it that. Its nickname was a throwback to the days before the Kessock Bridge linked Inverness to the Black Isle, when a small car ferry used to cross the Beauly Firth between North and South Kessock. The bridge had opened in 1982 and the ferry was no longer in use. The name had stuck, as had the area's reputation as the roughest place in Inverness. Joe wasn't sure about that. There were other areas with just as many problems, but the stigma of living 'down the Ferry' had remained.

As DI Black, the Senior Investigating Officer, approached the flats with the pathologist, he was trying to close the zip on a white paper suit that was several sizes too small.

Tear-resistant these crime-scene suits might be, but there was only so much force they could take.

"The wearer must be able to bend, reach and work without restriction," Roberts said, his voice low and monotonous, as if he was reading from a book. "Generous sizing ensures comfort during motion and offers more freedom of movement. The suit must be closed to protect the crime scene, and the tie, from contamination."

Joe tried not to smile. Roberts had recently completed his detective training and he appeared to have memorised the manuals in their entirety. Whether he could put all that he had learned into practice was still to be seen, and he wasn't doing very well so far.

The DI was wearing a paper mask and his large black spectacles had started to steam up. He wiped at them with a gloved hand, cursing under his breath. "Ah yes," he said, when the mist had cleared. "Galbraith, Roberts." He had given up on the zip; there was no way it was closing.

"Sir," Joe said, "I have a suit for you in the car. Roberts will – " Before he could finish, Roberts was gone, his tall lean frame sprinting towards Joe's car. Perhaps the boy would do all right, after all.

***

Betty MacLaren was sitting in the courtyard, oblivious to the rain, all hunched and fragile beside the fading tulips. She wouldn't come in. It was the walls, she said; the walls were listening. Boxes in the walls, listening and stealing her thoughts. Boxes and wires and recording devices. Janey crouched before her, a large black umbrella over her head. Didn't she want to come in and see her son? He'd be here soon. Betty shook her head and whispered: "Stephen takes my thoughts too, you know. Always has. Even when he was a wee boy, my thoughts weren't safe. I'll just see him out here."

The rain was getting heavier, bouncing off the picnic

tables. From the window, they were observed by a row of patients. They'd seen it all before, but there was nothing worth watching on the telly.

"You'll both get soaked," Janey said. She moved the umbrella across until Betty was in its shelter. "What about taking Stephen to your room? No one can hear you in there."

"The walls can! Listening, listening, listening." Betty put her hands over her ears. "Always listening."

"Betty, your lovely hair; you had it so nice for Stephen. Won't you come in?"

Such a big decision. Overhead, a seagull screeched. Betty looked perplexed. "Where am I?" she whispered.

"New Craigs Hospital in Inverness."

"New Craigs? Am I a dafty?"

"You've been a little unwell, but you're getting better. Come on inside. We'll give your hair a comb and a bit of spray. It'll be lovely again."

"Are you a nurse?"

"Aye, I'm Nurse Black – Janey. I gave you tablets this morning, remember?"

"No uniform; you could be anyone. How am I supposed to know?"

Janey smiled. "Betty, you're right. I liked my uniform. Now even I can't pick out the staff from the patients."

"Staff look madder than the patients. See that one with the ring in her nose; looks like a bull. Is she a nurse?"

"Aye, and don't get me started on nurses with body piercings or tattoos. I think you and I have a lot in common. So, are you coming in?"

Betty stood up. "Yes; I don't know why you're keeping me out here. I'm getting soaked."

In the long corridor, Stephen waited. Five minutes early. His mother didn't like that. Said he was trying to steal her time as well as her thoughts. A minute late and he was wasting it. Time was precious, didn't he know? She had a lot to be getting on with. Aye, Mum; course he knew.

Three minutes. That tightening in his stomach. He scratched at his neck with his bandaged hand. Better keep that hidden. She'd only go on about it. On and on and on. Another glance at his watch. It was time. Stephen pushed the ward door open and made for his mother's room.

The voice stopped him. He knew the voice; heard it almost every time he visited. Why couldn't he remember to knock on the office door as soon as he entered the ward? Why couldn't he just do as the notice said, and knock on the bloody door? Because thinking about his mother and the questions and the ranting and the rambling got him so wound up that everything else went out of his head. He turned to face the receptionist's pinched displeasure. She knew who he was. She knew what he was here for, but she had to stamp her authority all over him, every damn visit.

"Stephen MacLaren. Here to see my mother, Betty MacLaren."

"See that sign? It says knock on the door and tell staff you're here."

"Aye."

She stared at Stephen, her eyes and lips all narrow and her pointy chin jutting out. Ugly vicious cow. If she was waiting for an apology, she'd wait a long time, mother or no mother. She gave in first, turned away with a grunt, and went back to her lair to wait for her next victim.

His mother was on the chair in her room, so Stephen sat on the bed, keeping his bandaged hand in his pocket. Betty frowned and reached out to smooth the cover around him. "Leave it, Mum," he said. "I'll sort it before I go. Your hair's nice. How have you been?"

"I'd be out of here if the walls would stop stealing my thoughts. I make plans, you know. I've got timetables; I'm ready to just pack up and leave. It's all arranged in my head. I'm coming to visit you first. Just a few days; I know you need space in your own house."

"You can stay as long as you like, Mum." He'd

stopped telling her it was her house; there was no point.

She shook her head. "Can't stay long; Jean's waiting for me."

As if. Betty and her sister, Jean, hadn't spoken in years. They'd fallen out when Stephen was a boy and he'd never discovered why.

"Aye," she continued. "Jean's got that empty flat at the side of her house. She's been keeping it for me. Train leaves at twenty-five past ten; you're going to drop me off at the station. Better go early, so I can collect my ticket and find my seat. It goes straight to Kirkcaldy; I don't even have to change. And I can stay as long as I like. We're going on a coach trip all round the East Neuk. Fish and chips in Anstruther – best fish and chips in the world. The little harbour at Crail. The rock pools at Elie Ness."

Stephen smiled. "The East Neuk's grand."

"Have you been, son?"

Keep smiling. "Aye, Mum." You took me, you stupid old bat, before you and Auntie Jean fell out. I nearly froze while you wandered the narrow streets fussing over the cute wee houses. Couldn't understand a word the buggers said.

Betty frowned and shook her head. "What was I saying?" she whispered.

"Jean. The East Neuk."

She shook her head again. "It's gone." Her lined face crumpled. "They've taken it. Or is it you? This happens whenever you come." She banged her head backwards against the chair, startling him. "You! You're a thief too."

Stephen leaned towards her, his face serious. "I'm not a thief, Mum; I haven't taken anything. Will you tell me about . . . about Meg and Dusty? Please, Mum."

She smiled, and beyond the madness and the jagged network of lines, Stephen saw the ghost of his real mother. "Meg, Meg, Meg," she whispered, her blue eyes gleaming and her voice soft. "Pressing myself against her. That smell; I can smell it now." She closed her eyes and inhaled deeply.

13

"It's like . . . it's like earth and hay and . . . and love. That's what it is; it's the smell of love. Meg followed me everywhere, you know, always nudging at my pocket for a sugar lump. Didn't like Jean. She threw Jean in the water trough. Just me and Dusty, that's the only ones she loved. Just me and Dusty, sitting on Meg's broad back. Aye, Dusty the dog, sitting in front of me on the pony! Only if Meg was walking, mind. I didn't let Meg trot or canter. Dusty wouldn't have liked that. Oh, my little Dusty, with her wee speckled paws and her long pink tongue; that little black spot right in the centre, a titchy wee little black spot."

As the rain poured down the windows, Stephen listened. He had heard it all before, heard it so often he knew the words before she said them, but it wasn't the words. It was her smile. It lit the room and it lit his heart. He was a boy again, before . . . before all that.

When her stories were done and her voice was tired and a little slurred, Stephen got up to leave. He kissed her and she reached for his hands. He forgot about the bandage.

"Your hand," she said, her voice anxious.

"It's nothing, Mum; just a scratch."

"How?"

"Pruning. Tidying the garden."

"I remember a garden. On the island. An old shed. The painted fence. Remember the willows, how they bent in the wind? On and on, that wind. Nothing else would grow. Nothing but willows, sighing and murmuring constantly, backs bent against the perpetual wind." She shook her head. "And the beach, son; remember that beach, near the hill?"

"Forget that, Mum."

"How can I forget it? How can I forget what they did? The girl – "

"No!" Stephen's shout was out before he could stop it. His mother's bony frame jolted, her eyes wide and scared. "No," he repeated, falling to his knees before her, his voice now soft. "Don't think about it, Mum. Don't . . .

don't. What goes around comes around. You know that."

As the memories evaporated from her head, Betty smiled. "You're a good boy, Stephen, coming to see your old mother. Now, get out of here quick." Her voice dropped to a whisper. "It's quiet this week; I think they're on the lookout for new people."

***

Seen anyone suspicious? Was that a joke? He'd never seen anyone down here that wasn't suspicious, and if he saw such a person, he'd be very suspicious indeed. Sheriff Officers in and out, drug squad, social workers and cops. Hardly a day went by without something going on. But a suspicious death? How could he have missed that?

The old man in the back of the police car shook his head. He might be old, John MacMahon told Roberts, but there was nothing wrong with his eyes. Nothing. Twenty-one years he'd been living on the ground floor of the block of flats. Seen it all. A stabbing, four overdoses, countless fights and arrests, children removed by social services, parties so loud they made his false teeth rattle; he'd seen it all. Never seen a death on the stairs, though. Was it murder? Roberts was giving nothing away, but the constant flashing of lights inside the stairwell had MacMahon intrigued. Wouldn't be taking photographs if it wasn't suspicious, would they? And was that someone with a video camera going in now?

Murder – how could he have missed that? If he hadn't had to go to the doctor, they'd have their suspect by now. Nothing got past him. Nothing.

Roberts asked MacMahon if he knew the other residents in the flats, and the old man took off. He knew them all and had little time for any of them. No one here but junkies and alcoholics, prostitutes and nutters, teenage mothers and kids running wild. Starting at number two, he began to list them for Roberts. If he didn't know their name, he had a name for them. Aye, he had them all weighed up all right.

When MacMahon had finished assassinating the character of the man in number seven, Roberts looked at his watch and decided to stop him; this was going to take all day; he'd pass it to the uniformed cops. Before Roberts could interrupt, MacMahon had started on number eight. A woman with a dog. Late sixties, early seventies. Posh kind of woman. Out of place down here. Strange accent. No visitors. Seven or eight months she'd been in the flats. Nothing much to say. Didn't even know her name. She wasn't one for going out often, except to walk her dog. Nice wee dog.

Aye, he'd seen her go out this morning. About half past seven, just after he made his breakfast. Opened the kitchen blind and she was teetering around with the dog. Stupid high heels, she was wearing. Never saw her in high heels before. Always well dressed, with good shoes, sensible shoes. She was smart today in purple and black, hair done nice, make-up. Shame about those daft shoes. Was it her? Was she the victim?

"I couldn't say," Roberts told him, but the old man had already decided.

"Shame," he muttered. "Damn shame. How did I miss that?"

Roberts could have kissed MacMahon. The old man had given him the break he'd been waiting for, a chance to show his sergeant that he knew what he was doing. He asked Big Johnny Watkins if he'd seen Joe Galbraith.

The old PC shrugged. "Which one's he then?

"Bit shorter than me. Broader."

Watkins smiled. "That doesn't really narrow it down, son. Everyone's shorter and broader than you."

"Fairish hair. Tanned."

"Him that used to be a joiner? Aye; he was here a few minutes ago. Grumpy shite."

"He can be," Roberts said, "but he's good."

"A bit up himself."

"Aye, but he's still good."

Watkins shrugged his broad shoulders and winked at Roberts. "Whatever floats your boat, son."

Roberts was stumped. Didn't want the uniforms thinking he fancied Galbraith, but didn't want to diss him either. He settled for saying, "There's worse."

Watkins nodded. "That tosser, Jimmy Jackson, for a start."

On safer ground, Roberts agreed. "Don't even get me started on that bastard. D'you know - ?"

"Which bastard would that be?"

Roberts spun round to face Joe. "Not you, Sarge."

His face turned scarlet as Joe raised his eyebrows. Behind Roberts, Watkins sniggered. The old bugger must have seen Joe coming. "I was looking for you," Roberts said. "Got a minute?"

"Only if you've something worthwhile to tell me."

"I know where she lived."

The smile on his sergeant's face made Roberts' day. As he followed Joe towards the flats, he could still hear Big Johnny Watkins sniggering.

Chapter 2

As the bus shuddered over pot-holes and swerved round cyclists, Stephen's thin body was jolted and swayed. He didn't notice. He didn't see anyone else on the bus, though there were several, and he didn't even hear the driver arguing with a teenager trying to get a half fare. It was the willows. He closed his eyes and he was back on the island, the sound of the wind whistling through the trees. He could see their slender shapes on a stormy day, the wind bending them until they looked as if they were praying, just like the islanders. And beyond the willows, the hill. It had haunted his dreams for years, that hill, even after they had left the island.

The island; he wasn't sure why his mother had stayed there so long after . . . after all that had happened. They could have moved to the mainland to be closer to Auntie Jean and Uncle Colin. Maybe then his mother wouldn't have argued with Jean, and Stephen would have someone now to help share the burden of his mother's madness.

The driver had to shout Stephen when the bus reached the town. He stood in the street as people barged past him, as a sudden shower soaked him, as Davie Dobbs crept up behind him and stuck his tongue in Stephen's ear.

"Fuck off!" Stephen shouted. "You manky bastard!"

An old lady outside the Post Office tutted and glowered at Stephen. He felt his temper rise. How would she like it if she was just minding her own business and Davie Dobbs came along and stuck his tongue in her ear? He nearly shouted at her. Instead, he took a deep breath and told himself to get a grip.

"Bet you thought your luck was in," Davie said, his smiling face so smug. "Wee Julie or that tall blonde one I saw you with on Grant Street last week. Didn't see her face, but she looked a right – "

"Shut up about her. She's . . . it's not like that."

Davie smirked. "Whatever. Pint?"

Stephen hesitated. He wasn't keen on drinking during the day, and he really wasn't in the mood for Davie Dobbs. "I'm working early tomorrow."

"Thought you were on holiday for a couple of weeks."

"Day after tomorrow."

Davie ran his fingers through his long curly hair and winked at a couple of passing teenage girls. Stephen felt his temper rise again. Vain lazy git. Didn't even know the meaning of real work. Made his money from the misfortune of others. From cocaine to fake passports, hit men to false pedigrees, Davie Dobbs was your man. Stephen had required his services a couple of times recently, and there was still the matter of the car. Ach, why not go for a pint? What else was he going to do? Go home and brood. Think about his mother and the past. Wind himself up again. "Just one," he said.

"Sound. All work and no play, Stephen; not good for you; not good at all. I've told you, there are other ways of making money, and I'm just the man to get you set up."

Stephen raised his eyebrows. "Just the man to get me sent down."

Stephen shouldn't have let Davie choose the pub. He'd made that mistake before, and they'd had no peace, with Davie's dodgy mates constantly in and out, bumming cigarettes and pints, and generally making a nuisance of themselves. Born and brought up in Inverness, Davie Dobbs prided himself on his knowledge of the darker side of the Highland capital. There would be a reason he chose this pub; some lowlife that he needed to see. Davie did nothing without a reason.

"What you done to your hand?" Davie asked, as they sat down with their pints in a dark corner.

None of your business, Stephen wanted to say. "Fitting a new wing mirror on my mate's car – cut myself."

"Aye? Bad?"

Stephen shrugged. "I'll live."

"Speaking of motors, Crabs says he can get us one for this weekend, but it'll cost . . . Heh, Fingers McCreadie! How you doing, ya bastard?"

Davie's lowlife pals didn't come much lower than this smelly specimen, with his long greasy beard and scabby face.

"Dobbsie!" the lowlife yelled. "Haven't seen you since . . . ah, fuck knows? How you doing, man?"

"Yer seen' it, Fingers," Davie said. 'Yer seen' it', or 'you are seeing it' was the standard Invernessian response to a query as to one's health. "You know Stephen?"

Fingers shook his head and stuck out his right hand. "Put it there, mate."

Stephen hesitated. He didn't want to touch this person; he just wanted to leave. But Davie had something to tell him, something about Crabs and a car, and not before time. He reached for Fingers' hand.

"Ha ha!" Fingers roared as Stephen discovered the reason for the nickname. The bugger's right hand was missing three fingers. "Ha ha!" Fingers cried again, waggling his left hand in front of Stephen's face. Another missing digit.

Davie was giggling into his pint like a schoolgirl. Fingers was gazing at his hands, as proud as a new dad. Some bird with no teeth, hanging about behind Fingers, was almost wetting herself. Even the barman was smiling like a moron. Bastards. Stupid bastards. Wasn't that bloody funny.

"Take that as a lesson, Stephen," Davie said. "If you want to keep your fingers, don't you be messing about with broken glass."

That set off another bout of hysteria. Stephen

scowled, considered leaving again, then re-considered. He needed to know about the car. Lighten up, he told himself, and then he started laughing too.

***

Sharon MacRae might once have been a looker, but that was a while back. Lank bleached hair with several inches of black roots, pitted skin, a couple of missing teeth. Probably not even thirty-five, but sad as hell. "Whaisit?" she croaked.

"Police," Joe said, holding up his warrant card. "Detective Sergeant Galbraith; this is Detective Constable Roberts. Are you Mrs MacRae? Liam and Ryan's mother?"

Staring into her eyes, the pupils as tiny as pin heads, Joe saw that the question was causing her some difficulty. It wasn't worry; she wasn't concerned that two policemen were standing at her door asking about her children. She was just right out of it.

"Aye," she muttered at last, her voice barely a whisper.

"There's been an incident in the flats."

"Inci . . . " She nodded.

"Did you hear anything? See anyone here this morning?"

She just stared. And stared. "Nah," she said.

"Anyone in with you?"

"Nah."

"You won't mind if we come in for a look." Joe was in before she could object, Roberts behind him.

That smell. It hit Joe as he followed an unsteady Sharon MacRae down the long hall to the living room. It wasn't a dirty smell. Not even a particularly dirty flat. See some of the places he'd been in – man, you wouldn't even want to breathe, then you'd wipe your shoes on the way out. This one was all right. Untidy, but not minging. But that smell; the smell of deprived child. It was sweet and cloying and clinging, and it turned Joe's stomach. It always had. There was a memory there somewhere. Long ago. A boy . . .

"You been using, Mrs MacRae?" Roberts asked.

"Nuh." She tugged at her left sleeve, confirming their suspicions.

"You're out of your head."

"Am not." She collapsed backwards onto the settee, pulling a pink fleecy blanket around her. Roberts gestured towards the kitchen and Joe nodded.

"Someone with you this morning, Mrs MacRae?" Joe asked.

Sharon groaned and tried to shake her head. Roberts returned. "Nothing there, Boss."

"Right. The boys won't be coming home for a while. They're safe, but they can't come in right now." There was actually nothing to stop them coming in, now that the body had been removed, but Joe wasn't going to leave them in her care.

"Sound," she whispered. "Sound. Not feeling well."

"What's the name of their social worker?"

She groaned. They waited. Another groan, then she tried. "A . . . A . . . An . . . "

"Anne?" Joe asked. "Anne Morrison?" Joe had worked in child protection, so he knew the local Children and Families team.

"Tha's her."

"Okay; the boys will go to the Family Centre. We'll be back later to talk to you. Get yourself sorted. We'll see ourselves out."

She was asleep before they left the room. Roberts checked one bedroom, Joe the other. A quick look in the bathroom, then the hall cupboard. A lot of mess and nothing of interest.

Outside, Big Johnny Watkins had a wee white dog on a lead. He was trying to pull it away from the door, but it wouldn't move.

"This the hound that was making all that noise?" Joe asked. "Sounds a lot fiercer than it looks."

"Aye," Johnny said. "SOCO found it in the victim's

flat. It's not for leaving. How do you lift a dog with a broken leg?"

"Dunno. Carefully?" He wasn't about to try. "Roberts, you used to fancy the Dog Section . . . "

Though Roberts tried to lift it carefully, the dog yelped. "Sorry, little dog," he said. "You look so sad. Do you know what happened to your owner?"

Joe leaned close to the dog. It gazed up at him with dark eyes. "Maybe you could give us a clue. Save us a bit of time? No? Didn't think so. Roberts, give it to – "

"She," Roberts said. "She's a pretty wee Westie."

"Whatever. Tell uniform to call the SSPCA."

When Roberts was gone, Joe took out his phone. Two texts from his sister, Lucy; she was coming home on Friday after all. Odd. Last week she'd said she was staying in Edinburgh for the holidays, studying for her exams. She'd sounded terrible, and Joe had been worried. Probably something to do with that Sebastian Moore. Fecking Sebastian – what kind of name was that for a potential brother-in-law? Mind you, no one in the family had met him though they'd been going out for over a year; maybe it wasn't that serious after all. Joe hoped not. He sent Lucy a text and he didn't mention the murder; maybe they'd have it all sewn up by the weekend. Aye, that'd be right.

Liam's grubby wee face lit up when Anne Morrison, the social worker, told him where they were going. "McDonalds? No way! Can I have a Happy Meal and is Ryan coming too?"

Anne smiled. "Yes and yes. Where is Ryan?"

"With the GGs."

"The what?"

"Glendoe Gadgies. They're a really really tough gang . . . I mean, it's just some boys from Ryan's school. They're all right."

Joe had already clocked the GGs. Older than Ryan and heading straight for trouble. Ryan had grown a couple of inches since they came along. His wee brother soon cut him down to size. "Ryan!" he shouted. "Guess what? We're going to McDonalds. You're allowed a Happy Meal!"

"Retard," his brother muttered, as he shuffled towards Anne's car, the Gadgies laughing behind him.

From the back seat, Liam smiled up at Joe. "You won't forget to tell Mum where we are, will you?" Before Joe could answer, he added: "Will you look after her? Will you see that . . . that he doesn't come back?"

"Who?" Joe asked. He crouched down. "Was someone in the flat with your mum today?"

Liam shrugged, a tear creeping down his cheek. "I don't know. She sent us out early. I don't know who was in."

"Who were you thinking of?"

From the front seat, Ryan turned and glared at his brother. "Just shut the fuck up," he said.

Joe straightened up, rubbing the small of his back. "Your mother will be fine. We'll come and see you at the Family Centre later."

Liam smiled and wiped his nose on his sleeve.

"Poor wee sod," Joe said as he watched the car pull away.

***

Stephen got used to the smell, and the *craic* wasn't that bad. One pint led to another and then some more. While Fingers McCreadie was shouting endearments across the bar at the toothless bird, Stephen got a quiet word with Davie about the arrangements for the car. He nearly choked when he heard the cost, but that was the going rate, Davie assured him, and he would know. There was no way Stephen was handing that kind of cash over to Davie; he wanted to give it to the main man, see what he was getting. Plans were made.

They were all well on their way to inebriation when

Fingers returned from a fag break and mentioned a murder in the town. "Flats down the Ferry," he said. "Not sure which block. Some old dear, this morning. There's a few stories going around. Tortured and raped, according to Donny the Bong. Slack Susie said her hands were cut off, and Wee Johnny says she only had one leg in the first place."

Davie grimaced, then he laughed. "She'd have been hopping mad, then."

Fingers shook his head. "Man, have a little respect. Could be your granny."

"Nah. Saw her off long ago, dottled old cow. Shame someone didn't cut her hands off; would have stopped her whacking me round the lugs. You haven't got a granny down the Ferry, Stephen?"

Bloody. Stupid. Question. Stephen's good mood evaporated. If he had a granny, she wouldn't be living in Inverness, and she certainly wouldn't be staying down the Ferry. Breathe, he told himself. Breathe. "Why would I? You know I don't come from Inverness."

"You not from around here?" Fingers asked. "Where you from, like?"

"Nowhere really. I'm a nomad."

"And he's no half mad," Davie added. That caused a further eruption of hilarity. Stephen forced another laugh, finished his pint, and left.

On the High Street, he dodged the dread-locked chuggers, with their clipboards and nauseating smiles. It took some doing, persistent buggers. He'd side-step one, and another would appear from nowhere, undaunted by his fiercest stare and muttered insults. If he'd been sober, he'd have remembered to avoid the pedestrianised street. Not that there was much scope in the town centre for reaching your destination without being accosted. If the jakies weren't scrapping in the street, they were tapping you for money or peeing on your shoes, while their junkie pals serenaded dealers in the homeless hostels above the shops on Union Street. *Rapunzel, Rapunzel, throw us down a bag of smack and a tenner of blow.* It seemed the council couldn't be persuaded to limit the number of homeless hostels in the town centre, no matter how much the ordinary people protested. Ach, Inverness wasn't the same place Stephen had visited as a child. It had seemed idyllic then, a Highland haven of fancy shops and friendly people. Now, the town centre was a disgrace. Shops closing all over the place, and a general air of dilapidation and depression.

As he walked up the Market Steps, Stephen felt the familiar weariness in his legs. He should be fitter than this. He should be sober. He should be so many things. In a shop in the Crown, he bought a photo frame for his mother. He'd look out some old photos to take into the hospital. She'd like that. As he handed over the money, he held his breath and willed his hands not to shake. He didn't look at the girl, didn't thank her until he was at the door. Still, he knew that she knew that he was nothing but a useless drunken bastard.

***

There was stale tobacco and whisky on DC Jimmy Jackson's breath, and fear in his piggy, bloodshot eyes. Though the smell was hideous, Joe didn't loosen his grip on Jackson's egg-stained tie. He twisted it tighter in his hand, shoving his fist harder against Jackson's throat. "Give me the photo," he said again, in a voice one might use to a naughty child. "Now."

Defiance and cowardice battled in Jackson's eyes. Joe pressed the older detective's head against the metal locker. "Drop it."

As Jackson's fist released the photo, sending it fluttering to the ground, the door of the locker room opened. Roberts' eyes widened as he took in the scene. "DI's looking for you both," he said. "Briefing's starting."

"Thank you, Roberts." Joe untwisted his hand from Jackson's tie, and patted it into place. It hadn't looked very good before he got hold of it; it was never going to look good again. He picked up his photo, then he smiled at Jackson. "Touch anything of mine again and you're dead."

Jackson coughed, his face scarlet. "That was assault," he said, his voice a little higher than usual. "You saw that, Roberts. You heard him threatening me."

Roberts' eyes were on the cracks in the flooring. "Shocking state, this lino. Accident waiting to happen."

Jackson glared at Roberts, his eyes narrowing, until the younger detective looked up. Roberts smiled and held the door open. "Gentlemen, the briefing?"

"Fucking wee shites, both of you," Jackson said.

In the incident room, Joe was aware of Roberts staring at him with admiration and more than a little curiosity. He was aware of Jackson behind him, seething with resentment. The DI talked them through the photos of the body and the video of the murder scene, then he moved on to the video of the victim's flat. It was a mirror image of Sharon MacRae's home, but there the resemblance ended. The bathroom was spotless, a white net curtain blowing in the slight breeze from the open window. In one bedroom, the bed was made, the duvet smooth and pristine. In the other, just a couple of stacks of cardboard boxes. The living room was sparsely furnished, with a small green sofa, two low tables and a television. In the kitchen, the victim's small black handbag was hooked over the back of a wooden chair, and a mug and plate sat in the washing-up bowl. And not as much as a picture on the wall, an ornament or a framed photo.

The victim, Moira Jacobs, had been born in Durban, South Africa, seventy-two years ago. She'd been discovered at the bottom of the common stairway in her block of flats at 10.10 am by Neil Cranston, a postie who was new to the round. He wasn't a suspect. His time could be accounted for from the minute he left the sorting office, a trail of delivered items or cards with recorded times left in his wake. Paramedics had attended, but there were no signs of life. The victim had lived at number eight with her dog. It was found injured in the flat.

Moira Jacobs appeared to have suffered a single blow to the back of the head from a hammer that was recovered at the scene, and further injuries from a fall down the common stair. The weapon matched a set of tools on a wall-mounted rack in the cupboard by the front door. There was a chequebook, bank cards and eighty pounds in the victim's handbag, making robbery an unlikely motive. She'd been dressed as if she was expecting a visitor or going out. A flier on top of the fridge advertised a tea dance at the community centre that afternoon.

"A tea dance?" Roberts said. "In the afternoon? What the – ?"

The DI sighed. "A dance with tea. Just what it says on the tin. Since you're so interested, you can go along. Find out if she's been before. Who was there? Anyone expecting her?"

Roberts groaned. "Sir, can't uniform do that?"

The DI's face reddened. "We'll do it," Joe said. "I thought we might go to the Family Centre to speak to Sharon MacRae's sons. It's next to the community centre." He looked at his watch. "We could go there first, before the dance finishes."

"Big sook," Roberts muttered.

"Fucking big sook," Jackson hissed.

Joe ignored Jackson and winked at Roberts. "Might get you a bird."

"Aye?" Roberts brightened up. "Seriously?"

"All right, you two," the DI said. "Contain your excitement. Galbraith, what about the other neighbours?"

Joe filled the team in on the results of the door to door. Not that there was much to tell. Twenty-four flats, and only six people at home, including Sharon MacRae and John MacMahon. Despite the way the latter had spoken about the residents, it seemed that many of them actually worked for a living and were out for the day. No one else had seen or heard anything. They scarcely knew their murdered neighbour. Torn-faced, dour and fierce were among the more complimentary adjectives the neighbours used to describe Moira Jacobs. Uniform were doing door to door in the adjacent blocks of flats and surrounding houses. Joe suggested that he and Roberts go back to see Sharon MacRae and the other absent occupants after they'd interviewed the boys. The DI agreed. As he spoke, Joe noticed Jackson coughing loudly. Probably faking it, but Joe really hoped he'd done some damage to the bastard's throat.

There was little else of interest in the flat, the DI said, except this. As he pressed a button on his laptop, Jackson's cough got louder. Joe turned and stared at him. The older detective smirked and blew Joe a kiss, then he started picking his nose. Joe gave him his middle finger.

"This was found on the coffee table in the living room," Joe heard the DI say. "It's at the lab for prints. A bit out of place, considering there are no other photos in the flat." Joe turned towards the screen as the DI said: "Just one photo, on the coffee table. This could be important."

When Joe looked up, he felt as if a sledgehammer had rammed into his guts. What? He closed his eyes. When he opened them, there would be a different photo on the screen. There wasn't. It was the same photo. It was the hill.

"An island," the DI said.

Joe shook his head. It looked like an island, but it wasn't. It was a hill on the edge of the sea, with two rounded peaks, one lower than the other. Long ago, in another life, Joe had lived in the shadow of that hill, and he had hoped never to see it again.

He hesitated. Why say anything? No one would ever know. He needn't, but he did. "It's not an island," he said, his voice a little weak. He cleared his throat. "It's a hill, Ceapabhal; it's in the south of Harris, close to the village of Northton."

"Harris?" the DI said. "How do you know that?"

The back of Joe's neck was damp. He wiggled his shoulders and felt his shirt collar move. He wondered if it was wet. Could Jackson see it? "I . . . I lived there for a few years as a child."

"I suppose someone has to," the DI said. "MacKay, get on to the council for Moira Jacobs' housing application, and the NHS for her medical records. Jackson, try the local vets to see if the dog's registered with them. Get something for that cough while you're at it; euthanasia by lethal injection, preferably. Aird, there was a file box recovered at the flat; go through it and check the documents and correspondence. And get rid of that damn chewing gum!"

As Jackson giggled, DC Wendy Aird blushed. She'd been trying to stop smoking for months. Patches, chewing gum, electronic cigarettes; they weren't working. And Jackson was loving it. Waving fags under her nose and blowing smoke in her face at every opportunity.

The DI allocated some further tasks, then he looked at his watch. "We'll de-brief at eight pm. Let's get this sown up quickly. If I have to cancel another holiday, there's no telling what my missus will do. It could be very very messy."

***

A riot shield was required. Scenes from college raced through Roberts' head. It might have been called training, but it was terrifying. A baying mob throwing bricks and bottles, and Roberts had cowered behind the others, convinced that the tills in Tesco might be a better career choice. A change of career crossed his mind again now. They might not be wielding bricks and bottles, but they were just as frightening.

"When you said bird," Roberts said to Joe, his voice a little squeaky, "I wasn't thinking turkey. Look at the wattle on that one; I've seen better looking vultures."

The arrival of two relatively young men had caused a stir at the tea dance. The twenty or so women were ecstatic.

One of the three men looked relieved, another looked threatened, and the third looked like he didn't know where he was.

"No, thanks, dear," Roberts told the first woman to reach him. "Not allowed to dance on duty, I'm afraid." He fumbled in his pocket and pulled out his warrant card, wielding it in front of him, his own little riot shield.

"They're police!" the woman cried. "How exciting! I do love a handsome policeman. Go on, just one dance. I'm sure your boss wouldn't mind."

How Joe would have loved to tell her that he didn't mind. Seeing Roberts whisked off his feet and thrown around the hall, amid swinging strings of pearls and sparkly shoes, would have made his day, but he couldn't be certain they would stop at Roberts. "I'm afraid not, dear," Joe said, pulling out his own warrant card. "Who's in charge here?"

"Is it the council again?" another woman asked. "We've already told them it's not our shoes that are damaging the floor. Cheap polish – that's what it is. Police? I ask you. Have you nothing better to do with your time than harass pensioners enjoying a wee dance in their twilight years?"

"They're here about the floor!" someone shouted. "Imagine!"

Before Roberts or Joe could say another word, the pack had them surrounded.

"Council's sent them!"

"Damn disgrace!"

"Let's have a sit-in!"

"Stop paying our council tax!"

"Bastards." It was one of the men. He turned crimson. "Not you, officers," he added. "The council."

"That's enough," Joe shouted above them. "Calm down. Who is in charge here?"

There was a woman standing to the side, a little younger than the others, the only one who hadn't joined in. She looked as if she was enjoying herself, her smile turning to laughter as all the pensioners turned and looked at her.

"Guilty, officers," she said. "Jeanette Lowe. What can I do for you?"

"You can take us somewhere private for a start," Joe replied.

Unfazed by his abrupt tone, she turned to the pensioners. "How about a quick step while I help the officers? Elsie, get the music on. Come on. Let's face the music and dance!"

Grumbling, the pensioners moved away. The muttering continued as they sorted themselves into pairs.

"Might be the last time."

"Probably close us down."

"Parking tickets and harassing pensioners, that's all they're good for. Never solve a bloody crime, though, do they?"

Joe was about to answer them when Jeanette Lowe started singing. "There may be trouble ahead," she sang, along with Nat King Cole, then she quick-stepped out of the hall, followed by a bemused Joe and a relieved Roberts.

Much as she would have liked to help, Jeanette Lowe didn't know a Moira Jacobs, and she couldn't remember anyone of that description coming to the dancing. There had been a recent marketing drive, with fliers in the papers and posters in shops. Yes, that was one of the fliers, and there had been a call from a woman. Last week, maybe, shortly after the fliers went out. Strange accent. Difficult to place, but it could have been South African. She said she used to dance, and she might come along this week. Keen to know how many men attended, and disappointed to hear that women outnumbered the men at least six to one. Was that all? Did they want to tell her anything else about the mysterious Moira Jacobs? Disappointed with their response, she asked them if they were sure they wouldn't like a wee dance. They declined.

"There may be teardrops to shed," she sang, as she waved them off.

Chapter 3

Pure magic. There was no other word for it. Roberts had seen children interviewed before and he'd been less than impressed, but Joe was fantastic. Starting with the rapport phase, and some chat about Liam's friends and school; less than five minutes and Liam was laughing and joking as if he'd known Joe for years. Another ten minutes or so, then a seamless move to probing whether Liam knew the difference between make believe and real, between lies and truth. Moving gently on to his mother. The right language, open questions, nothing suggestive. And Liam sang.

There was a man called Mac. He'd been to the flat a few times. More times than two, but not as many as ten. Liam didn't like him. He was always staring at the boys. Ryan said Mac was probably a pervert and he'd smash his face in if he touched Liam. He was big with dark hair. Not big like fat, but big like long. Not as long as Roberts, though. Quite old, like about Joe's age. His hair was not long, not short, not straight, but not exactly curly. A bit like Roberts' hair, but shinier.

"Liam," Joe asked. "Did you see Mac this morning?"

Liam hesitated. He pulled at the zip on his hoodie. "Is my . . . is Mum in trouble?"

"No, but something happened in the stair of the flats this morning and we need to know who was in and out."

Liam thought about that, then he nodded. "He was near the flats, but I don't know if he went in. He was walking towards us, on the other side of the road, soon after we went out."

"Can you remember where you saw him?"

"The big road with the railway bridge."

"Thornbush Road?"

Liam nodded.

"Did he speak to you?"

Liam shook his head. "Had his head down, hurrying. Didn't even see us. He looked funny. A bit like you."

Joe smiled. "Do I look funny?"

Liam giggled and shook his head again. "Your clothes. That's what he was wearing."

"A suit? Ever see him wear a suit before?"

"Nah, usually a black hoodie and jeans. And he was carrying a flat black case today, like someone from an office. I wanted to go back home then, see that Mum was all right, but Ryan said they might be shagging."

"Do you know what that means?

"Sort of." Liam blushed. He pulled his zip down, then he looked up. "Well . . . not really. Big people do it; Ryan says he's going to do it soon with . . . with someone."

"And did you see Mac again?"

They hadn't. The boys had gone down to the water to see the boats. Sometimes they threw . . . sometimes they used to throw stones at boats, but they never did that now. Not ever never. Then they went to see Ryan's mate, Sean, and played on his PlayStation until they came home and saw Joe in his funny white suit. As for the next door neighbour, she had a grumpy face and a cute dog. He didn't think his mother had ever spoken to her.

Liam smiled as he slipped off the chair. He'd enjoyed his chat. If he could help them again, he told them, all they had to do was ask.

Liam might have sung, but Ryan wasn't even humming. He never saw no one. No one visited his mother. He was worried about nothing. They didn't do anything today. Just wandered about. Didn't see Mac; didn't even know if his mother had a friend called Mac. Couldn't remember his next door neighbour.

As Ryan left the room with Anne Morrison, Joe told Roberts he was annoyed with himself for his first dealings with the teenager. He should have anticipated that Ryan might be a witness, and tried to build a rapport.

Roberts laughed. "A rapport – with that? I don't think so."

"He's just a boy," Joe replied. "Mother's a junkie. Can't be easy for him."

"You are one sentimental copper, Sarge."

"Aye, right. C'mon; back to Sharon MacRae's before the boys go home. Let's shake her up a bit. See how quickly she squeals when she finds out we've got her down as a suspect."

"That's more like it," Roberts said with a grin.

Sharon MacRae was lying. She could try all she liked to pass herself off as confused, hung over, doped up or just plain thick; she was lying. It took a wee while to sink in that she couldn't watch Judge Judy and answer their questions. At last, she put the television off. That was about as helpful as she was going to get. Sitting next to her on the blue corduroy sofa, Joe asked again: "So, you sent Liam and Ryan out for what at 9am?"

"I've just told you," she said, then she lit her third cigarette. Joe could feel his sinuses clogging up. "Milk and a paper."

"Times? Daily Telegraph? Guardian?" Roberts asked.

Sharon got his sarcasm, despite her vacant act. Joe could see it in her eyes. Really hostile, but struggling not to show it. "Sun."

"And did they bring it back?" Joe asked.

"Haven't been home, have they? You've took them."

"Surprised you remember that. Do you usually put them out so early in the school holidays?"

"If I need something from the shop."

"Funny thing is, when the boys came back, they didn't have a paper or milk."

"Wee buggers spent the money. Do it all the time."

"Right, you sent the boys out. Then what?"

Her hand shook as she raised her fag to her mouth, eyes narrowing as smoke spiralled around her head. "I lay on the couch. Felt sick. Still do."

Roberts asked her again if she had seen anyone after the boys went out. How could she? She was sleeping. Had she heard anything? How could she? She was sleeping, until they came hammering on her door. Did she know the woman in number eight? No. That was unusual, Joe said – lived next door for several months and they had never spoken. Didn't sound very likely.

Sharon gave a shrug. "Maybe the odd grunt."

"Would that be you or her?"

Her eyes narrowed and Joe knew that she'd really like to tell him where to go. She shrugged again.

"See, Sharon, that poor woman doesn't look like the grunting type to me. More a 'good morning and how are you today?' type, wouldn't you say?"

"Aye, right. She's a miserable old boot. Doesn't have a smile or a word for anyone. Won't even let the boys near her dog."

"Is there a Mr MacRae?" Roberts asked.

"Not in this house. Got himself killed on the A9 a few years back."

"Sorry to hear that," Joe said. "What was his name?"

Sharon reddened. She ground her cigarette into the ashtray, twisting and turning until it was well and truly dead. "What's that got to do with anything?"

"Peter MacRae?" Even as he said the name, Joe hoped he was wrong. There were things he didn't want to think of; images seared into his brain that he never wanted to recall.

Sharon started picking at the arm of the chair, picking and picking, though there was nothing there. The longer he waited, the more Joe hoped her man had been someone else. She nodded, and he felt a rush of nausea. His first road traffic accident. Four dead. Grandparents and their four year old grandchild. Peter MacRae, drug dealer and serial wife beater, his car full of heroin and amphetamines. High as a kite, he'd failed to pull back in after a stretch of dual carriageway.

"Who gave you the gear today?" Joe asked. "One of Peter's mates?"

That slight flush on her cheeks again – gave her away every time. "I'm clean. And I have nothing to do with his mates."

"You certainly weren't clean when we called earlier."

"I told you, I was sick."

"You scored today, Sharon. Someone brought you the gear."

"Don't know what you're talking about." She wiped a shaking hand across her brow, then she scratched her arms, her leg, her neck. She was in for a rough ride. Time to get her really rattled.

"You need to see a doctor. We'll arrange that while you're at the station."

"The station?" Sharon straightened up as it finally dawned on her that Joe wasn't going to let her off easily. "What the hell – ?"

"Time we took you in. Two visits today and you've given us nothing. We know you had someone here this morning, not long before your neighbour was murdered."

"Murdered? But – "

"We know you're using, and that makes you desperate. Maybe desperate enough to kill Moira Jacobs."

Her eyes wide, Sharon shot off the sofa, hand over her mouth. "I'm gonna be sick . . . "

"Thank God she made it," Roberts said, as the sound of retching came from the kitchen. "What do you think? Here or the station?"

"She'll talk."

Joe was right. Sharon's tongue had suddenly loosened. She might be a low-down junkie, but she wouldn't kill someone. Couldn't even kill a fly. Yes, she had used this morning, but it was the first time in months. She'd been on a methadone programme; doing really well until today. Didn't have a dealer, but there was this guy she'd met at the chemist a few weeks ago. He'd been down a few times, but she hardly knew anything about him. Called himself Mac and he was in his early to mid-thirties.

"So," Joe said, "you meet a guy in the chemist. You know nothing about him, not even his real name, and you take him into your house to meet your kids. Why would you do that?"

Sharon shook her head. "I don't know. There was something about him. It was like . . . like as if he cared, and not in that way." She laughed, a dry, humourless laugh. "I'm a mess; why the fuck would anyone care like that? But I didn't invite him straight away. Met him a few times, in the chemist, in town. We just hit it off. We had a drink down here one night last week. I had too much and I ended up talking about being in care. Mac got upset when he heard I was abused. Asked what would make me happy, and I said a big hit of smack. Didn't even mean it. I really wanted to stay clean for the boys. Saw Mac in the town on Monday and he told me he'd be down on Tuesday morning with something to make me happy. Told me not to bother going for my methadone, said I'd not need it. Fucking stupid of me, I know, but I couldn't stop thinking about it then. I sent the kids out 'cos I didn't want them to see me like . . . like that."

Mac had come to the flat at the back of nine, not long after the boys left. She'd never seen him in a suit and tie. He said he was going to a mate's funeral. He was quiet and she put it down to his friend having died. She thought he would just give her the smack and go, but he didn't. He wanted to stay until she'd taken it. He said he'd never tried it, but he wanted to see what it was like.

"Did that not seem a bit weird?" Roberts asked.

"Too right. It got weirder. He got upset and

apologised when I was getting the gear ready." She shrugged. "That's the last thing I remember. Don't know when he left and I never heard another thing until you came to the door. The syringe was gone too."

"What did this Mac tell you about himself?"

"Bugger all. He seemed worried about the boys, wanted to know if the social worker was good to them and if there was any danger of them being taken off me."

Joe raised his eyebrows.

"Aye," Sharon said. "Funny way of showing his concern. Bastard."

"Where did he sit today?"

Sharon gestured to the chair in the corner. "He usually sat closer. He was weird today, distant. Not himself."

Joe rang the station and arranged for a SOCO to come and take samples from the chair and prints from the door handles. As he came off the phone, Roberts was asking Sharon if Mac knew Moira Jacobs.

"Don't think so. He didn't even know his way down here when I first asked him to come."

"Did you ever see them speak?"

She shook her head. Until then, Joe had been certain that she was telling the truth, but now he wondered. She had hesitated there, just for a second. "Are you sure about that?"

"Aye. But . . . there is something. A few weeks back, maybe the second or third time he came, I picked up some mail at the door when he was leaving. Postie had put two letters for Moira Jacobs through with mine. I gave them to Mac and asked him to put them through her letterbox."

"Do you think he went to her door, spoke to her?"

Sharon shrugged. "He might have."

Joe noted a description of Mac and asked Sharon to let them know if she remembered anything else, or if she saw him again. She agreed to come to the station soon to look at photos of dealers.

"You going to be all right?" Joe asked.

She nodded, lit another cigarette. "Just need a good sleep."

"Do you want Social Work to keep the boys overnight? It might – "

"No!" she shouted. "No way! I want them back." She dropped her head, started crying, started rocking. "I want them back now."

Joe put his hand on her shoulder. "I'll speak to Anne, tell her you're okay."

Sharon nodded, her head still down. "Ta," she said. She didn't look up as they left. At the front door, Joe stopped. He could still hear her crying.

***

Old men with moustaches and sepia clothes, unfamiliar houses, and great aunts that Stephen had never met. Grainy pictures of his mother and Jean on the farm, two or three of their brother, Daniel, killed in a car accident when Betty and Jean were young, and a few of Dusty and Meg. All his mother's memories, spread out before him on the table. He'd choose a nice one for the frame, and he'd take the rest into the hospital. She'd remember everybody, he was certain of it. She'd not remember what he'd just said, but the distant past was like yesterday to her.

At the bottom of the box, there was another packet of photos. Stephen knew he should leave the packet there, but the drink made him take it out. Shouldn't have opened that bottle of wine, shouldn't have finished it. He didn't even like wine, but there was nothing else in the house when his hangover started. That was the trouble with drinking during the day. If you got pissed in the evening, you could just go straight to bed, sleep through the worst of it. He'd tried going to bed when he finished the wine, but his stomach was giving him gyp. He needed food, proper food, but there was nothing in the house. Couldn't even remember his last proper meal. A couple of days ago, in the canteen at work? Proper meal? What a joke. Reheated macaroni and chips. Still, it would be better than nothing now. Stephen knew he should put the last packet of photos back in the box, leave well alone, but he didn't. He put it on the table and went for his jacket.

It was a warm calm night. As Stephen headed for the all-night Tesco, he tried not to look at the houses with lights. He didn't want to see families together while he walked the streets alone. In front of him, a teenager was walking a dog slowly, his head bent over his mobile phone. The dog kept stopping to sniff at gates and lamp posts, and the boy scarcely noticed, so caught up was he in his texting. Bloody texting. Online messaging. Emails. No one spoke to each other these days. Stephen realised then that his reluctance to look into houses was daft – the members of the 'normal' family were probably all in separate rooms on the internet or playing computer games. He crossed the street and hurried on.

***

Moira Jacobs had died from intra-cranial bleeding; a circular fracture of the skull, courtesy of the hammer blow to the back of the head, and two linear fractures from the fall down the stairs. Odd that the killer would use a weapon belonging to the victim. Perhaps the murder was unplanned. Perhaps someone Moira Jacobs knew, someone she feared or hated, had come to her door, and she'd gone for the hammer. There had been much speculation about Mac at the evening briefing. Odd that he had befriended Sharon out of the blue. And how often did your average drug dealer get upset when watching a punter inject? Had he given Sharon the heroin reluctantly – a necessary evil to make sure she wouldn't hear anything if he went for Moira Jacobs?

So many questions. Wouldn't be much sleep for Joe tonight. It was always hard to switch off during a major investigation, and the photo of Ceapabhal had unsettled him. The lab results on the photo had come up with a twist – two sets of finger-marks, but none of them belonged to the victim. Someone else had brought the photo to the flat and put it on the table. Was it the killer? And why? Why that picture?

Joe signalled left at the roundabout and entered Nairn's Fishertown, a maze of narrow streets of terraced houses and cottages. He still wasn't sure if his move to the small seaside town sixteen miles east of Inverness had been a good idea. Two years on and he often missed living in Inverness. Wasn't much fun going to the pub with the others when the shift ended, if you could only drink coke. But there were advantages. He was less likely to meet someone he'd arrested, or their irate girlfriend, when he'd had a few. There was PC Carla MacKenzie, based at the local station. They'd been seeing each other for a couple of months and it was going very well. The beach was fine for walking, the sea for sailing, and the town was fairly quiet. And best of all, Joe's mother couldn't just pop in whenever she felt like it.

Nothing to stop her phoning, though. Three messages on his answering machine. First was just to say hello, hadn't seen him for a while, hoped he was fine. The second was to tell him that Lucy was coming at the weekend. Family meal on Friday night; could he let her know as soon as possible if he was free? The third was a huffy reminder that he had a family that cared about him, and it would be very nice if he could just return a call occasionally. He checked his watch; eleven twenty – too late to phone her back. Shame.

After a pizza and a beer, Joe had a bath. As he closed his eyes and let the warm water relax his aching muscles, he thought again about the last time he'd spoken to Lucy. He'd asked her what was wrong, and she'd insisted it was just her exams. She was in her third year studying law at Edinburgh. She'd taken her time to decide what she was

42

going to do with her life, spending a year travelling and another working in a bar. Joe had never seen his parents as chuffed as they were when she chose law. He wished he felt the same. The thought of his wee sister taking instructions from the kind of people he dealt with every day made him shiver. Ach, maybe she wouldn't want to be a criminal lawyer. Anyway, it was good that she was coming home. If they cracked this case quickly, he'd take some time off, drag Lucy away from her studying. Maybe he'd take her sailing on Sunday. He'd been promising to take her out for ages. She'd have had enough of their parents by then; she'd need to get away. And then he remembered, and he felt sick. Sunday was the fourteenth of April. Lucy's birthday, and the one day of the year that Joe dreaded. He hadn't spent that day with his sister since she was sixteen, and he wasn't going to make an exception now. He'd think of something else.

He was towelling himself dry when he heard his mobile phone beep. A text from Lucy. *7.30 Fri. Bring Carla xxx*. Definitely something wrong. Three texts today and none of her usual stupid text acronyms. It made Roberts feel important when Joe had to consult the younger officer on their meaning. FFS? LMFAO? PIMP? Joe was certain Roberts was lying. Wee Lucy wouldn't say that, would she? Roberts always suggested a suitable response for Joe, but he was having none of it. He had a certain Jurassic image to preserve. It amused Lucy.

He read the text again. Certainly wouldn't be bringing Carla. Even if she wasn't on a late shift on Friday, he wouldn't be letting his mother anywhere near her. Joe's relationship with his mother had been strained for as long as he could remember. He'd left the family home in Melrose as soon as he turned sixteen, moving to Perth to train as a joiner. He was still too close to home. Almost every weekend, his mother was there, advising on décor and furnishings, house-keeping and cooking. Despite their difficult relationship, Joe let her do the cleaning and cooking in the little flat he shared with his friend, Matt. It would have been rude not to, when she seemed so keen to be involved. She left him alone for a time, that dark time when his world came crashing down and the very sight of her made him want to scream abuse. Lucy, just turned sixteen, took over the visiting and cleaning duties then. It wasn't right; Joe knew that, but, for a time, it had seemed like Lucy was the only brightness in his life.

When he left Perth and headed for a new career with Northern Constabulary, he expected some peace. His mother had hated her time in Harris; there was no way she would move north again. Wrong. He was no sooner settled in a flat in the Crown area than Lucy left home to go travelling, and their father retired from teaching. Joe's parents moved to Inverness and a house in Lochardil, less than two miles from Joe. He gave up the fight then – what was the point? His mother was back to doing his cleaning and ironing, bringing him casseroles and walking in whenever she felt like it. Until the day she walked in and caught him and WPC Suzanne Smith in a compromising position on the living room floor. She started knocking after that.

Their uneasy truce had continued until Joe moved to Nairn. His mother gave up then. She wasn't that keen on driving and she certainly wasn't wasting her time going through to Nairn just to skivvy for him. The standard of cleanliness in Joe's house declined, but it was worth it. He wasn't sure his mother would ever forgive him for the move, and Joe couldn't have cared less.

He thought about replying to Lucy. Maybe he should phone her, try again to find out if there was anything wrong, but he was suddenly overcome with fatigue. Perhaps he would sleep after all.

Joe slept. He dreamed of the island, of willows bending and whispering in the wind, of torrential rain and smothering mist, of whispered Gaelic and heavy mournful songs. He dreamed of the spirits of the restless dead, haunting the dark slopes of Ceapabhal. He dreamed of a small body, lying on the beach, in the shadow of the hill.

***

How many frozen meals would he need? Stephen wasn't sure how much longer he could stick around and listen to his mother. Though he loved her, it was so hard to keep going to the hospital with a smile on his face. He might just take off when his holidays started. His mate, Paul, had been on at him to come down to London, said he could get him a job in a call centre. The pay was rubbish, but the work was easy. A call centre? Stephen didn't fancy it, but it would keep him going for a while. He could kip on Paul's floor until he got sorted out. His mother would understand, wouldn't she? Probably wouldn't even notice he was gone. He grabbed a fish pie and a lasagne, a small loaf and a lump of cheese – that would do for now.

High above the houses, the moon was hiding behind bruised clouds, a multitude of stars sparkling. His hunger forgotten, Stephen gazed upwards and he was a boy again, watching the clear night skies on the island. Uncle Colin and Auntie Jean had given him a telescope and a book. He'd learned all the constellations and planets, and he remembered Colin sitting on his bed for ages waiting for a turn of the telescope. Not once did his uncle say that he couldn't see whatever Stephen pointed out, even when Stephen himself was sure he was imagining things.

Not for the first time, all that Stephen had lost hit him with such force that he almost howled into the darkness. Instead, he ran until he reached his mother's house, his breath coming in sharp, painful gasps. He unlocked the door and threw himself inside, a wave of dread rising and rising, choking him. He dropped the carrier bag by the front door and rushed to the living room. The moon had broken free from the clouds. Through the open curtains it shone upon the final packet of photos. Stephen grabbed it and fell to his knees. He scattered the photos on the patterned carpet until he was surrounded, until they were all around him, everyone that he had lost, all smiling up at him in their outdated clothes. He lay among them, in the sharp white light of the moon.

***

On the grass verge, a small boy sits on a rock. He looks up the road and sees a string of houses, sheds, ruins. He looks down the road and sees the hill, a huge dark lump. Sometimes, when the swirling mist comes, the top of the hill is gone. Sometimes the whole hill disappears. He likes those times. He'd like the mist to come now and hide him from the village boys, but it's a bright sunny day.

They're coming. He can hear them, though he can't yet see them; he can hear their laughter, their boasts. Someone's singing that Ghostbusters song, the one from the film that he hasn't seen, that he'll probably never see while he's stuck in this dump.

"Seen any ghosts, city boy?"

He jumps. Didn't expect one of them to come from behind. He doesn't turn, doesn't answer. A thump on his back. "Hey, I asked you a question. Seen any ghosts?"

The boy shrugs and looks down. The others are in front of him now. He can hear them, but he doesn't know who's talking. They all sound the same anyway.

"Dumb today, are you?"

"He's dumb every day. Someone's taken his tongue. Probably one of the ghosts in his house."

"Aye, Seonaidh Ruadh died in there. Hung himself from the rafters in the bedroom. Do you hear him, boy? Creak, creak, creak. Do you hear him when the wind blows and you're lying in the dark?"

"And Mairi Bhan. Throttled in the bath by her mad husband. Glug, glug, glug. Do you hear her? Do you hear her when you're in the bath?"

"He's never been in the bath!"

The biggest one comes from behind him, crouches down and pushes the boy's chin up with his hand. "You never have a bath, do you? You or your mother. You both stink. Filthy tinks from the city."

It's him that stinks, of boiled mutton and peat. It's him that sounds dumb with his stupid accent and his slow speech. But the boy says nothing.

"Who you gonna call?" one of them shouts.

"Ghostbusters!" they chorus.

"Come on! Let's go and see if Angie's tractor will start."

The biggest one pushes the boy over. "See you, tink."

He's lying on his back in the squashed rushes. Above him, there's something dark and terrifying in the clouds that race towards the hill.

Chapter 4

DI Brian Black was not a cheerful man. An eternal pessimist, he always looked tired, his skin pasty and mottled, his gut huge and his patience short. He wasn't a bad boss, just not the most inspiring of leaders. Joe was fairly certain he'd never seen the DI laugh, and he definitely hadn't seen him in a state of excitement. Until today.

There wasn't a hint of the usual impatience as DI Black waited for his officers to gather in the incident room. A sheaf of papers in his big hand, he was smiling at everyone as they came in. It was most unsettling.

"D'you think Mrs Black gave him one this morning?" Roberts whispered.

Joe shook his head. He'd seen the DI earlier and he'd been his usual miserable self. Whatever it was, it had happened suddenly and recently.

"Morning, officers," the DI said. "How are you all today?"

Stunned and a little nervous, they muttered a response.

"Good, good." The DI nodded. And smiled. "You'll all be sorry to hear that DC Jackson can't be with us today. He is under the duvet . . . I mean the weather." How the DI laughed at his little joke. "Not to worry, though. We shall soldier on without the benefit of his razor sharp skills."

Everyone laughed at that.

The DI waved the sheaf of papers. "Ladies and gentlemen," he announced. "We have our man!"

Moira Jacobs had lived in Elgin with one James Clancy for five years, he told the officers. Fleeing domestic violence, she had moved to Inverness. Clancy had been imprisoned for assault, and, while he was inside, Women's Aid had helped Moira Jacobs secure the flat in the Ferry. Clancy was released in the summer, giving him a few months to track his ex down and murder her.

"Sir," DC MacKay said. "Why did that not show up yesterday? Surely her name is stored as a victim on the database?"

The DI smiled some more. "Good question, MacKay, a very good question. Some plonker in Grampian Police had recorded the victim's name wrongly. I shall be having words about that. Right, I'm off to Elgin to bring Clancy in. And . . . " A few people ducked slightly as the DI's eyes swept the room. MacKay made himself taller, then slumped as the DI said, "Galbraith – you're coming."

Roberts slumped too. "You get to go and interview a suspect, and I spend the day contacting funeral directors?"

Joe smiled at Roberts. "Life's a bitch."

"Before you go, Sarge, you wouldn't like to tell me what was going on with you and Jackson yesterday?"

"For the fifty sixth time, Roberts, no."

***

Betty's gentle voice carried down the long corridor, reminding Janey of her granny. She had sung the same songs as Betty: old Scots ballads of pretty lassies and thwarted love. Today, it was *The Bonny Lass o' Fyvie o'*. Janey edged closer to the door, but Betty saw her and stopped singing. "Are you a nurse?" Betty asked.

"Aye, I'm Janey – Nurse Black. I've brought your paper."

Betty snatched the Press and Journal from Janey and glared at her.

Janey smiled. "You have a lovely voice, Betty."

"Don't you bother trying to get round me. I remember you. You had me out in the rain yesterday. I'm

49

going to complain."

"I found you in the rain, Betty. I took you in."

Betty looked sceptical. "When am I getting out of here?"

"The doctor says you're doing well. Maybe a couple of weeks and he'll let you home for the weekend."

"But I don't have a home."

"You have a house in Drakies, up near Raigmore Hospital. There's some photos in your bedside cabinet. Stephen brought them in. Will we have a look at them?"

Janey spread the photos out on the bed and waited. Betty stared at them and shook her head. "That'll be Stephen's house. He's doing well for himself, you know."

"What does he do?"

Betty shrugged. "Can't remember. Something important." She picked up one of the photos and peered at it. "Sleekit wee bugger! That's my mother's Toby jug in the window. My own son, bent as a nine bob note! Ma will be turning in her grave."

"Betty, it's your house, and your Toby jug."

"I'll be having words with him later."

"He's not coming in today. Anyway, I better get on. Enjoy your paper. You like that one – it's got the farming news."

"Thank you, dear. You're a good girl. Are you a nurse?"

"Aye, Betty; I'm still a nurse."

Betty didn't see the headline: 'Police appeal for witnesses in city murder'. It was the picture she noticed, and then she couldn't take her eyes off it. A dark-haired woman – just her head and shoulders. She was stern-faced, dour, as Betty's dad would have said. Well turned out, though; hair done nicely, but miserable as sin. She was . . . she was . . . Betty stared and stared at the picture and tried to remember. Shaking her head, she turned to the farming news.

Call Kay was on Radio Scotland, and the topic was gay ministers. "Oh yes, Kay, dear," a shaky old female voice said. "We had a very gay minister when I was young. He organised splendid parties and the most marvellous picnics for the children. Sometimes he even told a joke from the pulpit! You know, that was quite frowned upon at the time, especially in the Highlands. Yes, he was really very gay, very gay indeed. His wife was a bit dour, though."

There was a silence, quite a long silence for the radio. Kay coughed, thanked the caller and said it was time for the news. Joe laughed. He looked at the DI. Nothing. Completely oblivious. It would be a long journey.

James Clancy was not in a good place. Stuck in an interview room beside a lawyer with poor personal hygiene, opposite a glaring DI Black and a pensive DS Galbraith, he almost wished he was back inside. Prison had not been a happy experience, especially for someone with ginger hair, but coming out had not been easy either. There was something safe about being inside. You weren't protected from the bullies or the more sadistic screws, but there was security in the structured day, in the locked doors and the high walls. And there were no nagging women. Not that Clancy was about to tell DI Black that, of course. He had to concentrate on the positives about his relationship with Moira, relay the happier times. Trouble was, he couldn't remember any positives or happy times.

Yes, he'd heard about Moira, Clancy told DI Black. It was on the news last night and in the paper today. He was deeply upset. It didn't matter how they had split up, that she had got him arrested, had him sentenced, that she had removed more than half his belongings while he was inside. They had lived together for five years. He wouldn't want that to happen to anyone. Anything he could do to help, he would do it. He owed her that, even if she'd had him sent down for next to nothing.

"Next to nothing?" the DI roared. Clancy jumped, his knees banging off the table. "You held her arm in the door and slammed it repeatedly, breaking it in two places, then you punched her in the face twice, knocking out four teeth! Next to nothing? The Sheriff certainly didn't agree with you when he sent you down!"

Clancy squirmed. His knees started to shake and he had to hold them to stop them hitting the table again. "Well, when you put it like that. It's just . . . there were people inside for much worse. Really dangerous people."

"And you're not dangerous?"

He shrugged. "She just got to me."

"Got to you? The newsagent gets to me when I trip over a stack of papers left just inside the door. The doctor's receptionist gets to me when she offers me an appointment in two months' time. My son gets to me when he picks his nose and flicks bogies on the floor of my car." The DI's voice rose to a bellow. "But I don't go around breaking their arms and knocking out their teeth!"

Clancy couldn't stop himself. He leaned forward, his face serious. "But she was a snobby, condescending, hypocritical, nagging, superior bitch."

Oh dear, Clancy thought, as he sat back, his shaking fingers fiddling with his tight collar; so much for the positives. But wait, DI Black was smiling. Perhaps he had a wife like that at home.

DI Black kept smiling as he stared at Clancy. "So you killed her," he said, his voice calm. The smelly lawyer came to life. "Don't answer that," he instructed his client. Clancy couldn't have answered anyway. It had suddenly hit him; he was in deep shit.

Clancy, that slimy ginger git, had been a helpful source of information, to a point, before his lawyer came to life, DI

Black told the briefing that afternoon. The couple hadn't had a dog when they were together, so Moira must have acquired the Westie after the split. She had no family that Clancy knew of, no family and no friends. She was brought up in South Africa, but she rarely spoke of the past. Clancy knew that she had been a social worker before she retired. He didn't know what kind of social worker she would make, with her right wing views and her holier-than-thou attitude. Joe had tried not to smile when Clancy said that. Those who were fortunate enough not to have social workers involved in their lives thought they were all kind-hearted left wing liberals. That hadn't been Joe's experience when he'd worked in child protection. Moira Jacobs might just have fitted in very well.

Clancy and Moira had met at ballroom dancing classes. She fancied herself as a great dancer, but Clancy didn't rate her much. Too heavy on her feet, and always insisted on dancing in high heels. He wouldn't have told her that, though, for she had a fearful temper. He'd been surprised when Moira wanted to live in sin soon after they met. Wasn't about to ask her to marry him. He'd tried that once before and it wasn't for him, but a live-in housekeeper and bed-mate – that suited him fine. He knew Moira had been in England before she came to Elgin, but he couldn't say where. She had worked for Moray Council for a couple of years after they met, then she'd retired. She had never mentioned working in Harris or anywhere in the Outer Hebrides. Never volunteered information and he never asked.

There had been no incidents of domestic violence before the assault, no incidents of any kind – his record was clean. After he attacked Moira, he ran. Officers found him hiding in the woods behind the house, and he'd seemed relieved that they found him before Moira did. It was noted on his file that Clancy seemed far more scared of Moira than he was of the law.

"He did it," the DI said. "I'm certain of it. He's got

previous and not a shred of remorse – blames her for his sentence. More than enough motive. No alibi. He did it. We've just got to prove it."

Joe didn't share the DI's certainty. His instincts, for what they were worth, told him that Clancy was not lying. And there were just too many unanswered questions around Mac. "Sir," he said, "I wonder if there could be a link between Clancy and Mac." He didn't think there was, but he didn't want the DI forgetting about Mac.

DI Black nodded, a half-smile on his face. He was still in good form, although sparring with Clancy had dented his cheerfulness a little. "Good point, Galbraith. Definitely worth bearing in mind. Roberts, anything to tell us?"

Yesterday had been a quiet day for funerals, Roberts reported, with a yawn. In fact, it was so quiet he hadn't been able to find a funeral within fifty miles of Inverness. It didn't prove much. The Highlands covered a large area, and the Central Belt was only three hours away. Mac may well have been at a funeral.

Mackay had been in touch with the housing department again. They had nothing of interest relating to Moira Jacobs. She hadn't made any complaints about the neighbours and no one had complained about her.

DI Black assigned more tasks. MacKay was to get on to the prison, find out more about Clancy. Who did he associate with on the inside? Who visited him? Wendy Aird was to follow up the social work connection. WPC Scott was to get as much information as possible on Sharon MacRae. Joe said he could put Scott in touch with Anne Morrison, see if there was any reason that this Mac would target Sharon. Roberts was to check with the Crime Operation Group for dealers calling themselves Mac. Joe was asked to see DI Black in his office.

"You're in the shit," Roberts told Joe, as the officers dispersed.

Though DI Black wasn't small, his room was. There were

heaps lying everywhere – a couple of briefcases spilling their random contents across the floor, papers and files, newspapers and envelopes, painkillers and lunch boxes, training shoes and shorts. Training shoes and shorts? The DI wouldn't even walk across the road to the filling station for a sandwich. Joe glanced at the DI's gut. No, if anything, he had put on a few pounds in recent weeks. And the three bacon rolls he'd bought in Nairn on their way back from Elgin wouldn't help. Training shoes and shorts? He missed the DI's opening sentence, but his next words captured Joe's attention.

A trip to Harris? Joe looked at the DI as if he was mad. He wanted to be here, working on the case, not traipsing off to the Outer Hebrides.

"I'm only talking a day trip by plane," DI Black said. "Land in Stornoway before 9am, return at 5pm. June has checked it out – you'd have more than enough time – only an hour or so from Stornoway to Tarbert. One of the local officers will drive you down."

In Joe's head, it took days of travelling to get to Harris, days of throwing up in the toilets on the ferry, while his mother lay groaning in the lounge. Of course it wasn't days – the ferry only took a few hours, but that's how it had seemed in his young mind. His mother wasn't groaning on the last trip, the day they left the island. She was standing on deck, proclaiming it as the happiest day of her life. They had moved from there to the Borders for a short period, then to Brighton, where they'd stayed for a few years; perhaps that explained Joe's distorted memory of the distances involved. "But what would I do on Harris?" he asked.

"Find out more about Moira Jacobs." The DI's voice was tetchy. Ach, no one could expect him to sustain his good mood for much longer.

"Wouldn't it be better to see what I can find out from here? I could contact the local authority, see what they can tell me."

The DI was quiet as he thought about it. "Aye, you're

55

right," he said at last. "Budgets and all that. No point in rushing off until we know, but keep it in mind. You might have to go at short notice."

Great, thought Joe. Lucy had sent him a text that morning, reminding him that he would be disembowelled and disinherited if he didn't turn up for dinner with his folks on Friday night.

"Feasgar math, Comhairle nan Eilean Siar."

"Pardon?" Joe had been slouching in his chair. Now he sat up straight and looked at the computer screen. Aye, he had googled the right number for the Western Isles Council, and their official name was in Gaelic. No surprise, really. He asked for Social Work. Nothing doing; they'd never heard of Moira Jacobs. He asked for the Harris office. It was closed. He asked for Human Resources. The man he spoke to didn't think they had records going back more than ten years, but he'd have a look and call Joe back. As he put the phone down, Joe crossed his fingers and hoped the man would find nothing.

On a whim, he picked the phone up again. His mother sounded peeved. Nothing new there. Joe didn't need to be in the same room as her to know that she would be frowning, her brow all furrowed and her lips narrow. People said Joe looked like her, but he hoped they were wrong. Like a ferret licking pee off a nettle, Matt had once said, when Joe's mother found their flat in a particularly unclean state after a party.

"Sorry, Mum," Joe said. "I'm rushing, as usual. I hope I'll see you all on Friday night." Aye, right, he heard his mother think. "You'll have heard about the murder yesterday?"

"The woman – somebody Jacobs?"

"Aye. Moira Jacobs. Do you recognise the name at all?"

"No. Should I?"

"Probably not. I can't say too much, but I wondered

if she had a connection with Harris." His mother was silent. The silence stretched. "Mum?"

"Harris?" She said it as if it was Hades. "It was such a long time ago. The name means nothing to me."

"It was a long shot," Joe replied. "Well, I better go."

"Seven thirty on Friday. Try not to be late. I don't want another dinner ruined."

He resisted the temptation to tell her where to stick her dinner.

***

Fiona Galbraith's face looked troubled as she put a cup of coffee on the table. "Do you want anything else?" she asked her husband, her voice distracted.

"No, thanks," Raymond replied. He put his newspaper on the arm of the chair. "Everything okay?"

She nodded.

"What did Joe have to say?" He didn't have to ask who had been on the phone; her clipped tone had told him.

Fiona seemed to hesitate forever. A line of starlings lifted from the roof across the road. While he waited for his wife to answer, Raymond watched the birds tighten into a shimmering ball, then scatter in different directions, like fireworks.

"Nothing much," Fiona said at last. "Just work."

"Did you tell him Lucy's coming?" At the thought of their daughter's visit, his lips curved into a smile. He saw Fiona's eyes narrow a little, and he knew he'd been too enthusiastic. He let the smile slip from his mouth.

"I left a couple of messages for him last night."

"We'll do something nice at the weekend, all of us."

Fiona glanced at page five of Raymond's paper, her face still troubled. "There was a murder in Inverness," she said, nodding at the small column on the page. "Joe's involved in the investigation. Do you still think we'll all do something nice with Lucy?

Chapter 5

The predominant odour in the mortuary was disinfectant, laced with a tinge of death. It always made Stephen gag. He shivered. "I hate this place," he said to the mortuary attendant.

"You get used to it," the older man said. "How long you been working in the hospital?"

"Six months or so. It's all right, apart from this."

The man shrugged. "People die in hospital; just a fact of life." He laughed at his wee joke as they manoeuvred the trolley closer to the refrigerated drawers. "Murphy, MacDonald, Robertson." He pointed to the closed doors, naming them as if they were old friends. "This one's free, I think."

Stephen hoped it was. He'd come down one night and another mortuary attendant had taken great pleasure in opening several occupied drawers and sliding the deceased out, just to make sure they were really dead, before finding an empty one. The bastard was loving it, freaking Stephen out. It worked. After the first two cadavers, he had closed his eyes. That didn't work. Later, in his bed, he could still see the old man's gaping mouth and waxen skin, the child's bashed head and blue lips; he could still smell them. It wasn't that he minded the freshly dead, like the woman in his trolley. She looked peaceful enough. It was the ones in the drawers that bothered him.

The mortuary attendant waved Stephen off with his empty trolley. As he wheeled it back along the hospital corridors, Stephen glanced at the passers-by. Most people didn't look twice. They were either oblivious to the purpose of the trolley, or they were miles away, worrying about their sick loved one. Perhaps they didn't even see Stephen and his trolley, as they trundled along the corridor. The occasional passer-by noticed and knew. Some even crossed themselves as they scurried past.

Stephen looked at his watch. Twenty more minutes and he'd be on holiday for a fortnight. The phone in his pocket vibrated. Just as well it hadn't done that in the mortuary. A text from Nisbet. Stephen's heart start to race.

***

Raymond Galbraith liked handwriting. He stood back and admired the whiteboard on the wall of the garden shed. The board was split into twelve columns, each listing his monthly garden tasks in neat handwriting. People just couldn't write properly these days, since computers had taken over the world. He liked lists. And he loved his garden.

Fiona had wanted to move last summer, get a house with fewer rooms and a smaller garden, but he had resisted. Maybe they didn't need three bedrooms. Maybe they didn't need a living room and a sitting room and a dining room and a conservatory, but he didn't want to leave another garden. He'd left too many gardens behind.

Fiona wasn't keen on gardening. She had long since admitted that her initial interest had been a ruse in order to get to know Raymond. How could anyone enjoy all that hard, dirty work? She didn't mind having a nice garden, though, as long as someone else did the work. Anyway, she had said recently, maybe it was time to get a gardener.

Never. The thought made Raymond's hands shake as he opened a packet of dahlia bulbs. He might be retired, but he was perfectly capable of looking after his garden. What else would he do with his time? She wouldn't want him in the house, messing the place up or disturbing the cushions. And she wouldn't want him going out anywhere without her, in case he spoke to another woman. She wouldn't want him in the supermarket, getting in the way of the trolley. Damn! What would she have him do with his time if he had no garden? Fade away in his chair, just like his father? Drink himself to death, just like her father? Better not mention that. There would be a mighty rattling of bones if the family closets were suddenly opened. That wouldn't do at all.

There was a knock on the shed door. Fiona, with a cup of tea and a slice of cake. Ashamed of his thoughts, Raymond wiped his hands on his gardening trousers, smiled and thanked her. When she put the cup and plate down, he took her hand and pulled her close. She was beautiful, still so beautiful, and he was very, very lucky.

***

At the late afternoon briefing, DI Black had the preliminary results of the hammer examination. There was silence in the incident room as he delivered the news. Blood, hair and skin traces from three sources. One source was blood group A, as was the victim. One was blood group O. The third was blood group DEA 1.

DEA 1? An exchange of puzzled looks. No one had heard of that group. "No," DI Black said, after a long pause, "the third source is not an alien, nor is he from Clacton-on-Sea."

"Ha ha," said PC Mike Allen. Originally from Essex, he had met his Invernessian wife at T in the Park. Two years later, he found himself married and living in Inverness. He got on fine with the others, but no one ever let him forget where he came from, and drunken locals weren't too slow to point it out either.

"The third source is canine," the DI said.

The officers gasped. As Joe looked round the room at their shocked faces, he wondered why cruelty to animals often provoked more outrage than cruelty to humans.

"Bastard," one WPC said. "How could he?"

"I'd like to get him alone in a room with a hammer," Roberts said. "And a couple of Rottweilers. Bet he wouldn't be so brave then. Did Clancy have any obvious injuries?"

The DI shook his head and looked at Joe. Joe hadn't seen anything but his snivelling ginger head and his little manicured hands.

"He gave us blood and hair samples," the DI said. "Results will be back soon. We'll get him."

∗∗∗

It was as if someone with a sense of humour had taken Marty Feldman's eyes, Barbara Streisand's nose and Mick Jagger's mouth and combined them in Nisbet's face. His grey hair was long and straight, and parted in the middle. His clothes looked like rejects from Oxfam, and he smelled worse than the mortuary. As Stephen looked around The Fluke, he was relieved to see that none of his work-mates were there. They could come in any time, though. Should have picked somewhere further from the hospital, but he just couldn't wait to hear what Nisbet had for him.

Stephen ordered a pint. "What'll you have?" he asked Nisbet.

"Nothing, thanks. Don't drink."

"Soft drink?"

"Never touch the stuff."

"Water?"

Nisbet shook his head, looked round the pub, coughed, and gestured to a table in the corner. When they sat, Nisbet looked round again, then he slid his hand into his inside pocket. Could he be any more conspicuous? How he made a living as a private investigator, Stephen just couldn't understand, but he had come highly recommended by Davie Dobbs, and the results had been satisfactory so far.

Nisbet pulled out a few crumpled sheets of A4 paper, a birth certificate and a handful of photographs. He put the photos face down on the table and unfolded the papers. In a spidery scrawl, he had written some details. "It's all there," he said. "Everything I've got. Doesn't live locally – you'll see for yourself." He reached for the photos, but Stephen stopped him. "Not here," he said. "I'll just take them with me."

Nisbet winked and tapped the side of his nose, then he left. Stephen slid the photos and papers off the table and put them in his inside pocket. As he knocked back his pint, the photos burned a hole in his pocket, right through to his heart.

***

Joe stared at the pad in front of him and tapped his pencil repeatedly against the blank page. Had Mac targeted Sharon because she lived in the same block as Moira Jacobs? Did he need a legitimate reason to visit the flats? And those letters Sharon had mentioned – had Mac put them through Moira Jacobs' letterbox or opened them himself? Maybe something in one of the letters had given him an excuse to go to Moira Jacobs' door. A suit and a briefcase to complete the picture – an official with a purpose.

"Bugger off," he told his mobile phone when it rang for a second time. Third time, he glanced at the screen. Shit, it was Carla. He'd forgotten that she was coming to Inverness to get her hair cut. They'd arranged to go for something to eat, before someone had bashed Moira Jacobs' head in with a hammer.

"You're busy," Carla said. "Is it the murder?"

"Aye; I'm sorry." As he was speaking, Joe was reaching for the list of correspondence found in Moira Jacobs' flat. It wasn't a long list. She certainly wasn't a hoarder, and the small shredder in her spare bedroom had been well used. It was a cross-shredder, so there was no chance of putting anything back together again. Joe looked at his watch. "Where are you?"

"Heathmount, with a large white wine. Can you get away?"

Joe hesitated. He wanted to carry on, but he'd been in for almost twelve hours.

"It's all right if you can't make it. There's a cute guy at the next table giving me the eye. I'm sure he'd keep me company until I go for the train. Might even give me a lift home."

Though Joe thought she was probably joking, he wasn't taking any chances. He'd been at work long enough. "I'll be there soon."

"No need to rush – give me time to get the guy's number."

Joe retrieved a letter from Moira Jacobs' file. It was from CICA, the Criminal Injuries Compensation Authority, a body that awarded compensation to innocent victims of violent crime. The letter was dated early April, and it referred to a call from Moira Jacobs and a previous letter, which the victim had clearly not received. Her claim was obviously in the initial stages and the first letter had been sent to acknowledge receipt of her claim and to give her a note of her reference number. Was that one of the letters Mac had offered to put through Moira Jacobs' letterbox? Had he opened it? Had it given him the ideal excuse to go to her door?

As he drove up to the Heathmount, Joe turned his theory over in his head. It made sense. Not having had an acknowledgement from CICA, the victim phones them and they send out a second letter. Not knowing anything about the second letter, Mac goes to her door and makes out he's come personally from CICA. How would Moira Jacobs deal with that? Would she wonder why someone was coming out, when the second letter clearly said that they would write again when they had carried out some enquiries? Had she challenged him? Gone for the hammer to scare him off?

Joe paused at the door of the bar. Carla was sitting with a large white wine, reading the Guardian. Her choice of newspaper amused her colleagues. Not that her colleagues were stupid; well, not all of them. It was just that the tabloids provided instant, easy access to news, and they could be read quickly in the snatched moments available to police officers during their work shift. Or was Joe just being charitable? He watched her take a slow sip of wine. She put the glass down, her eyes still on the newspaper, then she licked her lips, her tongue lingering on her bottom lip, her teeth gently biting. Joe felt his stomach muscles contract. What did she see in him? He let the door close behind him. Carla looked up and smiled. Looking into her dark eyes, Joe's stomach flipped again.

Joe wouldn't have liked to speculate on whether the guy sitting at the next table was cute or not, but he certainly wasn't in any state to be giving anyone a lift home. In fact, if DS Galbraith was to see him getting into the driving seat of a car, he would have to take appropriate action. The guy looked disappointed when Joe kissed Carla and sat down.

"Nice hair," Joe said. On his way to the Heathmount, between thinking of possible scenarios involving Mac and Moira Jacobs, Joe had repeatedly reminded himself. Didn't matter if there was no obvious change in the hairstyle; you just had to mention it. Couldn't really go wrong, unless, of course, there had been a change of plan, and no haircut. He'd got into trouble with that in the past. But tonight he'd been careful. 'Nice hair', he'd said, not 'nice haircut'. That should cover all eventualities, although he was certain that her hair had been cut. Was that a new jacket she was wearing? Safest not to mention it, as that had also got him into trouble with others, when it turned out said item of clothing had been worn many times in his presence, including on the very first date, and how could he possibly forget such a thing?

"Like my new jacket?" Carla asked.

"You took the words right out of my mouth."

"Must have been while you were kissing me," the drunk at the next table sang, before lurching for the door.

Joe hadn't seen Carla for over a week. She'd been away the previous weekend on a hen trip to Dublin. She hadn't wanted to go; couldn't stand the bride, her second cousin, but family politics had left her with no choice. The weekend had been every bit as bad as she'd expected. The worse the tale got, the more Joe laughed. When Carla told him of the fate of the bride-to-be's Louboutin patent slide (an expensive slip-on sandal, apparently), he almost choked on his steak.

After copious amounts of champagne and cocktails, the hens had spilled out of a bar in the city centre. The inebriated second cousin had tried to get the others to do the can-can for passers-by. No one was taking her on, but she was undaunted. Kicking her leg high in the air, the Louboutin flew off her foot and landed on the roof of a passing bus. Never had anyone sobered up so quickly. Clutching her remaining sandal, she had chased after the bus, leaving the others to enjoy the rest of the night without her. They found her later in the hotel, sobbing over the fate of the Louboutin; it was now in the Liffey. She'd almost saved it, when it fell off the bus several streets later, but two drunken neds had reached it before her, and tossed it into the river.

It was a long time since Joe had gone out with another copper. Years of experience had put him off. But Carla was different. She wasn't hard and cynical like so many of his colleagues. Perhaps she just hadn't been in the job long enough.

"How's the murder inquiry going?" Carla asked as Joe drove home. "Or would you rather not talk about it?"

Joe was desperate to talk about it. As soon as they left the Heathmount he'd started turning it over in his head, and then he'd felt guilty that he was no longer giving Carla his full attention. He told her the facts but not his theory about Mac. Carla listened and said nothing until he was finished and had asked for her thoughts.

"Sounds like Mac has a grudge against social workers," Carla said. "Perhaps Moira Jacobs was involved in putting him, or someone he was close to, into care. He's found out where she lives and targeted Sharon MacRae to get access to the block of flats. The letters have given him some information about Moira Jacobs that has allowed him to go to her door, and he's made sure Sharon's out of it before he does that."

"That's exactly what I was thinking," Joe said. "I just have to persuade the DI that James Clancy is not the only obvious suspect."

"Persuade DI Black?" Carla had worked with the DI before. "More chance of Boris Johnson being the next Provost of Nairn."

Later, they took a walk along Nairn beach in the dusk. Despite the mild night, they passed few people as they walked. Moonlight sparkled on the water and silent birds flitted past in the half-light. It was only then that Joe mentioned the possibility of a trip to Harris.

"Harris?" Carla said. "Why?"

Joe told her about the photo. He hesitated before telling her anything else, but he knew there was no point in keeping it quiet. Carla was friendly with Wendy Aird; it would sound odd if Wendy told her, and he hadn't mentioned it. "Actually," he said, "I lived there for a while as a child."

Carla stopped and turned to face him. "Really? You kept that quiet."

"There's a lot you don't know about me." Joe tried to keep his voice light-hearted. He put his arms round her and pulled her close. "I once spent a whole summer dressed as Mickey Mouse."

"Cute." She kissed his nose. "There's quite a lot you don't know about me. My grandparents on my dad's side were from North Uist; I spent a lot of holidays there, and we used to go over to Harris for day trips. I loved it; all those gorgeous beaches. Nice place for kids to grow up."

Joe said nothing as he held Carla tight.

***

There was a knife in Stephen's heart, a twisting in his stomach. Was he going to throw up? He shut his eyes, breathed deeply, opened them and looked at the photos again. She was beautiful, really beautiful. For now.

He went downstairs to make himself a cup of tea. As he waited for the kettle to boil, he stared out into the darkness. Though he couldn't see it, he knew the garden was a mess. He should have kept it nice for his mother, but he hated gardening. Maybe he could get someone in to do it, but how would he pay for that? He'd spent most of his money on Nisbet. The little he had left was to sort out that business with the car. Was it worth it? Was all this really worth it? Stephen pulled down the blind, then made his tea and went back upstairs.

On a cork notice board on the wall in front of the desk, there was a group of three photos – two men and a woman. Beside them, there was a white sheet of paper with a sketch of a stick figure with long hair. Stephen tore the sheet of paper off the board and crumpled it into a ball. He threw it into the bin, then he picked out the best of the new photos. He pinned the photo on the board beside the others. Standing back, he stared at them. Quite the cosy wee family, the four of them.

"Fuck you," he hissed. "Fuck you!"

***

"Where's your father?"

The question is asked by a small girl with glasses who always sits alone at the front of the school bus. He doesn't know what to say. Maybe if he knew where his father was, he would tell her. The girl always gets on the bus before him, so he has no idea where she lives. Are the places beyond his village better or worse? Apart from Leverburgh and Tarbert, and the scattered houses in between, he's never seen the other villages. He's seen the signs that point to narrow winding roads and places with unpronounceable names. They must be better, surely, for they cannot be worse.

The boy looks at the girl and shrugs. She gives him a wee smile. "Mine's dead," she says. "Sank with his fishing boat before I was born. Granny says his carcass will rise from the sea on the Day of Judgement."

The boy feels sick. Their teacher told them all about the dead rising on the Day of Judgement, but that's not what bothers him. It's the memory of his mother on the school bus the next day, muttering and mumbling and breathing whisky fumes, as the village boys giggled in the back seats. Why had he told his mother what the teacher said? He had stayed in the playground that day until his mother came out, her face red and her legs unsteady. "I've sorted that woman," she told him. "There'll be no more of that shite. Go on, son; in you go."

The memory turns his face red. He looks away from the girl, rubs the condensation from the window and watches until he sees the road-end. When the bus stops, he jumps down and runs. Behind him, there's laughter.

Chapter 6

Fifty quid? The train reached Aviemore and Stephen was still in shock. Fifty quid! If he'd been organised and had booked two fixed singles a few weeks ago, the smug bastard in the booking office told him, he'd have got it for twenty two pounds. Well, if he'd known he was going to Kirkcaldy a few weeks ago, he told the smug bastard, he'd have booked it, but he didn't. Life doesn't work like that. Anyway, booking fixed singles was no use to him. How was he to know what time he'd want to come back? He might decide to stay a few days. Couldn't live his life to a timetable. The man had smiled, nodded, let him rant on, then told Stephen that Scotrail worked to a strict timetable, and the train was leaving in three minutes. Three minutes? Not even time to get a paper. Shit!

No seats either, until someone got off at Aviemore. Stephen pretended not to see the elderly man closing in from the other end of the carriage. The bugger might have a stick, but he was tanking it. Not fast enough. Stephen slipped into the seat, and the old man scowled at him as he passed. A minister sitting at the next table on the other side gave up his seat for the old man, then he scowled at Stephen too and left the carriage.

At least he had a seat, but he could do without the two old dears opposite trying to catch his eye, the Goth beside him listening to The Damned on giant leaking headphones, and the old man at the next table continuing to glare. And not even a paper to break the monotony.

Stephen closed his eyes and tried to remember the last

time he'd seen Auntie Jean. They had visited each other often when he was a child. They had fun then. Jean had always cheered his mother up. She was a typical Fifer – dour as hell on the surface, but kind and funny underneath. And her man, Uncle Colin, he was great. Betty said Jean had landed on her feet with Colin, though he wasn't much to look at. His parents had passed the family mansion to him and Jean when they got married. Perhaps a mansion was a bit of an exaggeration, but the house in Kirkcaldy had always seemed gigantic to Stephen as a child, with its huge rooms, high ceilings and long corridors. It was so big there was even a separate flat upstairs that they rented out.

Jean and Colin had no children. Something to do with Jean's tubes, Stephen's mother had whispered. Ever since she was a girl, she'd been doubled up and crying every month, bleeding like a stuck pig. Stephen shuddered as he remembered; too much information, Mum.

When had he last seen Jean? It was on the island; Jean had come over on her own. It was after the . . . after all that; he was certain of it. He remembered a cold winter day, him and his mum on the bus, going to meet Jean off the ferry. His mother had a half bottle of gin in a brown paper bag in her handbag, and the smell knocked him sick every time she took it out for a sly glug. She could hardly walk by the time they reached the ferry. He remembered the journey home and his mother singing at the top of her voice. Jean was mortified, especially when his mother tried to get her to join in. Maybe that was it – the last time; maybe that was the reason for the silence.

Stephen sat up straight and opened his eyes. Of course. Jean had come over with their Christmas presents; Colin wasn't well. It was towards the end of Jean's stay that he'd been taken. Stephen had been certain Auntie Jean would say something. He could go and stay with her and Colin. They would . . . he could . . . But Jean hadn't said a word. Over the years, Stephen had asked his mother when they would be seeing Jean. She was a toffee-nosed cow, his mother said; thought herself too good for them, and her man was nothing but a dafty. Eventually she told him to stop asking, so that was it until her mind went and Jean was back. The Jean that lived in his mother's head now was a saint. Nothing would be too much trouble for family. The flat would be waiting for her – Jean had promised it years ago. Had she really? Were Jean and Colin still alive?

Stephen bought a sandwich and a cup of tea just after Perth. Another mammoth Scotrail rip-off, but he was suddenly gripped by hunger and he couldn't wait.

Not long to go. They were in Fife now, stopping at Markinch. This was where Betty would always start reciting that poem, the one about the boy on the train knowing by the queer-like smell that the next stop was Kirkcaldy. There had been a hell of a smell in the town; he remembered it clearly. It was the smell of linseed oil from the linoleum factories. Although it had seemed really strong when Stephen was a child, that was nothing compared to the smell in Betty's day, when the linoleum industry was going strong.

The next stop was Kirkcaldy. As Stephen stood on the platform and watched the train pull away, he wondered if he was imagining the hint of linseed oil in the air. The memory could do funny things. Leaving the station, he went down through the War Memorial Gardens to the roundabout. Left or right? He wasn't sure. "'Excuse me," he said to an elderly lady. "Do you know if there's a big park near here?"

She stopped and leaned on her stick, her breathing laboured and her face pale. "Aye, pal," she said. "Beveridge Park." She nodded to the right. "Keep on along this road – cross at the lights and carry on under the bridge. Down to the roundabout, and the park's on the other side of the road. Cannae miss it."

He thanked her, then he asked her about the smell. Turned out there was still one linoleum factory in Kirkcaldy.

Colin and Jean's house was opposite Beveridge Park.

Stephen remembered how proud Colin had been of the park. He and Stephen used to play football there, then they'd take a walk past the tennis courts and round the pond, up the hill and down by the rugby pitches. Colin was good to Stephen, spent a lot of time with him. Maybe that was because of Jean's tubes and the missing children.

The house was big, but not a mansion, and there was a sad air about it that hadn't been there when Stephen was a child. The outside steps up to the flat were covered in bricks and broken slates, buckets and plant pots. No one living in the flat now, and it certainly wasn't ready for his mother. The garden was untidy, the hedges and bushes overgrown. There were leaves scattered everywhere, moss covering the paths and weeds growing through the stones in the parking area. Colin's polished Rover was gone. The pots at the front door were cracked and empty, and the brass nameplate on the door was so dirty that Stephen struggled to read the name. He wiped it with his sleeve. Henderson. The right name. He knocked and waited.

Stephen's mother might be completely off her head, but she had worn well. He couldn't say the same for Jean. Her short grey hair was thin and brittle, her eyes dull and crusty. She had skin like wrinkled old leather and breath like rotten eggs. Supported by two sticks, her back was so bent that she was several inches shorter than she had been. If it wasn't for the voice, Stephen might have turned and left.

"Aye, son. What can I do for you the day?" she said, and he knew it was Auntie Jean.

***

Leave it, Joe wanted to say; don't even think about touching it. He swallowed the words as Roberts bent down and picked up the photo. The young detective smiled as he looked at a fresh-faced Joe and another young man with sandy-coloured hair and a smattering of freckles across his nose. Both smiling, both so young and full of hope. Jackson's taunts, from Tuesday, rang in Joe's ears. *This your boyfriend, Galbraith? Another chippy? Aww, you make a lovely couple.*

Roberts passed the photo to him and said nothing. Joe stuffed it in his wallet, pulled out a fiver, and paid for their bacon rolls.

And Roberts had the cheek to call Joe soft. The detective constable looked as if he was about to cry as he crawled into the cage and knelt beside Moira Jacobs' Westie. She was curled in a ball, but she wagged her half-shaved tail as Roberts reached beneath the white plastic collar and scratched her ears. "The boss here has been worrying about you something terrible," Roberts told the dog. "Hasn't been able to sleep."

Joe shook his head and smiled at the bemused young veterinary nurse. They had been down the Ferry to speak to the residents of the last two flats in Moira Jacobs' block. Waste of time that was. On the way back to the station, after he'd scoffed his own bacon roll, then half of Joe's, Roberts had badgered Joe into going by the vets to check on the dog.

They'd seen the vet when they arrived. He told them he'd had to put a steel plate in her hind leg. He asked if the injury was caused by a road accident or a kick. He grimaced when Joe mentioned a hammer. "Aye," he said. "That would do it. Brutal."

Roberts straightened up and closed the door of the cage. "What will happen to her?" he asked the nurse. "Her owner has passed away."

"Cat and dog home, I suppose."

"Sarge," he said, "she'd suit you fine. Keep you company in that house on your own, and you could have nice long walks on Nairn beach."

"And what am I supposed to do with her when I'm working?"

"Dog walker."

"What's stopping you?"

"Landlord. Long hours. General aversion to exercise."

The nurse smiled. "Don't worry, guys; they'll be falling over themselves to take her home."

"So she won't be put down?" Roberts asked.

"Unlikely. We're the vets for the cat and dog home – I could let you know if she doesn't get a home."

That pleased Roberts. He had his card out of his pocket and in the nurse's hand before she could say another word.

They left, and found Inverness town centre at a standstill. Nothing new there. Joe tapped his fingers on the steering wheel and glared at Roberts. He'd distracted Joe as they left the surgery, going on and on about the dog. It would have been much quicker to go round by the Longman to get back to the station, but before Joe realised what he was doing, he was heading into town and couldn't turn back.

On his left, a taxi was trying to edge out into the traffic. "No chance, mate," Joe said, inching his car forward and blocking the taxi in. "When did you last give way to anyone? Buggers think they own the road."

The lights up ahead turned green, but no one moved.

"That nurse was nice," Roberts said. "Caring; I like that in a woman."

"A woman? She was scarcely out of nappies."

"Hardly. She was only a few years younger than me. She was keen, like."

"Can't say I noticed." The car in front of him inched forward. Joe revved the engine, then cursed as the lights changed again. The town centre was a joke. Between one-way streets and pedestrianised areas, it took forever to get anywhere. Just when you got used to the layout and direction of traffic, it changed again. Must be about time for another change.

"Aye," Roberts said. "She was keen. I can always tell.

I think that Anne Morrison quite likes me too. She's not bad for an older bird."

"Older?" Joe stared at Roberts. While he was staring, the car behind him beeped. He looked ahead and the traffic was moving. The driver behind beeped again as Joe stalled and missed the changing lights. Looking in his rear view mirror, Joe smiled. It was the taxi driver he had refused to let out. He looked at Roberts again. "Anne's about thirty five."

"That's what I said: older."

"Older than you," Joe said. "Not very much older than me. And a lot younger than lots of people."

"So, would you fancy going out with her?"

"No. Her husband probably wouldn't fancy it either."

"Carla MacKenzie might have something to say too."

Joe smiled and said nothing, as the lights changed again and he took off. He hadn't mentioned Carla to Roberts, but you couldn't keep anything secret in the police. Not that there was any reason to keep it secret.

"Have you ever seen Carla's mother?" Roberts asked, as Joe turned right into Strother's Lane.

"Bloody hell!" A woman with a pushchair stepped off the pavement, pushing her infant into the road in front of Joe's car. He slammed on the brakes, and opened the window to shout at her.

"Can't hear you," Roberts said. "Earphones. So, have you seen Carla's mother?"

"No. Why?" Carla's parents were divorced. Her mother had remarried a few years ago and moved to South Carolina, so Joe didn't expect to see too much of her.

"I was going with this bird once," Roberts said. "Really nice. Everything in the right place, and all going well. I was even thinking of proposing, and then I met her mother. Shit, she was a beast. I looked at . . . what was her name again? Shelley. Aye, I looked at Shelley, looked at the mother. Their features swam before my eyes, Shelley's face morphing into her mother's, like something from Dr Who.

That was it. Offski."

Joe laughed. "Have you ever wondered why you have such difficulty finding and keeping a girlfriend?"

"Aye. Often. And your point is?"

Joe shook his head and turned onto Longman Road.

"It's easy for you, Sarge. I've seen the way Mairi in the canteen looks at you. And there's that bird in the FPU – the one with the long black hair. She was definitely giving you the eye in the pub last week. I think Wendy Aird and Suzanne Smith both fancy you too."

Joe felt his cheeks start to burn. It wasn't the first time another cop had alluded to Joe's effect on their female colleagues, and it wasn't the first time he'd felt incredibly uncomfortable and entirely unconvinced. They were imagining it; they must be.

Roberts hadn't noticed Joe's embarrassment. "Boss, you couldn't give me the benefit of your age and experience, could you?"

"No, but I can give you the number of a bloody good therapist."

At the station, Joe found DI Black in bad form; James Clancy was blood group B, so he had not been hit with the murder weapon. The DI wasn't ready to give up on Clancy just yet. "He could have set it up," he said. "He could have been there with someone else. No alibi. Previous. Motive."

"Anyone checked his associates in prison?" Joe asked.

"MacKay's onto it. I was certain of this bastard. Certain."

"I've got a couple of theories about Mac and Moira Jacobs, based on what Sharon MacRae has told us." Joe outlined his theories to the DI. The older man listened and nodded occasionally, but he was having great difficulty forsaking James Clancy as the prime suspect. "Clancy might have paid Mac to do the dirty work," the DI said at last.

"It's a possibility. We just need to find out more about Mac."

June, the DI's secretary, knocked on the door and came in to tell Joe that Sharon MacRae was downstairs. As Joe got up to leave, the DI was pensive.

"You might have something," he said at last. "But I'd have staked my life on that bastard, Clancy."

***

"Oh Stephen, Stephen." Auntie Jean shook her head and peered closer. "Is that really you? Our Betty's Stephen? Oh, Stephen, Stephen."

Oh Jean, Jean, I'm bloody freezing out here. Are you going to let me in or what?

"Aye, Auntie Jean, it's me."

"Son, come away in."

Stephen followed his aunt into a house that didn't smell very good. He followed her tapping sticks down the dark hall to the small back room. There was no fire in the grate and the room felt damp and unused. When he sat on the same settee that he had sat on as a child, he was certain he saw a cloud of dust rise up around him. His feet rested on the same carpet, and on top of the same wall unit, the same games – Scrabble, Monopoly, Cluedo. Above the fire, nothing had changed. Three pictures – a herd of grazing Highland cattle, a twelve-pointer stag, a steam train. The nodding china milkmaid was still on one end of the mantelpiece, the carved wooden horse on the other, the gold carriage clock in the middle. Stephen wanted to get up from the settee and touch the milkmaid's head, send it nodding from side to side. He would be gentle, always gentle, Colin's voice behind his shoulder telling him not to let herself catch him touching that. When they heard Jean coming, Stephen would stop the nodding head and jump back on the couch, himself and Colin sitting there, trying not to laugh.

"Colin's dead." Jean was sitting in the chair by the fireplace, staring at the floor.

"Dead?"

"Aye, son. Dead."

It shouldn't have been a surprise. Although everything in the room was the same as it had been, the colour and life had been sucked out of it. Sucked out of Jean too, leaving her shrivelled and dry, alone in a house of faded shadows.

"When?"

"Seven year back."

"I'm sorry to hear it."

Jean shrugged.

Is that it? Forty or so years of marriage and just a shrug?

"What's doing with you, son? What brings you here?"

"I . . . it's . . . well, it's my mother, really."

There was something in Jean's eyes. Shame? Fear? Stephen couldn't tell.

"Is she dead?" the old woman asked.

Whatever fleeting emotion Stephen had seen, it was gone. She might as well have been asking if his mother had seen the latest episode of Coronation Street.

"No." He should go.

"What is it then?"

Fifty quid for his ticket. Fifty quid. He was going to get something out of the visit. "She . . . she's not very well. It's like her . . . her mind, really."

Jean laughed. The old bitch laughed. Not that it was much of a laugh, just a dry cackle. "Her mind? That'll be the drink then."

Call a spade a fucking shovel, why don't you, Auntie Jean? She had always been direct, but not in this callous way. "Aye," he said, his face colouring. "Her mind's gone, and the drink probably didn't help. Neither did everything she's been through. But see the funny thing about it – in her head, you're the bees' knees – best sister a girl ever had. She thinks you're saving your flat for her, when she gets out of hospital. Spends all her time planning the bus trips you'll go on together. Oh, the catching up you're going to do when she gets out. She's got all the photos ready for you –

Gran and Grandad; Dusty and Meg; Daniel. Every time she looks at them, it's 'Jean this' and 'Jean that', and fucking 'Wait until Jean sees this'." He hadn't meant to swear or get angry. This was supposed to be a good thing, seeing Jean. There weren't many good things left.

"I'm sorry, son," Jean said, her voice flat. "I'm sorry that I'm no' the Jean that lives in her head, but I never will be. That Jean disappeared long ago, thanks to her."

"What did she do? Was it the drinking, that time that you came on holiday?"

"No, and it wasn't the shame of seeing you taken off her, right in front of my eyes."

"Shame?" Stephen cried. "If it was so shameful, why didn't you take me? Why could I not have come and stayed with you and Colin instead of . . . of . . . " He couldn't find the words for them, those people he'd been forced to live with. "That's what families do."

"Families?" She had fairly come to life now, the old boot. Sitting forward in her chair. Pointing. "Families? Don't talk to me about what families do for each other. You haven't a clue."

"No, I haven't, because no one would tell me. I had an aunt and an uncle that I adored. Suddenly, you were gone, and no one would tell me why. I was just a child, for fuck's sake."

The adore bit got to her. There was shame in her eyes then. Maybe even a tear. "Stephen, son; you were special to us too." She nodded her head. "You know that. You were . . . you meant the world to . . . to him."

"Him? Can you not even say his name? He was your husband for long enough. You were happy together."

She nodded her head. "We were, once upon a time. For years, the Colin in my head was a good man. No one better. Looked after me, and the house. Earned a good living. Didn't even mind that I couldn't give him kids. And you know how good he was with kids – he'd have loved . . . just loved . . . " Her voice caught in her throat, squeezed tight. No more words.

The carriage clock ticked, just as it had when Stephen was wee and hiding behind Jean's chair, waiting for Colin to come and find him.

"So, what happened?" Stephen's voice was quiet, though he wanted to shout.

The chair seemed to grow around her as Jean shrunk into herself. All wee and hunched and crooked, her head nodding from side to side, just like the china milkmaid. He should have pitied her, but his anger wouldn't make way for anything else. "What fucking happened?"

She shrank some more. Muttered. Shook. Said nothing.

Stephen stood. "I might as well go. This was a waste of time."

"What was it?" she whispered. "What did you want from me?"

He saw himself in the mirror on the wall behind her. No sign of the boy that had stood on the chair pulling faces, sticking his tongue out, holding magic writing up to the mirror. Stephen shrugged. "I don't know, really. I'm . . . I'll be going away soon. I just wanted her to have someone when I'm gone."

He bent and picked up his rucksack. He straightened, and Jean had grown. She was huge now, too big for the chair, her temper filling the room. "She had someone all right," she shouted. "She had Colin! She had my man! On that very sofa and me sleeping upstairs. You want to know why Colin was so fond of you? You really want to know?"

No. Stephen backed away from her. Up against the door. Fumbled behind him and pulled it open. No. He backed into the hall.

"Whore! That's what she was. That's what she always was. A whore!"

An explosion in his head. The rucksack clattered to the floor. He was back in the room, the door kicked closed. In the mirror above Jean's chair, crazy, crazy eyes.

Chapter 7

Liam MacRae wanted to be a cop, his mother told Joe. He'd talked about nothing else since he met Joe and Roberts. Ryan was disgusted, called him a traitor and a wanker. He'd get called worse if he joined up, Joe told Sharon. She was looking rough today. Well, rougher. She hadn't used again, she said, but she was struggling. Liam was scared to leave her in case Mac came back. He'd agreed to stay with her pal in Innes Street just now, but he wasn't happy, wanted to come with her.

"No sign of Mac?" Joe asked.

Sharon shook her head. "Didn't see him that often. Could be a couple of weeks without a sign of him. Don't want to see the bastard."

"I know, but I do. You'll let – "

"Aye. I'll let you know."

Joe had read all the information they had on Sharon MacRae. Could have written the script himself. Alcoholic mother; father unknown. Sharon and two older siblings removed when she discloses sexual abuse at the hands of the mother's latest boyfriend. Not enough evidence to prosecute. Mother stands by the boyfriend and doesn't want Sharon back. Reading that had made Joe's hands shake. What made some women put a feckless abusive bastard before their own children? Was it society's fault? Skewed values? Anyone could get pregnant, but not everyone could keep a man. Was that what it was all about? Sharon goes from foster placement to foster placement. On her third placement, she claims her foster father is touching her. Children's hearing members are appalled at the suggestion that this decent professional man would abuse a child. Dissenting member of the hearing thinks another child placed in the same household hinted at abuse last year. Not enough evidence for prosecution. Psychologist suggests attention-seeking disorder.

Meanwhile, her brother ends up in a secure unit and her sister disappears. Placement after placement, until Sharon turns sixteen, when she moves to a homeless hostel. At seventeen, she meets the newly divorced Peter MacRae, convicted drug dealer and wife-beater. Sharon loses a baby at five months – a fall down the stairs. Soon, she becomes wife number three. A child is born, followed by another two miscarriages, a second child, frequent falls and occasional visits to the hospital, where she blames her injuries on clumsiness.

After Peter MacRae's death, Sharon manages to keep her addiction hidden from social services for a couple of years. An anonymous neighbour (sounds like an elderly man) reports her for neglect, by which time Ryan has been missing school and getting into trouble. Things come to a head when he and another boy push an old man in a wheelchair into the middle of Academy Street and leave him there. Causes a huge pile-up. The man escapes unhurt, but very shaken, and Ryan is lucky to avoid a secure unit.

The case is referred to the Children's Reporter. Sharon tries to fight the grounds of referral, claiming that Social Work have exaggerated and misrepresented her situation. No solicitor will take the case on, so Sharon accepts the grounds, and begins to go through the system again.

Children's hearings, review meetings, child's plans, and general interference in her life by a shower of condescending middle-class bastards. The children's hearing members don't like that outburst by Sharon. Bad enough using that language, but using it in front of the children shows a lack of moral fibre. Doesn't she know they're there to help? Doesn't she realise they have a wealth of experience in these matters? Aye, Sharon asks, and how many of them have been through the care system? How many of them know what it's like to live on benefits? How many are former drug users? What exactly qualifies them to sit in judgement upon her? There are no answers for Sharon.

All that keeps the boys from going into care is a half-decent paternal aunt. They're placed with her from time to time, while Sharon is on and off heroin, in and out of unsuitable relationships. A series of social work reports disclose a lack of willingness by Sharon to accept support and engage with services, and an appalling decline in the standard of English of those being admitted as social workers. Social workers do a lot of wandering about – mostly wandering about Sharon's ability to be a 'protective factory in the childrens' live's' [sic], while the children frequently wonder. They wonder from home to the shop to the play park, and sometimes this wondering goes on very late at night. Sharon's life is subjected to a level of scrutiny that would shame MI5. Even when she's clean and able to function well, she's criticised for having a night out or buying clothes for herself. Once, she goes to Glasgow for a weekend with two friends, leaving the children with their aunt, where they have a great time. It just goes to show, according to social workers, that Sharon is incapable of putting the boys first. Heaven forbid that she should actually dare to have a good time.

And so on, until the case is passed to Anne Morrison. Common sense prevails, as does proper English. Matters improve. A methadone programme, regular attendance at school by Ryan, acceptance of support by Sharon, and the children with her for several months. All going well until the mysterious Mac appears on the scene.

Joe saw Sharon's eyebrows rise a few times as she looked at the pictures on the screen. She would know quite a few of the dealers, he suspected. When they were done, she shook her head. "He's not there," she said, her voice flat. "The bastard's not there."

It wasn't far from the station to Linda's house on Innes Street. Sharon and Linda had been friends since school though their lives had taken very different paths. Linda was single and a chef, working off-shore, three weeks on, three weeks off. They could go for long periods without seeing each other, but Linda had always stood by Sharon. Their relationship had been strained when Sharon was using and in the habit of turning up and asking for money. That hadn't happened for many months, and Linda was keen to help out as much as she could.

Liam's relief at seeing her made Sharon feel guilty. "Hey son," she said. "You okay?"

He nodded. "Me and Linda made biscuits and I'm allowed to take them home. Do you want one?"

"Too right," she lied. "I'm starving." The biscuits smelled good, but Sharon might as well have been eating cardboard. Her appetite had disappeared along with Mac. She protested when Linda insisted that she and Liam stay for food. All she wanted to do was go home and lie down, then she remembered her empty fridge.

When they walked home, much later than Sharon had intended, Liam made his mother promise not to tell Ryan he'd been baking. "We'll say we bought the biscuits in the Co-op," he said. "Ryan won't know."

Thinking of the misshapen biscuits, Sharon could hardly stop herself from laughing. "No," she said, her hand covering a grin. "He'll not know. Liam, son, you didn't tell Linda we had nothing in the fridge, did you? I'd have made something. There was cheesy pasta in the cupboard, and beans."

"I just said you didn't really like cooking in pans with those wee bits of grass and real meat, like she does. That was all. Then she asked me if I'd had bolly knees before and I said no. Was that the wrong thing to say?"

"No. You were just being honest. And the grass stuff is called herbs. I can get some if you like."

Liam nodded. "I'm glad Linda gave us the rest of the bolly knees to take home. Did you like it?"

Sharon nodded.

"So why did you give me yours when Linda wasn't looking?"

"Sore tummy, but it's better now."

"Would you be able to make those worms to go with it? I liked trying to wind them round my fork the way Linda does, and sooking them up through the gap in my front teeth."

"I'll try."

"What were you doing at the police station, Mum?"

"Talking to DS Galbraith."

Liam's hand tightened in hers. "You're not in trouble, are you?"

"No. Just helping him out."

"Wish I had come with you," Liam said. "I don't think Galbraith's a tosser, no matter what Ryan says. And Roberts is cool, even if he's a bit of a fool." Liam laughed. "That was a poem, Mum, wasn't it?"

"Aye, son; it was."

"Anyway, I'd like to help the police. I'm going to be – " He stopped as a figure slipped out of a doorway on Grant Street and stood in front of them. Sharon's heart started racing.

Mac looked different, kind of tired and deflated, and much smaller than before. Sharon tried to smile, but her mouth wouldn't comply. Liam stood in front of her, as if to protect her.

"Sharon, Liam," Mac said. "How're you doing?"

"Fine," Sharon replied. "We're in a hurry."

"I won't keep you. Just wanted to say I'll not be down for a while. Might have to go away."

"Probably for the best," Sharon said, before she could stop herself.

Mac raised his eyebrows. "I saw Ryan before, in the shop with his cousin. Said the police were asking questions about me."

"I . . . I never told them anything," Sharon said.

"Neither did I." Liam's face turned red and he slipped behind his mother.

"What did they want to know?" Mac asked.

Sharon shrugged. "Just asking questions about my neighbour."

"What about your neighbour?"

Liam had shuffled round to Sharon's side. She looked down at him, unsure what to say. "Eh, suspicious – "

"She was slaughtered," Liam said. "Her throat was cut and her head was nearly off. There was blood and brains covering the stairs and the landing. Her legs were chopped into little pieces, and Mr MacMahon ate a bit of her liver on toast."

"Liam!" Sharon said. "That's not true. Who told you that?"

"Ryan; he was whispering it to me in bed last night."

"He's talking rubbish. There was a suspicious death on the stairs, not long after you left. The woman who lived next door to me."

"Aye? That's a shame. Never saw anything myself. I'll maybe drop in and tell the police before I go."

Aye, right, Sharon thought.

"Maybe see you if . . . when I get back," he said.

Don't bother, Sharon wanted to say. She said nothing. Just nodded and walked on. At the bend in the road, she looked back. Mac was still where they had left him. He looked just as sad as Sharon felt. He had seemed like a good friend, and she didn't have many of those.

When she was certain they were out of sight of Mac, Sharon took her mobile phone from her pocket. No credit. She thought of using 999, but it wasn't an emergency, and Mac had said he hadn't seen anything. He might be a bastard, but Sharon was certain he had nothing to do with her neighbour's death. She could go back to the station, but it was getting late now and she wanted to pick Ryan up and get the boys home. DS Galbraith had probably left by now. She'd go back down to the station tomorrow.

Liam tugged on her hand. "Are you sad, Mum?"

She tried to smile. "No. I've got my best boy and his biscuits, and enough bolly knees to last a week. Why would I be sad?"

"I'm not sad either. I'm as happy as . . . as . . . a really happy person. I don't think he'll be back, do you?"

Sharon shook her head. She was certain that she would never see Mac again.

***

Joe didn't notice the solitary figure waiting to cross the road. When he stopped at the Shore Street roundabout, he didn't see Mac cross behind his car, head down and shoulders slumped. He didn't see him pause at the corner and look across the roundabout, back the way he had come. He didn't see him lower his head and move on. Joe was too busy watching the road and thinking about his telephone conversation with the outreach worker from Inverness Women's Aid.

Margaret MacLennan had never really got to know Moira Jacobs, who was quite different from their usual client, not least because the abuse appeared to be an isolated incident. Most of their clients were escaping serial abusers, to whom they had often returned after seeking help. Although Margaret was there to provide support at any time, Moira had only asked for help with the application for criminal injuries compensation. Margaret was aware that Moray Women's Aid had helped Moira to secure accommodation; she hadn't accepted any support or help to deal with the effects of the assault. Margaret wasn't aware of Moira having any problems with anyone since she settled in Inverness. She had never mentioned anyone bothering or following her. She wasn't that happy with the flat in the Ferry; that was why she got the dog. She'd have liked a bigger dog, but she couldn't cope with having to exercise it. At least the Westie would bark if anyone tried to break in.

Margaret had provided Moira with a range of Women's Aid leaflets and information on abuse, but she wasn't sure that Moira had even read them. She hadn't kept them, thought Joe; they had found nothing of that nature among her belongings. When asked if she had any thoughts on Moira's violent death, Margaret said that, without wishing to make assumptions, abused women were at greatest risk of being murdered either at the point of leaving, or having left, a violent partner. Interesting, Joe had thought, but they'd need a lot more than that to get Clancy.

Joe pulled out and indicated right. He followed the roundabout, exiting left at Waterloo Place, and crossing the Black Bridge. The bridge was neither black in colour nor official name. It was the Waterloo Bridge, but Joe had never heard anyone call it that. The original early nineteenth century wooden bridge that connected the village of Merkinch with the burgh of Inverness had been dark in colour, hence its local name. That bridge had been replaced in 1896 with the present light coloured metal bridge, but the name had stuck.

On Grant Street, Joe parked in front of the Nip Inn. The smokers outside the pub eyed him with suspicion as he locked the car. Did one of them grunt? Probably not the best time for a confrontation. Was his profession really that obvious, or did the clientèle of the Nip Inn have more experience of CID than most? Aye, and who was guilty of stereotyping now?

Grant Street was a depressing area at night. If the buildings weren't boarded up, they were shuttered. Although it had always looked a little shabby, it wasn't so bad during the day, when the shops and businesses were open and there were people about. As Joe made his slow way along Lower Kessock Street and under the railway bridge, then onto Thornbush Road, he was thinking about Mac. Only one householder had noticed him passing the morning Moira Jacobs died. She had commented to officers that he looked out of place in his suit, with his briefcase. She thought he might be an insurance man, but why didn't he have a car?

How had Mac felt that morning? He was hurrying, the woman had said, hurrying with his head down. Liam had also said that. What was he thinking as he hurried towards Sharon's, a little bag of happiness in his briefcase? Did he also have a photo in there? And if he did, why that photo? Joe's stomach churned at the thought of the photo. Shit, it was so long ago; why did it still get to him?

There was no one outside the flats. Perhaps they could smell pig too, these people. A shadow on the stairs inside caught his eye, and Joe hurried to the door. Relieved that the woman coming out wasn't someone he had interviewed during the door-to-door, Joe thanked her and slipped inside.

Some officers got their best ideas discussing a case together. An idea thrown into the room, tossed around, changing, growing, until a theory was reached that might lead them to the culprit or the reason for the crime. Although Joe was a good team player, and could join in with the rest of them, he got his best ideas alone. That was when the answers came to him.

And now he stood at Moira Jacobs' door in the fading light and he asked why. Why had someone, Mac or Clancy or someone else, why had they bashed her head in with a hammer? It hadn't been carefully planned, Joe was certain of that. If the killer had known he wanted her dead when he went to her door, when she invited him in, presuming that she did, then why kill her with her own hammer on the common stair where anyone might come across them? She had been hit at the top of the stairs and pushed downwards, the culprit dropping the hammer as he left. Had he stopped at the bottom of the stairs or had he hurried away in a panic? He'd avoided standing in the blood that had congealed around the victim's head. The footwear marks found in the blood had been matched to the paramedics.

Joe tried to imagine Moira Jacobs in life, but it was difficult. Never before had he delved into a life so barren, into such an empty flat with so few personal effects. How could she live like that? She didn't intend to stay long in the Ferry, he guessed; she hadn't even unpacked all her boxes. Perhaps the criminal injuries compensation was going to jump-start a new life, or maybe she thought she'd meet a replacement for Clancy at the tea dance.

He thought of all that he'd been told about her. She'd worked in Moray for a couple of years, in the older people's team, before retiring. None of her colleagues had got close to her. They knew nothing about her, except that she didn't have a great manner with the elderly. Too brusque and unfeeling. No one was sorry to see her go.

One thing Joe was certain of, Moira Jacobs wasn't going to go down without a fight. What would have happened in Elgin if Clancy had stuck around after attacking her? He ran. He hid. They found him cowering in the woods. He was terrified of her. He wasn't going to risk coming back, was he? And if Joe was wrong, if Clancy had sought her out, surely he just wanted to talk. Perhaps he wanted his furniture back; perhaps he wanted to apologise. And perhaps Moira Jacobs went for the hammer first. But why was someone else's blood on the hammer? Why was the dog attacked? There were no answers coming to Joe tonight, none at all.

Outside, in the bare excuse for a play park, two boys had tied a girl up with police tape. The boys ran when they saw Joe.

"Tossers!" the girl shouted after them, shaking herself free from the loose tape. She kicked it, then she sat on the bench and took out her mobile phone.

"Shania," she said, "you'll never guess what Winkie and Daniel just did to me. Tied me up with that police tape. Aye! They did!" She giggled. "Aye, it was quite good. Come down later and they might do the same to you."

***

Stephen was dying. It was a heart attack. Rolled into a tight ball on his bed, his heart was hammering in his chest and his breath was gone. He tried to pull air into his lungs, but they wouldn't inflate. He was dying. He had gone to bed as soon as he'd got home, his body and his mind exhausted. He had fallen into a deep sleep almost instantly, then he had woken with a start. Had he heard something? Was someone in the house? Before he could get up, he'd felt a strange sensation running through his body. The muscles around his eyes were contracting, strange tingling spasms shooting down his limbs. Sweat started to pour from him, sweat and fear. His head was on fire, his limbs shaking, his gut contracting. It was no more than he deserved. Surely death was the best that he could hope for now. A quick, painless death. But this wasn't painless. It wasn't quick. It was terrifying.

He rocked back and fore, back and fore, his body hot, his body icy cold, his head clanging with every noise outside, every car, every shout. Time was speeding, rocketing, erupting. Then crawling, hanging, stopping.

A series of agonising spasms ripped through Stephen's gut. He'd have to get up; he'd have to go to the bathroom. But how could he? His legs were like jelly. Sweat and tears poured from him as he sat up and put his feet on the floor. Legs were useless. Legs were soft, pliant rubber. He was going to go where he was. It was going to pour from him, right there on the carpet.

Stephen had never known pain like it. Could a heart attack do that? He would never know how his legs carried him to the bathroom. But did they? Had he walked, or had he crawled on trembling hands and knees? He must have crawled, for now he was on the bathroom floor and he was reaching up to the sink and hauling himself onto the toilet.

There was no strength left in his body as he slumped on the pan. But he was breathing, and his heart was no longer pounding. What use was that, though? His bones had melted and sweated out of him. His eyes couldn't see properly and his ears were ringing in time to the bathroom fan.

It was the worst thing Stephen had ever known.

***

The rain is torrential and the wind is howling, banging the lid of the wheelie bin against the wall by the back door. There's no moon tonight and the sky is as dark as coal. Outside his window, there's loud gushing and gurgling as the wind forces the rain water back along the rone pipes. In the garden, the willows are murmuring, bending and swaying. Inside, above his bed, the rafters are creaking and groaning, the house as shaky and noisy as a train.

It takes all his courage to leave the bed, to tiptoe across the bare floor, to open the door. Across the landing, his mother's door is open, a soft light spilling out. He wonders if she's still awake, but it's ages since he heard her come to bed; it was before the storm took hold. She had opened his door, peeped in, whispered something. She sometimes did that, but he could never hear the words. He thought they were good words tonight, soft words that fluttered into the darkness, across the room, caressing his neck and head. They would have soothed him to sleep if the storm hadn't come.

He peeps round his mother's door. She's alone. She's asleep. Her arm is flung out to the side and her hair is spread in dark curls across the pillow. Her book is still in her hand, resting on the quilt, just her thumb keeping the place. He wants to take it from her so the pages don't get bent. He wants to crawl in beside her, into the crook of her arm. He wants to sleep there, with her warm breath on his neck.

But he daren't. Disturbing her might make the bad words come, send them slamming into him like bricks, bashing and hurting until he'd have to run and cower under the covers, his pillow over his head.

As if his thoughts have disturbed her, his mother's arm moves. Her nose wrinkles. She pulls her hand from the book and rubs her nose, her eyes still closed. He backs away, across the cold landing, into his room, a little of her light following him. It guides him to his bed. He hears the sound of coughing from his mother's room. The noise of a switch and the light is gone. The room is so black, and the storm so loud.

But he knows. It's not the wind that's making the rafters creak; it's the ghost of Seonaidh Ruadh, hanging, creaking back and fore, back and fore. And the sound of water, it's not from the rones; it's Mairi Bhan, gurgling as her mad husband throttles her in the bath. It's dusty under the bed, dusty, but safe.

Chapter 8

Flora MacDonald was standing in front of Inverness Castle, her dog by her side. She wasn't alone. There were others hanging about, but none of them had a seagull perched on their head. Cast in bronze, Flora had been there since 1899, gazing westward after her hero, Bonnie Prince Charlie.

As Joe made his way up the hill at the front of the castle, he wondered what the tourists made of the large white vans parked behind Flora. Perched on a rock above the River Ness, the 19th century castle housed the city's courts. The buildings weren't open to the public for anything other than court business, but tourists often mingled with the great unwashed in the castle grounds. Many a photo opportunity must have been ruined by the prison vans. As for those not yet in custody, they were huddled around the steps at the side door, gasping on hurried cigarettes as if it might be their last, their voices ringing out in false bravado. And along the wall opposite the door, girlfriends and sisters, mothers and grannies, all frowning and looking far more worried than their men.

DI Black had not been pleased to hear that Joe had a court citation. In the middle of a murder enquiry? The citation came in months ago, Joe reminded him, and the case had already been put off once. It was a sheriff and jury trial in a child sex abuse case and no one wanted it put off again. Anyway, Joe might only be gone for a couple of hours. The DI had looked at Joe as if he was simple when he said that. Who went to court and came out after a couple

94

of hours? It was a big black hole that swallowed up police officers for days at a time. Most of those days were spent waiting to give evidence in cases that never went ahead, and, on the rare occasion that a case did proceed and an officer gave evidence, more often than not they were chewed to a pulp and spat out, disheartened and cynical.

Joe hoped that his days of being chewed to a pulp in court were long gone. He remembered the District Court when he was a traffic cop. He might have been on the same side as the fiscals but it didn't stop them tearing strips off him later for the standard of his notebook or his evidence. And that was after being mauled by the accused's solicitor, often a second year trainee with aspirations to be the next Donald Findlay. He remembered one Justice of the Peace asking him if he wanted a seat and a glass of water after one wee shite of a solicitor, a female who looked about twelve, had finished with him. If it wasn't for his partner on duty that night, Joe might have given up. Old Bob Hanley, a traffic PC for thirty years, told him to imagine a big steel toe capped boot descending from the sky and stamping on the fiscal and the solicitor, grinding them into the ground like insects. Failing that, just imagine them with no clothes on, but go easy with the imagination when it came to Maggie Sutherland, the almost retired PF. It wouldn't do for Joe to throw up in the middle of giving evidence. Several years on and Joe was more at ease in the witness box. He'd learned the importance of taking good notes and statements. And if there were blows, he could take them and stay standing. Not much hope for you as a cop otherwise.

Joe could have seen the case far enough too. They had Moira Jacobs' medical records and there was a lot of reading to do. Maybe they'd get some clues as to where she'd lived and worked before Moray. The full post-mortem report had also come in. Not a lot to add to what they already knew, except that the victim's gall bladder had been removed fairly recently – just a couple of months ago.

There was nothing else remarkable. Tea and toast in her stomach, two healed fractures in her arm, and a four piece dental bridge in her mouth, the last two courtesy of James Clancy. Well, the injuries were courtesy of Clancy; unlikely that he had paid for the expensive dental work, unless Moira Jacobs was clever enough to have made off with his money as well as half his belongings.

The DI was threatening to bring Clancy in again. He'd come in voluntarily last time; unlikely he'd do that again. They'd have to have something more on him before he was brought in formally. Joe remained unconvinced about Clancy. Sharon MacRae had come in this morning shortly before Joe left for court. He couldn't believe it when he heard that Sharon had met Mac the previous night, just minutes before Joe had parked on Grant Street. He'd asked Sharon if she'd noticed a bandage or an injury on Mac's hand, but she said he'd kept his hands in his pockets. Joe was interested to hear that Mac had looked tired and rough. Maybe his conscience was bothering him. Not so good that he was thinking of going away. The sooner they found him, the better. Joe had left Sharon looking at CCTV. If Mac went through the town when he left Grant Street last night, surely they'd get lucky. Hadn't had much luck with the CCTV for Tuesday morning. Just a grainy image of the back of someone in a suit with a briefcase on Grant Street, and no sign of him on his way back from the Ferry.

There were three others in the small witness room in the court. Joe recognised two of them as victims of the accused, a sixty-year-old alleged child abuser. The witnesses were sisters and Joe had taken their statements when he worked in the Family Protection Unit. He smiled at them, then he sat down and lifted a National Geographic magazine. Joe didn't read the article on Icelandic volcanoes. He just looked at the pictures and remembered the sisters' doubts about giving evidence. It was twenty years ago. How could that man be charged after twenty years? Anyway, maybe it was their fault. Maybe they had led him on, at six and eight years old. He had worked in a local park. He'd bought them sweets, pushed them on the swings, promised their mother he'd keep an eye on them, then taken them round the back of the summer house. They hadn't said no. They hadn't even screamed. Maybe it was their fault.

Joe remembered their reaction as they discovered they weren't alone. There were seven victims, their stories all so similar. He remembered watching as the façades the sisters had built around themselves crumbled. Shock. Anger. Realisation that their adult problems might be down to this man that had stolen their childhood innocence.

When he heard that the Sheriff was having a coffee break, Joe slipped out of court and phoned the Western Isles Council. The man he had spoken to previously in Human Resources was off sick, and no one else knew anything about old staff records. Joe asked to be put through to the Harris office. This time someone answered – a man with a soft island voice that took Joe way, way back.

Ten minutes later, the bar officer came to the door and gestured to Joe. The Sheriff was back on the bench and Joe would be called shortly. He thanked the Harris man for his help and switched off his mobile phone. As he waited in the court foyer, he could feel his heart thumping. It wasn't the thought of giving evidence that bothered him; it was the thought of a trip to Harris. Moira Jacobs had worked there.

***

A sudden idea loomed in Betty's head, startling her. All this time she'd been blaming the walls for stealing her thoughts, blaming Stephen, blaming the nurses. It was the television. She could hear it everywhere, all day long, even in her room. Trying to sleep and it would come creeping under the door, sidling up to the bed, sneaking into her ear. Gulp. One swallow and her thoughts were gone.

Ear plugs, that's what she needed. Keep the television out and her thoughts in. She'd ask the nurses to phone Stephen and tell him to bring some. Her fingers in her ears, Betty left her room. There was someone with a name badge beside the nurses' office, but she couldn't be a nurse, not with that hair. Pink and purple and grey; looked like a woolly jumper that Jean had as a girl. Mum washed it in hot water and it came out just like that one's hair. No, Betty wasn't asking her to speak to Stephen; she'd just get it wrong.

When Janey came out of the office, Betty was sitting on a chair with her fingers in her ears. "Are you a nurse?" she shouted. Janey nodded. No point in saying anything.

"I want you to phone my son. Tell him to bring me some earplugs."

Janey mouthed: 'Wait.' She went back into the office and returned with the Press and Journal in one hand, a small box in the other. Taking Betty's arm, she steered her back to her room. She closed the door and held the box out to Betty.

"I can't take it from you," Betty said. "If I take my fingers out of my ears, my thoughts will go too."

Janey shook her head. "It's okay," she said, her voice loud. She took an aural thermometer from her pocket. "This will keep them in."

"What is it?"

"It puts a special barrier in your ears. Lasts a couple of hours."

"Will it last while Stephen's here?"

Janey nodded.

"Okay." Betty took one finger out. "Get it in quick!"

Janey inserted the thermometer. When it beeped, she told Betty to take the other finger out and repeated the procedure. Betty looked chuffed. "That feels good. I wish you'd told me about this before."

"It's new." Janey didn't tell Betty that they had done

this the day before yesterday. "You're at the forefront of science. It only works once a day, so take these earplugs for later."

"Thanks. I'll put them in when Stephen leaves."

"Here's today's paper. Do you want to give me those for recycling?" There were a couple of papers on Betty's bedside cabinet. Betty lifted them and offered them to Janey. As the nurse reached out, Betty snatched them back. "Wait. There's a picture in one of them – a woman. I want you to cut it out for me." She dropped one of the papers on the bed, held up the other. "There, on page one. That woman."

Janey frowned. It was the murder victim from the flats down the Ferry. "Do you know her?"

Betty shook her head. "No. I just want to keep the picture."

"But . . . " Ach, it wasn't worth arguing. She probably just looked like someone that Betty knew.

Betty stared at the picture. She stared and stared. "Careful," she said, when Janey started to cut it out. "Mind her nice hair."

The picture was in Betty's pocket when Stephen came. She didn't mention it to him, just patted her pocket every now and again to see that it was still there. Stephen was a good boy. He brought a beautiful photo frame with a picture of her and Daniel, her beloved, lost big brother. And he brought more pictures. There was Dusty and Meg; Jean and all the family; even old Uncle Bert with the great big moustache. Betty and Jean had been scared of that moustache. It wiggled when Uncle Bert laughed. They were sure it had a life of its own, like the hairy black caterpillars in the woods. Sometimes Bert dozed in the chair and she and Jean crept closer, watching and waiting. The moustache didn't move much while Bert slept; just a few hairs wiggling here and there. Betty and Jean decided it must be asleep too.

Towards the end of Stephen's visit, Betty felt the barrier in her ears begin to fade. Just as well Stephen was going soon. In a way, she wouldn't mind him getting her thoughts today because they were happy thoughts, and he was looking sad. It would be good for him to have some nice thoughts, but it was good for her to keep them too.

Stephen didn't take any of Betty's thoughts. She put the earplugs in as soon as he was gone and she kept them there, even when she went for her food. She kept them there and she laughed to herself. She didn't see the others watching her and wondering. She just ate her food, and laughed and laughed at the antics of Uncle Bert's moustache.

***

The Banishment of Sebastian Moore began as the 13.05 left Edinburgh Waverley. For fourteen months and five days he had been in Lucy Galbraith's head. Not any longer. The photos were burned; the cards were in the bin; the jewellery was on eBay; his number was deleted from her mobile phone. If he rang her or sent a text, she would change her number. Perhaps she should do that anyway. Perhaps by keeping the same number, she was inviting him to contact her. But he hadn't, had he?

By the time the train reached Haymarket, less than five minutes from Waverley Lucy had started to go over the events of the last few weeks. Fifteen minutes later, crossing the Forth Rail Bridge, Sebastian Moore was firmly back in Lucy's head. The trolley was coming. Would alcohol help or hinder the situation? It wouldn't help her finances. Best wait until later and drink at her parents' expense. She bought a coffee and decided there was nothing else for it.

Criminological Perspectives – Lucy looked at the text book and groaned. She had chosen Criminal Law, Criminology and Family Law as her 3rd year honours subjects. She'd enjoyed them all at first, but lately she wasn't enjoying much. Did she still want to be a lawyer? And if she did, what kind of law? For her first two years she'd had her mind set on social welfare law. She was doing voluntary work with the Citizens Advice Bureau, and she'd done a placement at a law centre in Glasgow. Thought it was settled until she'd gone to sit in the criminal courts for a few days. Her plans were up in the air. She didn't fancy the conveyor belt crap of the lower courts; couldn't think of anything worse. How many different ways were there to try and mitigate the stupidity of your guilty clients? No, it was the High Court of Justiciary that brought her back day after day, when time and classes allowed. She'd slip into the public benches, where her fellow addicts, mostly pensioners, would nod, move to make room, pass her a mint. They'd point out the best and worst of the lawyers, the toughest and softest of the judges. She'd share their anticipation, their excitement, as the court rose and the drama began. She'd marvel at the cross-examination skills of leading QCs, at their poise and gravitas, their skill and cunning. She'd lean forward, hold her breath, smile. And then she'd glance to the side or behind, and see the harrowed faces of the victim's family as lawyers made light of the suffering of their loved one, or tried to shift the blame for death onto the emergency services, rather than the erstwhile crow-bar wielding thug now smirking from the dock. She'd cough, raise her notebook and start writing. People had to know she was there for a proper reason. She wasn't voyeuristic and shallow. Really, she wasn't. But it was so addictive. And exhausting. Maybe selling houses or drafting wills would be easier. Lucy didn't know how she'd ever decide. In the meantime, a chapter on the Future of Policing beckoned. At least it would give her and Joe something to argue about.

***

The DI was pleased to see an unscathed Joe back from

1 the early afternoon. He was delighted to hear Joe's news. Donald MacLean, the man Joe had spoken to in the Harris office, was certain that Moira Jacobs had been a social worker on Harris many years ago. He didn't remember her, but the name had lived on. If he misbehaved as a child, his mother would threaten him – 'Moira Jacobs will come for you,' she'd say. 'She'll take you to *Hiort.*'

"Where?" Joe had asked.

"*Hiort* – St Kilda. It's a group of uninhabited islands forty or so miles from the Hebrides. Bad boys were threatened with exile to *Hiort*, and Moira Jacobs was just the one to take you."

Joe had asked Donald how old he was. He was thirty-two, just a year younger than Joe. Was his mother still alive? No, she died a few years back, but Donald knew someone who could help Joe. Her name was Morag MacDonald and she had worked in social work for many years. Trouble was, she was very old and she could hardly walk. She was in a care home in Harris, and there was nothing she liked better than a visit from a young man.

"You need to see this Morag MacDonald," the DI said. "What about Monday?"

At the afternoon briefing, the DI delivered the DNA results. The unknown person hit by the hammer remained unknown, the DNA unmatched. Nothing to link the hammer to James Clancy, but . . . three of Clancy's hairs had been found on the floor of Moira Jacobs' hall. His prints were nowhere in the flat, but he'd been there.

"He's brought someone else with him to do the deed," the DI said. "Cowardly bastard. One of his prison mates, maybe? MacKay, what did you find out about his time in the nick?"

"Not very much," MacKay said. "Saw himself as a cut above everyone else, but desperate not to show it. Tried to stay in the background, keep his head down. There were a couple of nutters in with him that wouldn't be averse to this sort of thing for the right price, but nothing to show that he ever spoke, far less colluded, with them. One of them is still inside. Other one got out before Clancy, but he'll be on the DNA database."

The DI nodded. "Keep digging. The screws weren't there all the time, and these nutters have greedy wee brothers and cousins that haven't yet come to our attention. And get a search warrant organised. That wee shite won't recognise his own home if he ever gets out again. Galbraith, you're coming with me to bring him in."

Joe looked at his watch. Half past three. Dinner was at seven thirty. Wouldn't normally bother him to miss it, but he'd really like to see Lucy.

The road to Elgin was busy and the journey slow. The DI hardly drew breath as he drove. First, he lamented the demise of Northern Constabulary. For two weeks they had been part of the national force, Police Scotland. It was too early to say how it would all work out, but that didn't stop the DI imagining. Low morale, cuts, closures and catastrophes. All the funds going to the Central Belt. No appreciation of the particular problems of Highland policing. Largest division by area in the country; least well resourced.

The economy was next, then the housing market. The DI had been trying to sell his house for two years. Nothing doing. That was followed by a rant about bankers and their bonuses. The most obvious subject came next: the independence referendum in 2014. Joe hadn't made his own mind up yet; the last thing he wanted to hear was the DI's opinion. He switched off.

Just outside Elgin, Joe switched on again. A dispute at the DI's golf club, and someone had been stealing someone else's tea. Joe had always got the impression from his boss that whisky was the drink of choice at the golf club. He was about to say so when the DI mentioned that he had a preference for zero-friction tees himself, but the ones that were stolen were hardwood. Joe laughed, and got a glare for his trouble.

***

Clancy was in the hot seat again, and he wasn't half crapping himself. His solicitor had advised him to say nothing, but he couldn't stay quiet. His hair in Moira's flat? He didn't even know where she lived until she died. Even then, he'd only seen the flats on the news; he had no idea where they were.

"Come on, James," the DI said, his voice pleasant. "You were at the flat. How else can you explain those three hairs of yours that we found in Moira's hall?"

Clancy looked at the DI with suspicion. "You took my hair last time I was here. How do I know you didn't plant it?"

The DI laughed. "You've been watching too much American television, James." He glanced at the typed report in front of him. "The hairs were lifted by our scene of crime officers at or around 12.30pm on Tuesday. You were interviewed the following day. When those hairs were found, we didn't even know you existed."

"Three hairs? How does a scene of crime officer find three hairs?"

"They were lifted by special suction equipment."

"A hoover, in other words," Clancy said, with a sneer. "You've emptied Moira's hoover bag! No wonder you got my hairs – she stole the damn thing from me."

"How many months since she left?" Joe asked.

"I don't know; I was inside. She didn't send me notification of her change of address."

"It was last August. She probably changed the hoover bag once or twice since then. Anyway, we have our own 'hoover', with a brand new bag for each crime scene. As for her move, you had ways of finding out where she moved to, and when. You had her watched from inside."

Clancy looked like he might cry. "Why would I do that? I didn't want to see her again. I hoped she'd leave. I didn't want her to take my furniture with her, but I was delighted to find that she had gone. The last thing I wanted was a forwarding address."

The DI took over. "You didn't want to face her again, after what you did to her, James? Terrified of her, weren't you? But you were happy for your prison mates to help you get rid of her."

Clancy groaned and put his head on the table. "How many times?" he muttered. "How many times?" He looked up and shook his head. "I didn't have any prison mates and I didn't want Moira to die."

The DI leaned forward. "You didn't want her to die? Went wrong, did it? You just wanted to get your belongings back, but it went too far."

"I haven't been there! How many times do I have to tell you . . . you . . . people that I haven't been there?"

"Temper, temper, James," the DI said. "You'll be slamming my arm in the door next. Tell me, did Moira take any tools from your house?"

"Tools?"

"Tools. You know, the things you use for DIY. Screwdriver, hammer, pliers, spanner. That sort of thing."

Clancy shrugged. "I dunno. I haven't felt much like DIY since I got out."

"Did you have these kind of tools?"

"Aye. There's a set in the shed. Matching blue handles – Moira bought them for me one Christmas. She was the romantic type."

Joe coughed to cover up a snigger. "Matching blue handles? Interesting."

"I certainly wasn't interested," Clancy replied. "It was one of the worst presents I ever got. The Christmas before that, she bought me a suitcase. A big horrible green thing. I always hated green. Hope she took that with her."

Though Clancy was nervous, there wasn't a hint of

discomfort when the tools were discussed. Clancy was either very cool, or he hadn't a clue how Moira Jacobs had died. Joe didn't tell him that Moira had taken the suitcase. It was found in her hall cupboard, full of bed linen. Probably Clancy's spare bed linen.

"So you didn't like that tool set?" the DI said. "Resented her for buying it?"

Clancy shrugged. "What more can I say? DIY is not my thing. I didn't like the tool set. It wasn't much of a present. How would you like it?"

"I wouldn't complain. Come in handy. Especially . . . " the DI leaned toward Clancy, staring right into his eyes. "Especially a hammer."

"A hammer, a screwdriver – they're just tools. I don't know why you're so interested in them. I don't . . . " The penny started to drop and Clancy's lower lip followed it, the colour draining from his face. "Oh no." He shook his head. "No. Not a hammer. No."

Joe knew then. Clancy was innocent. The DI wasn't giving up though. "The hair, James; you still haven't explained the hair."

Clancy's lawyer was bored stiff. So stiff, he'd hardly moved since they started. He looked at his watch. "I think you've done the hair to death. There's nothing more my client can say."

"I'll decide when your client's said enough," the DI replied. "He hasn't even started." He leaned towards Clancy. "We've got enough here to charge you. You did it. Not only did she 'get you arrested', but you get out to find she's taken half your belongings. Doesn't matter that she may well have been entitled in law to those belongings. You were raging, wanted to get them back, wanted to get back at her."

"It was more than half!" Clancy cried. "Every day I miss something else. How would you like to come home and find your house plundered? She even took my new living room carpet. It was only down a month before I was

106

arrested. I bought it. My carpet!"

The lawyer straightened up. He smirked. "And what colour would your carpet have been, Mr Clancy?"

"Eh . . . blue with a light coloured fleck."

"Gentlemen – the colour of Ms Jacobs' hall carpet?"

The DI was stunned into silence. Joe felt a little sorry for him. "Blue with a light coloured fleck," Joe answered.

The lawyer's smirk turned to unadulterated delight, as he looked at his client. "Mr Clancy, we're out of here."

Chapter 9

Lucy gazed out on suburbia, on the perfect grass and regimented hedges, the polished cars and the jet-washed paths. Though she loved coming home to her parents, she couldn't understand why anyone would want to live here when they could have retired to the country, bought an old house with some character. There were so many lovely rural areas around Inverness. But they needed to be near facilities, her father always said; they weren't getting any younger. Besides, he loved Inverness; he felt safe and at home here. And her mother always shuddered at the thought of the countryside; she'd tried that. Never again.

"I don't know why you keep looking out," Lucy's mother said. "He'll not come. He's got more important things to do. Always has."

"Well, he is investigating a murder, dear," Raymond said. "It can't be easy. Lucy, would you like to see my pictures from the Inverness Flower Show? I won five prizes last year – two for my cacti. They're in the Floral Hall now; we'll go and have a coffee there. Maybe tomorrow; what do you think, Fiona?"

Fiona nodded and said nothing.

"I'd love to see your pictures, Dad," Lucy said. "And the cacti." She sat beside him on the settee, moving closer until she could smell the after-shave and earth. When she couldn't sleep, she thought of that smell. Lately, she had thought of it often. Speaking of smells, there was a hint of burning meat coming from the kitchen. That shifted Fiona.

Joe closed the front door and sniffed the air. Roast beef and more than a touch of impatience. In the lounge, Lucy and Raymond were sitting on the couch, both smiling. Lucy's eyes were glowing, but they looked huge in a little gaunt face. Her long dark hair, usually so shiny and healthy, was lank and dull. They hugged, and she was just skin and bone. What the hell had happened?

"I hear there's been a murrdurr," Lucy said, in her best Taggart accent, as she stepped back and looked at Joe.

He shook his head. "If I had a tenner for every time I've heard that."

"Sorry. Not very funny – who was the victim?"

"A woman in South Kessock. We, or rather the DI, thought we had our man today, but it turned out otherwise."

"Any other leads?" Raymond asked.

Joe took off his jacket and laid it over the arm of a chair. He put a bottle of wine on the coffee table and sat. "Not really," he said. The CCTV had come up with nothing. Mac must be keeping to the side streets, like a rat. Joe looked at the door to the kitchen, lowered his voice a little. "There might be a Harris connection."

Raymond looked surprised. "Harris?"

"Aye, I'm going across next week. Was going to fly over for the day on Monday, but the DI wants me to take the ferry, stay a couple of nights."

"Harris," Raymond repeated. He smiled, yet Joe knew the sadness in him.

"Can I come?" Lucy asked.

The coward in Joe almost agreed immediately. It would be so much easier for him to go back to Harris with someone else, and someone he was close to. But Lucy? In Harris? He saw the same doubt in Raymond's eyes. "You'd hate it," he said. "Nothing for you to do, and I'll be busy all the time."

"The weather's supposed to be good next week, so I could amuse myself. And I've got loads of reading to do."

"I wish . . . " Raymond said, then he stopped. With a

109

shake of his head, he dismissed his wish and smiled. "You should take Lucy. You'd both have a lovely time."

"I'll have to check with the DI," Joe said.

Lucy grinned. "I can't wait."

"Can't wait for what?" Fiona asked from the doorway. She didn't see the look that passed between Raymond and Joe. She didn't see Raymond press Lucy's arm. "She's excited about seeing my cacti," Raymond replied. "Joe's here."

Joe stood and kissed his mother. He handed her the wine. With her other hand, she lifted his jacket from the arm of the chair. "I wish you'd hang your jacket up when you come in. You know where the hooks are."

One day, Joe told himself. One day, he might just do that, when the child in him stopped getting pleasure from baiting his mother. Fiona took the jacket out to the hall. "It's lovely to see you, dear," she called. "Come on through; the food's ready. It's been ready for quite a while."

"You staying tonight?" Lucy asked Joe, when they sat at the dining table. Fiona and Raymond were in the kitchen,

He shrugged. "Hadn't really thought about it."

"Go on," she said. "Please."

"Cruella might not approve."

Lucy laughed. "Nothing new there."

Fiona appeared with a platter of sliced meat, Raymond behind her with a dish of roast potatoes. Their father smiled to hear their laughter. Their mother frowned and looked suspicious. She went back to the kitchen for the vegetables, then she sat.

"Dad," Lucy said, "it's all right if Joe stays tonight, isn't it?"

Raymond was still smiling. "Goes without saying. Bed's always made up, isn't it, Fiona?"

Fiona placed her napkin carefully on her lap before she answered. "I suppose so. I still don't see why he had to move to Nairn, though – it was just silly."

Lucy saw Joe's eyes narrow. He looked so like their mother when he was annoyed, though Lucy would never tell him that. He opened his mouth to respond and Lucy jumped in with a story about her friend, Emma, who had just returned from the Philippines. Fiona's pettiness forgotten, the other three groaned. The tales of Emma's mishaps and misadventures were legendary. They had never met her, and, on occasion, they had even voiced doubts whether anyone so silly and accident-prone could really exist.

"She exists," Lucy told them, before anyone got a chance to say otherwise. "I'm going to bring her up here one day. She's very attractive, Joe. If things don't work out with you and Carla . . . "

Joe frowned. Fiona raised her eyebrows. Raymond coughed. Lucy knew she'd be quizzed later.

As for Emma and the Philippines, on arrival in Manila, she had befriended a local woman and child in a play park. In her usual trusting way, Emma took the woman up on her offer to visit their home for refreshments. The chilled fruit juice was amazing, the after-effects even more so. Emma was found five hours later by a policeman, wandering in another park on the opposite side of the city, her purse empty. Luckily, Lucy, said, she still had her passport.

"Lucky she still had her kidneys," Joe said.

When Fiona and Raymond had gone to bed, and another bottle of wine had been opened, DS Joseph Galbraith got to work on his sister. She denied there was anything wrong, other than stress over her exams. It took three more glasses before she gave in.

"All right," she said, as Joe poured the last dregs of the bottle into her glass. She settled back against the cushions on the sofa and tried to smile, clutched the glass tighter, gulped her wine. "It's a fair cop, Joe. Sebastian and I are finished."

"I'm sorry," Joe said. When he saw the tears glistening in her eyes, he wanted to kill Sebastian, and not just for having such a stupid name. He had been really worried about Lucy tonight. She was drinking too much and eating too little, her voice too loud and her eyes so sad. "You were too good for him."

Lucy frowned. "You never even met him."

"Wasn't for want of trying. He was always conveniently busy whenever I was in Edinburgh, and you never brought him home. Why was that?"

Lucy shrugged. "Coincidence that he wasn't around when you were. As for taking him home, remind me how often Carla's been here, or any other girlfriend? Don't forget, for years Mum thought you were gay."

Joe smiled. His mother's growing fears and imaginings about his sexuality had given him such pleasure at the time, but seeing her face when she had walked in on him and Suzanne had been even better. "Point taken. Do you want to talk about it?"

Lucy drained the last of her wine. As she put the glass on the table, Joe saw that her hand was trembling. "Nothing to talk about. We just decided we weren't right for each other."

"There's more. I know there is."

Lucy hugged her knees. She avoided Joe's eyes. "Always the detective, Joe; always over-analysing everything."

***

At first glance, Stephen thought Jimmy Spaz a little too refined, perhaps even effeminate, for auto theft. He was standing beside a row of garages, under the light of a street lamp, deep in the murky depths of the Hilton estate. He was smoking a cigar as Stephen and Davie Dobbs approached. In his 40s, tall and thin, with longish dark hair swept back from a handsome face, he didn't say a word, just ground his cigar underfoot, and turned.

He had a ragged scar twisting down one side of his face, from just below his eye to under his chin. It looked as if a drunken Fingers McCreadie had stitched the wound in the dark, using knitting needles and wire. And he had the coldest eyes that Stephen had ever seen. Silvery grey, large and piercing. He lifted the nearest garage door just enough for the three of them to slip inside. There was a small vehicle covered by a tarpaulin. Beside it, a Neanderthal the size of a mountain was perched on a stool beneath an angle-poise lamp reading *Harry Potter and the Deathly Hallows*. He looked up, put the book down. "Where's the notes?" he asked, in a Cockney accent.

Davie nudged Stephen. Stephen patted his jacket pockets, his jeans. Where were the notes? He'd brought them; he'd definitely brought them. Lifted them from the kitchen table before he came out, didn't he? Oh shit; he was turning into his mother. Stephen glanced at Davie; he looked fragile. It wasn't often anyone made Davie Dobbs uncomfortable, but Jimmy Spaz was in a league of his own.

"That guy, is he foreign?" Stephen asked Davie, as they walked down Oldtown Road ten minutes later. It was a cold night and Stephen's breath steamed out and dispersed in broken trails.

Davie shrugged. "London? Foreign enough for you? Gives me the creeps. Never speaks and no one knows much about him. Just appeared one day with his henchman. Two evil bastards, they say. Doesn't look foreign, though, does he?"

"Just wondered. Spaz – an unusual surname."

Davie's laughter startled a woman walking on the other side of the road with her dog. "It's not a fucking surname, ya spaz!"

"Ah," said Stephen. "Anyway, how surreal was that? Harry Potter meets Scarface, in a garage in Hilton."

"This muggle nearly shit himself when you couldn't

find the money."

"Muggle?"

"Never mind."

"I scared myself a bit. Forgot it was in my map pocket for safekeeping."

"Ooh, your map pocket. With your compass and your Kendall Mint Cake?"

Stephen was about to respond when he noticed three neds crossing over from the other side of the road. Two had hoods pulled up over peaked Burberry caps and joggers tucked into white socks. The third, in the middle, was taller, meaner, with a leather jacket, skinny jeans and a bottle of Buckfast. They stopped in front of Davie and Stephen, stretched across the pavement. The middle one passed the Buckie to his mate. "Got any fags?" he asked.

Davie laughed. "Do I look like a fag machine?"

"More like a fucking faggot, if you ask me. Out for a wee stroll with your bum chum."

On either side of him, his mates sniggered, nudged him, offered words of encouragement. Davie waited until they shut up, then he looked the guy up and down. "That's good coming from you, son. What's your sister wearing the night, since you've obviously picked her jeans up instead of your own? It's that shite." He nodded at the Buckfast. "Addles your brain. Now, why not be a good wee tranny, and get out of my way."

"Fucking tranny?" Skinny Jeans shouted. "Fucking tranny? You're fucking dead!"

The bottle was smashed against a wall, the jagged remains passed to Skinny Jeans. "Fucking get him!"

Davie's hand slipped into his pocket as Skinny Jeans approached, Buckfast dripping down his arm from the jagged bottle. Stephen saw a glint of metal in Davie's closed hand. Fuck's sake.

The bottle was a couple of inches from Davie's nose when the ned on the right grabbed his mate's arm. He was no longer sniggering, just staring at Davie. "Victor," he said, "that's Davie Dobbs."

Skinny Jeans, aka Victor, froze. "Davie Dobbs? Is he right? You Davie Dobbs?"

Davie stared at him. Said nothing. Took his empty hand from his pocket. Victor passed the bottle to the ned, wiped his hand on his jeans, offered it to Davie. "No offence, man."

"Get ta fuck!" Davie roared. They were gone.

While Stephen picked up the broken bottle and dropped it into a wheelie bin, Davie smiled, squared his shoulders and puffed out his chest. Just what he needed after the Spaz experience; he was still a force to be reckoned with.

When they reached the junction with Balloon Road, Davie nodded to the right. "Going to see a mate along in Morvich Way. Want to come for a toke?"

Stephen shook his head. "Going home to pack."

"Where you off to, like?"

Stephen shrugged. "Dunno. See how it goes tomorrow. I'll decide then." He reached into his pocket. "Here." He passed a small digital camera to Davie. "You won't mess up, will you?"

Davie rolled his eyes. "Does a squirrel love his nuts? It's the Dobbsmeister you're talking to, not Nancy Drew." He patted his pocket. "Got the key. Get the wheels at ten down the Carse. Then – "

"How do we know Jimmy Spaz will deliver? He's got my money. What if he doesn't turn up with the wheels?"

Davie patted Stephen on the shoulder. "Honour among thieves, my boy; there will be wheels."

Davie watched Stephen walk away. He was an odd one. He didn't like Davie; that much was clear. Not that Davie would lose any sleep over it. He wasn't sure any of his associates actually liked him, but he was damn sure they respected him. Not Stephen; he saw himself as a cut above everyone. And there was a certain refinement about him at times. Though he drank and cursed with the rest of them,

115

it didn't come naturally to him. And then there was the rage; fuck's sake, that rage. Didn't take much to spark it, a word or a look was enough, and you could see it burning in Stephen's dark eyes. Though Davie liked to press Stephen's buttons just to get him going, he wouldn't fancy being on the wrong side of that rage.

Ach, he thought, as Stephen disappeared round a corner, what the fuck? They came, they went, these people. He was nothing more than a means to an end to most of them, and that was fine by him. But what was Stephen's end? What was he up to? After the photos were taken tomorrow and the car was passed to Stephen, what then? Davie shrugged and turned away. Less he knew, the better.

Stephen hung up his jacket, then he leaned against the wall and slipped slowly down until he was sitting on the floor, his head in his hands. He glanced towards the dark stairs and shook his head. The spectre of last night's attack was waiting for him up there. It hadn't been a heart attack – he had researched it on the internet, and it was a classic panic attack. A panic attack? Surely they were only for wimps and women? Apparently not. It could come back any time, and the thought terrified him. He'd sleep on the settee.

As he lay fully-clothed on the settee, his eyes on the yellow sliver of moon that peeped through the gap in the curtains, Stephen thought about the life he should be living. A good job and a car, a home of his own, a wife and children. Worrying about the state of the economy, making up his mind about independence, moving to a good catchment area. Not creeping around in the gutter with freaks and scum.

Aye, and whose fault was it? Who put him there? Bastards. They took his life, the life that he should have had. They fucking took it. And they were going to pay.

***

Galbraith. He writes the name on a piece of paper over and over, pressing harder and harder until his pencil tears the paper. He whispers the name again and again. He doesn't like it. It's too posh, too different. And he doesn't like them, the Galbraiths, the Perfect Ones.

Mr Galbraith with his strong brown arms, always digging, digging, digging. Always planting and pruning and tidying, always building and painting, wiping away every trace of the old man that had lived and died next door. The garden was much better when the old man was there. The boy could hide in the long grass. He could follow the trails of voles and mice. He could watch his own house without being seen, watch until it was safe to go home.

And Mrs Galbraith with her jug of orange juice and her pink plastic tumblers. With her fancy wooden table at the back door and the fringed parasol that sprouts from a hole in the middle of the table. How often the boy has wished that the wind would catch that parasol and send it crashing through the Galbraith's kitchen window. But that would never happen, for Mr Galbraith is far too careful. The parasol lives in the painted shed. It only comes out when Mr Galbraith is certain that the conditions are just right, and it always returns to the shed at the end of the day.

The bikes are in the shed too, ready for the perfect children. The bikes and the swing ball. The small trampoline and the paddling pool. The go-kart and the plastic sledges. All ready to come out whenever the perfect children want them.

Freaks. That's what they are. No one in the village lives like them. So why are they not bullied and taunted? Why? Because perfect Mr Galbraith is a teacher at the secondary school in Tarbert.

He tears the paper to shreds, then he throws the bits up in the air and they fall around his bed like snow.

Chapter 10

The scent of lavender tickled Joe's nose. He opened his eyes and all he could see was flowers. The curtains, the bedding, the walls: flowers of all shapes and sizes. Matching colours, of course; shades of lilac and pink and white. Ghastly. He reached for his watch and knocked a bowl of pot-pourri from the bedside cabinet to the floor. It was only ten past six. Shit. Another couple of hours would be great, followed by a good breakfast. He hadn't had a decent sleep or a proper breakfast all week. He turned over and snuggled down.

No chance. Moira Jacobs was firmly in his head and she wasn't about to leave.

Joe left a note for his mother, thanking her for a lovely evening. It had been a lovely evening. Maybe, just maybe, he would consider bringing Carla next time. He must be going soft.

He spent a couple of hours going over Moira Jacobs' file. The medical records hadn't yielded much. Until the last year or two, she'd been a healthy individual. Hadn't even registered with a medical practice in the Western Isles. She'd been with a practice in Slough for three years, although there were few appointments, then a spell in Newcastle and another in Dumfries. In 2007, she had registered with a practice in Elgin. Visits to the doctor were rare until 2010, when her stomach started playing up. In 2012, she had moved to a practice in Inverness. Her stomach problems had intensified and her gall bladder was removed in Raigmore Hospital a few months later. Joe added the surgical ward to his list of things for Roberts to follow up next week.

DI Black wasn't quite ready to give up on James Clancy, he had told Joe the previous evening. Even if there was an explanation for Clancy's hairs on Moira Jacobs' carpet, he had said through gritted teeth, he wasn't convinced that Clancy wasn't there, or that he hadn't orchestrated the attack. He wasn't for accepting Joe's analysis that Clancy had not known how Moira Jacobs died, and that the hammer came as a complete shock. Even if Joe was right, the DI eventually conceded, it didn't mean Clancy didn't have something to do with it. Maybe he set it up, but hadn't wanted to know the details of the murder. The DI couldn't quite let go.

Joe sipped a cup of coffee as he looked over the report of the search of Clancy's house. Nothing of any significance. Like Moira Jacobs, there was no sign of a computer or a mobile phone. He went through Clancy's bank statements. Nothing out of the ordinary. Living on a modest pension from his days as a civil servant. No mortgage on the house; no large payments into or out of his account. As for the records of his telephone calls – he didn't have a wide circle of friends. Most of the calls in and out were to the same Aberdeen number, and mostly in the morning. He looked down the list of calls to Tuesday, the day Moira Jacobs was killed. He could hardly believe it – there was a call from James Clancy's home to the Aberdeen number lasting from quarter past nine in the morning to half past ten.

A woman answered the phone. She was either drunk or she had just woken up.

"My name's Detective Sergeant Galbraith of Northern Con . . . I mean, Police Scotland – Highland and Islands Division," Joe said. "Sorry to bother you, but I wonder if you know a James Clancy."

Joe had to hold the phone away from his ear until the woman stopped shrieking.

"Hello," he said, when her wail dropped to a whimper. "Are you there?"

"Yes," the shaky voice said. "I'm here. What's happened to him?"

"Nothing! I'm sorry; I didn't mean to startle you. He's fine. He's been helping us with . . . with something and I notice that your phone number comes up often on his itemised bill."

"Oh thank God. I'm a nurse, on night shift, so I was fast asleep when you phoned."

"I'm sorry. How do you know Mr Clancy?"

"He's my brother."

"And your name?"

"Mary Robertson. Is James in trouble?"

"I don't think so. I just wanted to ask you about a particular call. It was on Tuesday morning – do you remember if James called you then?"

"Tuesday? I definitely spoke to him earlier this week. He usually calls around nine or nine-thirty in the morning – he knows I go to bed shortly after that. Wait – I remember – I was on the phone to James when the window cleaner appeared at the window and gave me a terrible fright. James said my screeching nearly burst his eardrum. He's a terrible one for exaggerating, is James. Wait, I've got the window cleaner's receipt." Joe heard her rustling papers. "I always keep my receipts. Here it is – yes, it was Tuesday."

"Can you remember how he was that day?"

"Same as ever. Painful corns, the pitfalls of second-hand cars, the latest twist in Eastenders. Just the usual."

"It was a long call for that time of day."

She sighed. "Tell me about it. Sometimes I get into bed while he's talking and I start to fall asleep. Don't think he even notices. Poor James – doesn't have much of a life. Not since . . . well, I'm sure you know about his . . . his trouble."

"Aye. It can't have been easy for you, for the family."

"Well, it's just the two of us now. My man passed on

a few years ago, and there's no one else. Neither James nor I were blessed with a family of our own. He's my big brother, and it was such a shock. He was always so gentle. Devastated, he was when his wife left him for someone else, after years of marriage. Then he met that Moira, and she gave him such a hard time. It's no excuse, but she'd drive anyone to . . . well, maybe not to violence, but to drink or another woman. I really don't know what kept them together. She's such a dissatisfied, nagging type of woman. Still, I didn't expect that from him. I was glad she'd disappeared when he got out, even though she took so much from the house. It was for the best, really. I hope she's not terrorising another poor soul now."

Oh dear. Joe's ear was about to get another blast – he'd be ready for it this time. "You said Tuesday was the last time you spoke to James?"

"Aye, I'm off for the weekend now, so I'll be phoning him this evening."

"Is it unusual for you not to speak to each other for several days?"

"No, not at all."

"And you can't remember anything unusual about that call?"

"Not unless I fell asleep and missed something. Detective Sergeant, can I ask what you're investigating?"

Joe delivered the news and braced himself.

"Oh my God!" she cried. "My boss says I'll miss my own death notice, since I never buy a paper or watch the news. Oh James! Why did he not phone me and tell me? Ach, he's a kind soul, really; he wouldn't want to worry me. Oh dear, oh dear." She sniffed. "Poor Moira – I wouldn't have wished that on her. I feel so bad now for miscalling her."

"You weren't to know. When did you last see or hear from Moira?"

"Weeks before the . . . the incident with James. We didn't speak often. I tried calling after James was taken away, but she wouldn't speak to me. I just gave up. The next I knew was when James got out and told me she was gone. Oh dear, maybe if I had tried harder . . . maybe . . . "

"You couldn't have done anything," he cut in. "Do you know anyone who might have wanted to harm her?"

There was another wail. "No, but it wasn't him! Not James! No, he wouldn't do that. Has he been charged?"

"No. Just helping us out. Do you know if he made any particular friends or acquaintances when he was in prison?"

There was no one, Mary Robertson told him. James took nothing to do with the others. He got a black eye once from another prisoner – something to do with biscuits or milk. Something silly. After that, he had tried to keep his head down.

Surely the DI would see sense now, Joe thought, when he came off the phone. Clancy was so stupid and so innocent, he hadn't even remembered that he had an alibi.

***

Stephen held his mother's coat close and breathed in the faint scent of the perfume that she used to wear. He remembered their last day out together before Betty was hospitalised. They'd gone to Strathpeffer, and Betty had loved the Victorian buildings. They'd eaten in the café at the old railway station, before exploring the shops. It had been such a nice day, the only downside Stephen's recognition that his mother's mental health was declining again. She'd greeted strangers as if they were old friends, her conversation rambling and far too personal. She laughed when an old man tripped and hurt his knee, and she cried leaving the café. He had known, as he drove her home, that it wouldn't be long before she was back in New Craigs. And it wasn't.

As Stephen turned to leave Betty's room, he noticed the Kirkcaldy book on her bedside cabinet. He'd bought if for her for Christmas. There was a newspaper cutting marking her place. Would she notice if he moved it?

Probably would – just when he least expected it, her mind was sharper than his. He looked again at the cutting, then he edged it out a bit.

"Stephen," his mother said from the door, "what are you doing to my book?"

"Just looking. I'm glad you're reading it."

"It was a good present, son; I like the pictures. Station Hotel's in there; that's where I used to work."

"Turn around and I'll help you with your coat." When his mother turned, Stephen pulled the cutting from the book and shoved it in his pocket.

New Craigs was situated on a hill high above Inverness. Behind the ward, they sat on a bench and looked out past the football pitch and over the town. Betty pointed out the rounded tree-covered Tomnahurich Hill. She told Stephen the tale of a fiddler that fell asleep on the side of hill. When he awoke, he found himself in a fairy palace. He played all night for the fairies, emerging to find that a hundred years or more had passed in his own world.

"Imagine," she said, her eyes alight. "A fairy palace. Jean said there was no such thing as fairies, but I knew. I heard them. I saw them! Well, I saw their wings among the dandelions. Weren't going to risk coming anywhere near Jean's muckle great feet, were they? Maybe you'll take me there, Stephen, when you get the time. Maybe we'll fall asleep on the side of the hill, leave all this behind."

"Sounds good. Are you glad you moved to Inverness?"

"Moved? Don't be silly; I'm just here on holiday. I always wanted to come back. We had a holiday here with Uncle Bert and Auntie Alice when we were kids. We hardly ever got holidays – farmers don't take holidays, my dad would say. Anyway, we came here and I loved it." She shook her head. "Ach, it could have been anywhere, really, but I always liked Inverness. It's kind of you to pay my hotel bill. Food's quite good and the staff are nice. I ordered tea for when we get back."

Stephen smiled. Inverness had seemed so exciting as a

child. They had come over from the island occasionally to meet Jean and Colin. When they moved to the town, Stephen had gone looking for their old haunts. The cinema and the swimming pool were gone. There was a cinema complex out at the retail park, and a new pool with flumes and waves, geysers and bubble jets. If it wasn't for Tomnahurich Hill, they would be able to see it from where they sat.

"Oh." Betty shook her head. "Oh, Stephen, you're right; I did move to Inverness, I think." She looked perplexed, her thin hands shaking in her lap. "Did I do the right thing? That was a nice flat in Glasgow. Maybe I should have stayed there."

They had moved to the south side of Glasgow from Harris, and Stephen had never liked it. He'd always felt a vague sense of menace in the air. "You did the right thing," he assured her. "It's much nicer here." His thoughts were racing. So many questions for her, so much he needed to know, but he had to be careful. She was in good form and he didn't want to spoil that.

"Son," she said, "do you remember when she took you away?"

Bloody hell. Maybe she was stealing his thoughts. The idea made him shiver. Wouldn't want his mother inside his head right now. "Aye, Mum; I do, as if it was yesterday."

"Remember the wind?"

He nodded and frowned. It had been such a dark day. There were rocks on the road, thrown up by the churning sea as it raged against the land. And white foaming spume, lifted from the top of the waves and scattered for miles. And he had been taken.

"Jean was there. She could have stopped it."

"Why didn't she? Why couldn't I have gone to stay with her?"

"I don't know. Maybe it was him, Colin; maybe he wouldn't let her."

Result. "What did you think of Colin, Mum?"

Betty shrugged. "Queer sort of bloke. Good with kids, I can't deny that, but he wasn't my cup of tea. Too soft – never stood up to Jean."

"You weren't close to him?"

Betty giggled, and Stephen's heart thumped. Did he really want to know? She giggled again.

"Mum?"

She looked around, as if Colin or Jean might be hiding behind the bench. She leaned towards Stephen. "No, I wasn't close to him," she whispered. "But I said I was, just to annoy them all."

Stephen forced a little laugh. He tried to keep his voice light, conspiratorial. "Who did you say that to?"

Betty started to count on her fingers. "One – her that lived next door – can't remember her name. Two – her . . ." Betty's face was suddenly distorted, as if someone had shoved a pile of shit under her nose. "Her . . . her man." She spat the last word out.

Stephen's mouth was dry. "And what did he say?"

"Called me a tart." Her tone had changed, the humour gone. "Then I told Jean – stuck-up cow – didn't half bring her down a peg or two. That'll teach her not to help her family. Poor Colin; how he protested his innocence, but she was having none of it. She probably never forgave him. We'd always had a giggle behind her back, Colin and I; it was easy to make her believe it was something more."

"So it wasn't true – you weren't close to Colin, not like that?"

She shook her head. "Wouldn't have touched him with a barge-pole."

A hundred questions raced through Stephen's head. Why had she told such a devastating lie? Why had Jean believed it? Why had his mother not brought this up before? Why? Why? Why? He wanted to stand, but he felt as if his legs might give way.

"Will we go in?" Betty asked. "It's cold when you sit too long."

Stephen forced himself to his feet and found that his legs held him up after all. Betty stayed where she was. She looked up at Stephen, her eyes shiny. "Why, Stephen? Why did they do it?"

"Forget them, Mum. We're all right as we are – we don't need them. Come on – the tea will be ready. We don't want it to get cold." He held out his arm and she took it.

There was something in Janey's eyes that Stephen didn't often see. It was beyond kindness; it was an understanding, a respectful realisation that anyone might one day sit where Betty sat, believing she was on holiday, the hospital a hotel, and everyone else there to wait upon her. And Janey waited upon her so well, taking her hat and coat, bringing tea and cakes, smiling, her eyes shining with that thing that Stephen wished he could feel.

"I used to work in a hotel," Betty told Janey. "Station Hotel in Kirkcaldy. Did I ever tell you that, Stephen?

Stephen sighed, then forced a smile. "No, Mum."

"Aye, a bit more upmarket than this place. Not that I'm complaining, Stephen; I wouldn't want you wasting your money. This place will do me fine for now. I wore a uniform, you know. Not like you lot nowadays."

"Don't get me started on uniforms," Janey said. "I better go – others to see to."

"Give her a tip, son. She won't be earning much."

Stephen smiled at Janey. "I'll see to it on my way out." Janey gave a mock curtsey and left.

"I used to get tips," Betty said. "Spent them at the cinema – me and the girls, after work. Dad didn't want me to go out in the town – thought I would come to no good. He didn't even want me to work in a hotel, but Mum persuaded him, said I wouldn't come to any harm in the hotel or the cinema. Little did she know about me and Robert Banks in the back row." She giggled and sipped her tea.

"You had a cinema in Kirkcaldy in those days?"

126

Stephen said, though he knew the name and description of every cinema in the town, and every last film she saw there.

"Cinema?" Betty snatched a cup cake from the plate. "We had the Rio, the Raith, the Carlton. Oh, the fun we had. Did I tell you about – ?"

Aye, Stephen thought, you told me, but he let her tell him again.

When she finished talking about the cinemas, Betty yawned. "You better go, son," she said. "Unless you want to get a room here?"

"No, Mum; I've a lot to do. Listen Mum, I might . . . I might have to go away for a while. It's . . . to do with work. I'm not sure how long I'll be gone."

Betty nodded. "I understand, son. That's the price you have to pay when you get to the top."

Stephen held her tight, too tight, then he left.

Outside, Stephen leaned against the wall. His head had been a mess before he came up, but now it was all over the place. Jean, Colin, his mother . . . they were all dancing round in his imagination, weaving in and out of each other in grotesque formations. He shook his head, tried to clear it. His phone rang. It was Davie.

"Dobbsie," Stephen said. "How's it going?"

"Never mind Dobbsie. Thinking of changing my surname to Bailey."

Tosser. "What you talking about?"

"Duh – the photographer."

"You being discreet?"

"Do vacuum cleaners suck? Got the wheels. Got loads of pictures. Meet you at Charleston, at the school, in ten minutes. You can drop me off in town, then it's all yours. And guess what? There's a bird too – twenty-something and very tasty."

And then Stephen's head was clear. She was here. She was here!

127

Chapter 11

Fiona Galbraith could stop traffic with one raised eyebrow. Both perfect eyebrows were raised now. "Is that why he moved to Nairn? To be near this Carla?"

"I don't think so," Lucy replied. "They've only been going out a couple of months."

"He hasn't mentioned her, but then . . . " Fiona looked hurt as she stared into her empty coffee cup.

"He's only just told me. I had to drag it out of him." Not strictly true, but necessary. Joe had mentioned Carla in an email before he'd asked her out. He was nervous about it; punching above his weight, he'd said.

"So you haven't met her?"

"Hardly. I would have told you."

"Well, I'm glad one of my children confides in me."

"Wait until he needs help with the grandchildren," Raymond said. "It'll be a different story then."

Fiona shuddered. "Is that supposed to make me feel better?"

Raymond laughed and lifted the car keys from the table. They had just finished lunch in the Floral Hall café "Ready?"

"Does anyone fancy a walk?" Lucy asked. "I haven't been to the Islands for ages."

All eyes were on Fiona, the decision maker. She smiled. "Why not?"

The Ness Islands were linked to each other and to both sides of the River Ness by a series of pedestrian bridges. As they walked through the forested pathways,

Raymond had so much to tell them. He pointed out different shrubs and trees, some imported, some native. He told them that one of the original chain suspension bridges had been washed away in the flood of 1849. "They didn't maintain it properly," he said. "Great shame."

They sat on a carved wooden bench and watched five ducklings take to the river with their mother. The water shimmered around their tiny forms as they bobbed and paddled. A slender branch dipped down close to the water, and the ducklings took turns reaching for the small green leaves, tentative at first, then bolder, until they were stretching right out of the water to grasp their target. The mother duck moved away and the branch was forgotten, five pairs of little legs paddling to catch up.

"What's the collective noun for ducks?" Lucy asked her father.

"Depends where they are. That is a raft of ducks. In the air, they would be a flight. On the ground, a badelynge."

"You made that last one up."

"I certainly did not, and I shall prove it when we get home."

"No need to wait until then." Lucy's phone was out of her pocket. A few twiddles and taps of her thumbs, while Raymond and Fiona looked on in wonder. Lucy grimaced. "Damn. You're right. You're always right."

Raymond had been a history and modern studies teacher. He was a wealth of information on everything from the Picts to the Patagonian economy.

"Dad," Lucy said, taking his arm, "how do you remember all these things?"

Raymond shrugged. "They just stick in my head, but only if they're interesting."

"Fascinating," Fiona said, taking his other arm.

"Are you making fun of me?" he asked.

As they returned across the last suspension bridge, Raymond suggested they take a short-cut past the Archive Centre. Opened in 2009, it was a remarkable place, he said.

They had burgh records going back to the fifteenth century. Behind his back, Fiona shook her head. Lucy smiled.

"Come on," Raymond said. "It'll not be open today, but there's a sign with the opening hours. I really must make time to go there again soon."

Fiona didn't hear the car; she was examining the sole of her shoe with suspicion. Mud? No. She turned from the road and began to scrape her shoe on the grass. Disgusting. She'd forgotten why she didn't like walking or dogs. Irresponsible owners – they should be shot. She turned back just as Lucy screamed.

***

Joe was updating the whiteboard with the details of places Moira Jacobs had lived when he got the call. Lucy was hysterical. Something about Dad, something about a car that hadn't stopped, something about the Bught. He heard the siren of an ambulance in the background.

Lucy was in the waiting area at Accident and Emergency, shivering and tiny. Her smeared mascara and pale face reminded Joe of her Goth phase, when she was fifteen, and came to see him and Matt in Perth. Joe's friend had tried really hard not to laugh. Matt would have hated to hurt Lucy's feelings, but she had looked so funny in her long leather coat and Docs, her skinny legs in fishnet tights, and a huge studded dog-collar around her neck. She was going to get her hair bleached that weekend, she told them, and a black stripe down the middle. Much as Joe enjoyed annoying his mother, he knew that, if he didn't talk her out of it, Lucy would never be allowed to visit him again. Somehow, he couldn't quite remember how, either he or Matt had changed her mind. The Goth phase hadn't lasted long.

Now, Joe held her tight. He couldn't bear to ask the words, to hear the answer. When she pulled away from him, he tried so hard to keep his face composed.

"Mum's with the police," she said, as Joe wiped the mascara from her cheeks.

He nodded. Still couldn't ask.

"And Dad's being examined."

The relief.

"He was conscious in the ambulance, but he looked awful. He was in such pain. Joe, how could someone do this and not stop?"

He was alive, and Joe could breathe. "Listen," he said, "the more you can remember now, the greater chance there is of catching whoever did this. Did you see the car?"

"It all happened so fast. One minute, Mum was complaining about dog shit on her shoe. Dad started to cross the road and I turned to wait for Mum. I heard the car, but I didn't see it coming. I just heard a . . . a thump, a sort of crunch, and Dad . . . " She hugged herself and rocked a little. "He made a noise; not a scream, just a cry. By the time I turned, he was lying twisted in the road."

"And the car?"

"I don't . . . I didn't look up until it was nearly at the corner."

"And what did you see?"

"It was so fast. Silver, I think, but I don't know the make. Just a fast, silver car, and then it was gone, and Dad was moaning and Mum was screaming."

"You didn't see who was in the car?"

Lucy shook her head. "Joe," she said, "do you think you could just be my brother for now?"

It was a silver car. Fiona saw it too. She had looked up, but it was too far away to see the number plate. It looked quite small, insignificant. She felt bad; if she hadn't been examining her shoe, maybe she'd have seen it, maybe she could have pulled Raymond out of the way. But wait; if Raymond wasn't such a damn geek, and if he hadn't wanted to go by the Archive Centre, which was actually closed at the time, and if he'd been more careful when crossing the road, everything might have been all right. Joe felt angry with her then, but he didn't show it. It was just her way of coping, but she could be so hard. She went to get a cup of tea, and Joe and Lucy went to see their father.

Raymond looked awful. Was it really just a broken leg, and a few cuts and bruises? He assured them it was. "I feel a right idiot," he said. "Shouldn't have been standing in the road. Are you all right, love? Is your mum okay?"

Lucy sat on the bed and took his hand. "Never mind us, Dad. We weren't hit by that cowardly little bastard. Why didn't he stop?"

Raymond smiled and squeezed Lucy's hand. "Scared, probably. Maybe just a boy. He might turn himself in yet."

"If he does, I hope . . . I hope Joe beats him up in the cells. I hope he breaks every bone in his body."

Raymond laughed. "Just as well you'll both be over in Harris soon."

Lucy shook her head. "I can't go now. I'm not leaving you."

"I'm getting home tomorrow. Mum and I will manage. It'll be good for you to go."

Lucy looked doubtful. "We'll see."

A frowning nurse came and told them it was time to go; Raymond needed rest. As they left, Raymond asked to speak to Joe alone. Lucy looked worried, but she left them to it. Raymond's hurried request was no surprise to Joe; he'd been expecting it ever since he'd mentioned the trip to Harris.

Joe stayed in Inverness again that night. He'd have loved to go home, to spend the evening on his own, to spend all of Sunday the fourteenth of April on his own, but he couldn't leave Lucy and Fiona. They got a takeaway and watched a bad film. Well, Lucy and Joe watched. Fiona just sat and stared into space. Around midnight, one of Joe's colleagues phoned. A damaged silver car with false number-plates had been found in a parking space at the old Craig Dunain hospital, just a mile and a half from where Raymond had been hit. The former psychiatric hospital, built in the mid-nineteenth century, had been closed for years, and the buildings were being converted to flats. A car of the same description had been reported stolen earlier that week in Kirkhill, a few miles outside Inverness. The owner was an elderly lady who had kept it spotless and unlocked, the keys always in the ignition.

"How do you know it's the car?" Joe asked.

There was a silence. It wasn't so easy giving this kind of information to one of your own. "Eh . . . your father's prints are on the bonnet."

Joe dreamed of Matt. They were sitting at the top of Birnam Hill and Matt was scratching diagrams into the earth, trying to explain the off-side rule. Joe was no more interested in football in his dreams than he was when awake, but he indulged Matt, paying attention to his friend and nodding from time to time. When Matt was certain Joe had it, they both stood. Only then did Joe look at the view. It wasn't Perthshire; there were no forests, no snaking rivers, no rolling green hills. Just scorched brown earth and a scattered village, a grey sea and black jagged rocks. It was Harris. He was on top of Ceapabhal. And beside him, Matt was fading.

"No," he shouted, making a grab for his friend's arm. His fingers slipped through Matt. He was just a grey shadow. And then there were hundreds of grey shadows before Joe. He turned to run, but he was surrounded. Faceless and cold, they closed in on him, the spirits of the restless dead.

***

Are Sundays worse or better than school days? He's not sure. His mother's often sick on a Sunday morning. Sometimes, while she's retching in the bathroom, there's loud snoring coming from her bedroom. He doesn't like that, doesn't want to see who's in there. Today, the snoring sounds like a pig, so he dresses quickly, takes the stairs three at a time, grabs a slice of bread and two biscuits, runs out the door.

From behind the byre, he watches the villagers come from their houses, a steady flow of gloom. The men first in their black hats, black suits, black coats. They start the cars and then the women and children come. The boys look so funny with their blazers and their hair combed flat, their steps slow and their eyes down, the girls and the women with their heavy dark coats and silly hats. Though he hates the wind, he often hopes for a strong gust on a Sunday morning, and a hat or two blown over the rooftops and into the ditch. Not today. There's a breeze, but it's not a hat-lifter.

And then the village is as quiet as a ghost town. It'll be like that all day, even after the villagers return from church. He won't go home yet, for the pig might still be there. If his mother likes this one, the man will soon be sitting at the kitchen table tucking into a fried breakfast, in the hope that it'll bring him back with his carry-out another night.

At the end of the village, before the gated track that leads to the hill, there's a track down to a small curved beach. He likes to go there on a Sunday when there's no danger of the boys being there, when there's no one to hold his head under the churning waves, no one to laugh while the sea and sand pours up his nose.

On the beach, he searches for the right stones, weighs them in his palm. Too light and the breeze will catch them, too heavy and they won't bounce. The sea is calm today, perfect for skimming. And he's away. No one can beat him. No one can come close. Champion of the village. Champion of Harris. Champion of the world!

He's watching his third stone bounce once, twice, three times. It's going to be the best. Four, five. The very best. Voices. He turns away from the shore. Damn. The stone was going as far as Uist, he knows it was, but he's missed it.

It's the Perfect Ones, all four of them. Squealing little daughter; clean bright son; sober pretty mummy; smiling teacher daddy. He doesn't know which is worse, the Perfect Ones or the bullies. For in their own way, they all rub his nose in the sad loneliness of his life.

134

Chapter 12

It wasn't much of a birthday. They hadn't forgotten Lucy; Joe gave her a beautiful necklace from The Jail in Dornoch, and her parents gave her money and a Karen Millen jacket she'd been fancying for ages. She had cards and presents from her friends in Edinburgh, and there was a never-ending stream of texts to her phone. Still, it was such a dull, long morning, just waiting. Lucy was on egg-shells, tiptoeing around Fiona, with her short temper and massive bags under her eyes.

Joe kept out of the way. He was exhausted; hadn't got back to sleep after the dream. He was desperate to be gone, to get back to work, anything to take his mind off his father, off Matt. But he wanted to collect Raymond from the hospital, see that he was all right. He spent half the morning pacing in the garden, trying to find some weeds or a ragged bush that needed trimming. There was nothing to be done; Raymond had it all under control.

Just before lunch, Joe got the call to collect his father. Raymond still looked awful, but he was in better form than Fiona, who had tidied away her ornaments and half the furniture. There had been endless questions. How was he going to get around the house? How would he manage to the toilet? Would he scratch the skirting boards with his crutches? Joe left them to it. He spent a few hours at the station, achieving little, then he went home to pack.

He didn't get far. Went to the attic to get his suitcase and he found Matt's box. As he picked it up and brushed away the dust, his fingers remembered every knot in the

135

wood, every crack in the grain. The box would outlive Joe, its design and construction perfect, the work of a true master, top of the class. Joe smiled as he remembered Matt's surprise and his pride. He was the only one in their class that hadn't recognised his own genius. The packing forgotten, Joe took the box downstairs and opened it in the living room. He lifted out a crumpled Rangers top, a stack of photos, a mug and a mouth organ, and then the doorbell rang.

Even the distorted glass door panel couldn't make Carla look unattractive. Joe hadn't spoken to her for a couple of days, hadn't told her about his father's accident. No doubt someone else had done that for him. Carla rang the bell again.

It wasn't that he didn't want to see her. Even now, even though he didn't know when he had last felt so low, he couldn't stop the butterflies in his tummy. He just didn't want her to see him like this. She rang the bell a third time. He took a deep breath, fixed on a smile, and answered the door.

Carla had been out for a run, and she'd just stopped off to ask after his father, to see if he needed anything. And though Joe had thought before she came to his door that he needed nothing and no one, he found that he actually needed her very much.

Joe made coffee, then he followed Carla into the living room. She glanced at the box, at the ragged pile on the floor, and said nothing. He knew he didn't have to say anything either; he didn't have to explain. But maybe it was time.

The Rangers top he and his friends had given Matt on his eighteenth birthday; it was faded and thin, the seams strained by almost constant wearing and washing. The 'Sexy Lover' mug Matt had got from Christina in the chip shop, his first conquest. It had pride of place on the fireplace of Matt and Joe's wee flat in Perth, long after Christina dumped Matt for a brickie from Buckie. A Celtic supporting brickie from Buckie – oh, the shame. Despite her act of betrayal, no one was allowed to touch Christina's mug. Joe had felt a sense of duty towards the mug whenever Matt was out and the boys were in. He was too late to stop Colin Watson peeing in it the night Robby Brown fell asleep in the toilet and no one could get in. The mug had scrubbed up all right that time, but it was beyond repair when Lucy knocked it off the fireplace one Sunday night as she demonstrated her latest judo move to Joe. Matt returned from his granny's and wondered why Lucy was standing in front of the fire, why she wouldn't sit down. She was there in the morning when he got up. As soon as he was gone, she'd hit the shops. Found the mug on special offer, so she bought two, just in case. Carla laughed as Joe pulled an identical mug from the box.

The mouth organ that had terrorised Joe and the neighbours for weeks. Musical, Matt was not, but he persevered until the night the man from upstairs cornered him in the common stair. There were no threats; everyone liked Matt too much for that. Just a sob story about the neighbour's early starts, and the promise of a few pints. Matt couldn't resist a sob story, and he was getting fed up with his lack of progress anyway.

And the photos of Joe and Matt's first holiday abroad – a trip to Magaluf. On the third night, Matt had sloped off from the night club with a girl from Swansea, leaving Joe to make his own way back to their apartment, where he'd enjoyed a great sleep without Matt's snoring. Returning to the apartment in the morning, Matt had gone for a shower. As he stepped out of the shower and reached for the towel, in a bathroom that looked much tidier than the one he'd left the previous night, a sleepy young lady came into the bathroom and screamed. Thinking Joe had got very lucky last night, Matt smiled and covered himself up. Leaving the bathroom, he met another two young ladies in the kitchen area. They screamed. Guessing that Joe probably wasn't that lucky, Matt realised: he had stopped off a floor too soon; he was in the apartment below.

It was left to Joe to return the towel and retrieve

Matt's clothes later that day. It wasn't easy trying to tell three German girls with very poor English why his friend had been naked in their apartment. Terrified that he would be arrested, Matt had refused to go out, sending Joe on regular forays for food, drink and surveillance of the apartment below. Two days later, Joe saw the German girls leaving with their suitcases. While Matt had been in hiding, Joe had met a lovely girl from Yorkshire, on holiday with her parents. He considered not letting on to Matt that the Germans were gone, but that would be too cruel, particularly as they only had two more days in the sun.

Matt was dead, Joe told Carla, just in case she hadn't already worked that one out. He'd died nine years ago today, on Lucy's sixteenth birthday. Joe still felt responsible. If only he'd stayed in Perth that weekend, instead of going to Melrose for Lucy's party. If only he'd been there when Matt walked home from the pub, and two doped-up crack-heads stopped him and asked for his money. He'd have laughed, Matt. Money? Didn't have a penny on him. He'd given the last of it to two girls in the taxi queue. Hadn't even known them, but he'd stopped to talk, felt sorry for them when he heard that one of them had lost her purse, that they'd no money to get home. The girls had come forward when they read about Matt's stabbing. The irony was, if he'd only met the neds first, Matt would have given them his money without any threats. It was just his way.

If it hadn't happened, Joe told Carla, he'd probably still be a joiner in Perth. He'd enjoyed his trade, never thought of joining the police until after Matt's murder. He'd got to know a couple of the policemen who were involved in the investigation. He used to see them in the pub after the trial, and it was one of them that suggested a career in the police, and, by the way, Northern Constabulary was currently recruiting. By then, Joe hated Perth and he hated his life. He hated his mother too, but he kept that from Carla.

Fiona Galbraith hadn't wanted Matt at Lucy's sixteenth birthday party. She suspected that Lucy fancied Matt. Why else would a fifteen year old girl want to spend her weekends at that disgusting flat in Perth? No, she wasn't going to encourage Matt by inviting him to the party. Joe wasn't that bothered. He told Matt it was a family party, that he didn't really want to go either. Wouldn't be much fun. And Matt thought nothing of it. It was only afterwards, in Joe's muddled, grief-stricken head, that Fiona began to share the blame.

Carla listened. The only observation she made was to mention, with a smile, that she'd wondered about the photograph in Joe's wallet. She didn't tell Joe what he already knew. She didn't say that it wasn't his fault, that there was nothing he could have done about it, that there was no point in going over and over it and beating himself up. She didn't say any of that. She just listened. If she noticed the shadow of tears in Joe's eyes, she said nothing.

And later, when the packing was done, and Carla's breathing had settled into sleep, Joe stared at the ceiling and smiled; it was safe to remember.

***

Stephen's head was sore and heavy. It was the smell of the ink in the small unventilated room, as he churned out print after print. He couldn't stop. He knew that he should leave now. It was only a matter of time before they came for him. Maybe if he hadn't started all this. Maybe if he'd put his hatred aside and gone south. He could have come up from time to time to visit his mother.

He looked at the small photo in a frame on the corner of his desk. Him and his mum on the esplanade at Kirkcaldy, leaning against the sea wall, eating ice-cream. The memory always made him laugh. Two seconds later and the picture could have been so different. They hadn't noticed that the tide was in, covering the grey sand and lapping at the sea wall. Just as Jean lowered the camera, a sheet of seawater came over the wall and soaked Stephen and his mum. How they had all laughed. Why hadn't they just moved from the island then? They could have settled in Kirkcaldy, close to Jean and Colin. His mother was a different person when they were off the island. What made her keep going back? But Stephen knew. He had the old photos spread out on the desk. All he had to do was look down at them, and he knew.

As he turned to leave the room, Moira Jacobs caught his eye. There were several pictures of her on his wall, but the one that stood out was the greedy cow clutching a lottery ticket as she left the Co-op on Church Street. He still couldn't quite believe that she had just turned up like that; hadn't even had to pay Nisbet to find her. It was just meant to be.

He smiled at Moira and went downstairs. The keys for the garage and his mother's car were hanging on a small wooden key rack beside the back door. *Home Sweet Home*, it said on the top of the key rack in coloured lettering that had faded over the years. Stephen remembered getting the bus by himself to Tarbert to find a birthday present for his mother. It was a choice between the key rack and a tea cosy, but he thought Betty had a tea cosy somewhere in a drawer. So he chose the key rack, and she had loved it, treasured it, even if their home and their life in Harris turned anything but sweet. The key rack had gone up in every home since then. The rack wobbled as Stephen removed the keys, then he opened the back door.

Stephen had made a SORN declaration to take the car off the road while his mother was in hospital. Must be six months or more since it was last driven. To his surprise, the car started first time. His body tired and aching, Stephen closed his eyes and reclined the seat. As he listened to the sound of the engine, he wondered if the lightness in his head was down to lack of sleep. If it wasn't panic that kept him awake, it was racing thoughts, compulsive thoughts, intrusive thoughts. So often recently, he seemed to have no control over his head, especially in the darkness of the night. Was he taking after his mother? Was it hereditary? Had his card been marked before birth? Maybe there was nothing he could have done about any of it. Maybe none of it was his fault.

He felt his mind start to calm, his body relax. He could just sit here, stay like this, with the engine running. Let it all be over. What a beautiful peaceful thought, the first peaceful thought in months. So tempting . . .

Nah. He wasn't ready for that. He sat up and turned off the engine. First thing tomorrow, he was going down to the station to get a ticket to London. Time to get out of here.

***

He usually pays for his Sundays. Someone always sees him, though he tries to sneak home. He'll get it on Monday. Maybe not on the school bus, when Duncan the driver is watching in his mirror, but they'll get him in the playground, or later, in the village.

'Heathen', 'Catholic', 'Jew'. The words they hiss mean nothing to him. He wants to ask his mother about the words, but he's not risking another drunken trip on the school bus, another rant at the teacher.

One Monday afternoon, when he jumps off the school bus and runs, they run too. Surrounded by the pack as they make their way down the village road, he's jostled back and forth between them, pushed by this one, shoved by that one, kicked by the smallest, punched by the biggest. One day, he tells himself, as blood runs from his nose and drips on his grey jumper. One day, he'll get them back.

A shout from behind stops the bullies. As he holds his head back and pinches the top of his nose, the others start to scatter.

"Touch him again and you're dead," a voice shouts.

And that is the end of the beatings. And though he can now walk through the village or on the beach without being attacked, and though he'll never again have to hide his bloody clothes from his mother, how he wishes it hadn't been the Galbraith boy that stopped it.

141

Chapter 13

Scullamus and Strollamus, Mol, Luib, the Quirang, the Old Man of Storr: Skye was a magical island. As they drove in the shadow of shimmering, jagged mountains, Lucy felt as if she was in a Tolkien novel, journeying to Middle Earth. It was just what she needed. For the first time in months, she felt at peace.

The decision to go with Joe hadn't been easy. "You're best out of there," her brother had said. "It'll be a minefield for a day or two. By the time you come back, she'll have settled down." Their mother did not adapt well to change, and the more people she had around her at times of stress, the more difficult she was likely to become.

"Harris?" her mother had said when Lucy finally found the courage to mention the trip. "Why on earth would you want to go to that place?"

"The forecast's good, and I'd like to spend time with Joe."

Her mother was quiet, clearly pissed off that Lucy wanted to spend time with Joe, but relieved at the thought of getting her out of the way until things had settled down. Lucy had waited to see which would get the upper hand. At last her mother had smiled and nodded. "That'll be nice for you both," she had said. "But Harris? Yugh."

Joe had feared a rough crossing, so he was relieved to see the ferry approaching Uig on a calm sea. He loved sailing; there was nothing else that gave him the same sense of freedom, the feeling of being so completely alive. He'd been out in some wild conditions, yet he had never suffered seasickness on a yacht or a dinghy. So why did the thought of a ferry journey have him almost throwing up? He was certain that the memory of childhood seasickness was planted deep in his brain, and the slightest movement of the boat was going to resurrect it. Seasickness was not the only unpleasant childhood memory that had surfaced in recent days, but Joe was managing to keep the others at bay. For now.

In the ticket office, while Joe queued, Lucy browsed the leaflets. She chose one with a map of Harris in the centre, surrounded by stunning beaches with golden sand. As she put it in her pocket and made for the toilet, she felt a tug on her jacket. She turned, expecting to see Joe. Instead, the shoogly rack of leaflets, firmly attached to the cord of her jacket, clattered to the floor. The leaflets went everywhere, assisted by the breeze blowing through the open door. Lucy couldn't go after them without dragging the rack with her. At the top of the queue, Joe turned and shook his head, mouthing something that looked very like 'what the fuck?' Didn't come to help her though, did he? Lucy grabbed the cord of her jacket and tugged. It wasn't giving up the rack that easily. She pulled the jacket off and crouched on the floor among the leaflets.

"Can I help?" a male voice asked.

About time, she thought, looking up. Shit. No. She'd hoped for a kindly old man, or a teenager, not a frigging sex god. She considered telling him she didn't need his help, but that would just be silly. Without someone's assistance, she was either going on holiday without a jacket or with a leaflet rack. She smiled, her face red, and let him help. In seconds, her jacket was free, the leaflets were gathered up, and the rack was upright. And Joe was still at the top of the queue.

Lucy forgot about the toilet and headed back to the safety of the car, fanning her glowing face with the leaflet as she weaved her way between motor-homes and very

143

long vehicles. Joe wasn't far behind. He was smirking as he got into the car. "You couldn't think of a more subtle way to attract his attention?"

"You know me," she replied. "If it's worth doing . . . and he was definitely worth doing."

"Better watch himself. I'm not having any old skank chatting up my wee sister."

"Skank? Get with it, Joe. A skank is a lower-class female, usually dirty, sometimes promiscuous, often ugly and always tacky. I think we can rule him out on most of those criteria, although I expect that, with looks like his, he may occasionally be forced into promiscuity. Anyway, there wasn't much chatting up going on." She couldn't even remember if she'd thanked him. "And since when did you have a say in matters of my heart? I haven't even met Carla. What if I don't approve?"

"How could you not? She's a police officer."

Lucy raised her eyebrows. "Birmingham Six, Guildford Four, Maguire Seven, PC Simon Slimeball Reid. Need I say any more?"

Joe had to concede that his sister had a point, at least about Constable Simon Reid. The Christmas before last, at a party in Inverness, Simon Reid had made a play for Lucy. Phone numbers were exchanged. There might even have been a kiss behind the pub, although Lucy was admitting nothing, except that she was looking forward to a date before New Year. It was Roberts who broke the news to Joe the following Monday; Simon Reid had been engaged for two years; he was getting married in March. Roberts had offered his services, just to ensure that Lucy wasn't too disappointed. One look from Joe and he didn't push it.

***

The MV *Hebrides* left Uig on a sparkling sea, a deep churning furrow in its wake. Lucy stood at the railings at the back of the boat and watched as the white houses that clung to the green slopes around Uig Bay diminished. Was the magic over? Gazing to the north-west, where the distant hills of Harris loomed out of the sea, Lucy hoped not. She'd felt so good today. Even the ticket office incident made her laugh now. She needed laughter. The Banishment of Sebastian Moore would be so much easier if there was laughter. Lucy zipped up her jacket and leaned against the railing. She loved the gentle motion of the boat and the feeling of the wind in her hair. Didn't know how she'd look by the time they arrived; she didn't really care.

Joe had refused to come outside. He was lying down in the lounge and he wasn't going to move from there until they reached Tarbert. "You've got to be kidding me," Lucy had said. "You're not coming out on deck? But you love sailing; you sailed to Orkney last month."

"It's not the same."

"It's a boat, on the sea. How can it not be the same?"

"You wouldn't understand." He had found himself a seat in the corner. Lucy looked at the row of small children in the next seat. They might look sweet now, but it was all show. Another five minutes and they'd be running riot. He wasn't going to get a minute's peace. "How about coming for a coffee?"

Joe shook his head. "It's only an hour and forty minutes to Tarbert; I – " He was interrupted by a welcome message in English on the ship's tannoy, followed by another in Gaelic. Before the announcement was finished, Joe was lying down, his jacket folded under his head, his eyes closed. "Bye," he said.

At the top of the stairs, Lucy had turned to look at Joe. His eyes still shut, he was oblivious to the little boy creeping up on him with a water pistol. Served him right.

A large white bird glided high in the sky, neck outstretched and huge wings barely moving. Lucy watched its graceful flight. Suddenly, the bird plunged downwards. Wings folded back, it hit the sea and disappeared. Captivated, Lucy waited. It seemed to take forever to surface. She laughed and watched the bird take off again. Binoculars would be good.

"Try these."

Lucy turned, and he was there, the guy from the ticket office, wearing a red goretex jacket, zipped up to the neck. He offered Lucy a small pair of binoculars. "It's a gannet, diving for fish. Amazing to watch."

Lucy didn't want his binoculars or his company. She wanted to ignore him. But she could hardly refuse, could she? His smell was on the binoculars. Aftershave or soap, or just him, just his own scent, dragging her in? Get a grip, she told herself, as she watched the bird soaring and diving, again and again.

When the gannet was all fished out, and it had taken off into the distance, Lucy handed the binoculars back. "Thank you," she said. "And thanks for earlier. Thought I was going to have to leave my jacket behind."

"My pleasure." He put the binoculars in his pocket, then he offered his hand. "John MacKay."

"Lucy Galbraith."

John repeated her name as he took her hand. His voice was soft but his handshake was firm. He stared at her with deep blue eyes and her stomach flipped. Shit; how had she come to be this idiot?

"So, Lucy Galbraith, what takes you over to Harris?" John turned his back to the water and leaned against the railing. "Holiday?"

"My brother was coming over for work. Thought I'd keep him company."

"Your brother?" Did she imagine his relief? She didn't think so, for he didn't really try to hide it. "Where are you staying?"

"Northton."

"What on earth kind of work takes your brother to a place like Northton?"

Shit. "Oh . . . something really boring. Health and safety sort of work."

"Can't imagine there's much call for that sort of thing in Northton."

"We're staying there; he's travelling about." Time to get off that subject. "What about you?"

"Just a short break. I'm a freelance writer and editor. I've been going over to Harris for years; it's a great place to write, and to unwind. I was planning a few days in Lewis too, then going home by Ullapool, but I forgot to book the ferry. It was full, so I've had to leave the car. Not to worry, though – the CalMac staff gave me the number for a car hire firm in Tarbert, so I'm sorted. Right, now that you know all about me, tell me all about you."

Escape. Was it possible? Seasickness? How quickly could it come on?

"Where are you from?" he asked.

"Mostly grew up in the Borders, in Melrose. I live in Edinburgh now."

"Thought I could detect a slight English twang. Just a hint."

Lucy was shocked. "We lived in Brighton for a while when I was very young, but I haven't really got an English accent, have I?"

"It's barely noticeable. I've got a good ear. Spend a lot of time listening to birds."

Lucy laughed. "Really?"

John blushed. "I specialise in nature writing. That and the environment. Helps if you learn to distinguish one bird call from another."

"I believe you. Hint or not, the accent will have to go. There are more than enough English accents at Edinburgh University."

"What are you studying?"

Lucy hesitated again. This time, she wasn't thinking of a way to escape; she just couldn't face listening to the usual nonsense about lawyers. She'd started her studies quite proud of herself, with the naïve idea that she was going to do some good for society. The widespread hatred of lawyers had come as a bit of a surprise to her. She soon learned to lie, she and her friends outdoing each other with elaborate charades and exotic occupations. But that was before; that was when she was whole and normal, and still capable of humour and fun. Seemed so long ago. She told him the truth.

"Cool," he said.

Quickly, before he remembered the tale of his great-aunt, ripped off by an unscrupulous lawyer, or his mate's divorce that would have been amicable but for the scumbag solicitors, she asked him to tell her about his work. "Must be interesting being a writer."

"Everyone thinks that, but it's getting harder to make a living at it. I spend most of my working life proof-reading and editing other people's writing, and most of it is drearier than you could ever imagine. Still, at least I can work anywhere, and Harris is one of my favourite places. I'm working on a – "

Above the sound of the boat's engines and the wind, there was a sudden unusual and urgent bird call. It rose in volume and intensity until it sounded like a giant flock of angry geese. Lucy looked up into the sky, then down into the water. John laughed, patted his jacket pocket and took out his mobile phone.

"Hi mate," he said. "Not bad. Yourself? No, not tonight. I'm on the ferry to Harris. The view's stunning." He wasn't looking at the scenery when he said that; he was looking at Lucy. "Aye – next week, maybe. Cheers.

"See these things," he said to Lucy. "Can't get away from people. I wouldn't mind tossing it over the side."

"You could just switch it off."

He laughed. "What a novel idea!" He did just that. "And I'm not switching it on until I get back to Uig."

"And which of your birds was that?"

He blushed again. "It wasn't a bird; it was just a mate."

"I meant the ring tone."

"Of course you did. That was the call of the red-billed

148

hornbill; a small bird found in sub-Saharan Africa."

"With a red bill?"

"You know it?"

Lucy shook her head. "The clue was in the name."

"Ah. I'm not making a great impression, am I?"

Lucy didn't tell him that he was making a much better impression than she wanted him to. It was time to go.

Upstairs, Joe's eyes were still closed. Lucy thought of prodding him, and then decided against it; he'd looked so tired all day, and he'd hardly said a word during the journey. She went for a coffee, and watched as the ferry made its way up East Loch Tarbert, a large sheltered inlet that separated North and South Harris. On the lower edges of ragged, rocky slopes, tiny white houses clung to the barren land. And not a scrap of sand in sight.

When the boat reached Tarbert, Lucy waited for Joe at the bottom of the stairs to the lounge. He was last down the stairs, and he looked relieved, and a little less tired. Lucy smiled. "You slept?"

Joe nodded. "Almost all the way."

"Did the wee boy get you with his water pistol?"

"Nah; showed him my warrant card and he buggered off. What did you do?"

"Watched some birds and drank some coffee."

They were a couple of steps down the stairs to the car deck when Lucy heard someone call her name. She turned and saw John in the doorway. "Have a lovely time on Harris," he said. He smiled and waved.

***

In the school holidays two brothers from the village come to his door and ask him out to play. They're not the worst of the village boys, but they've often been part of the group, watching, laughing, saying nothing. There has been no trouble now for weeks. The older village boys will go to secondary school later this year. They're not stupid. They don't want to risk the Galbraith boy telling his father what

149

they've been up to; they don't want to start secondary with a black mark against them.

But they can't erase history that easily from the boy's head. It might be a trick. He tells the brothers he's not coming out, closes the door and watches them as they run up the track to the road.

"Why don't you go out and play with them?" his mother asks.

He shrugs. It would upset her if she knew, and he hates upsetting her. "I like staying in with you."

She laughs, but it's a kind laugh. She's laughing a lot these days. Something has changed, but he doesn't know what it is. There's been no snoring from her room for weeks, no retching from the bathroom, no harsh words hissed in a cloud of whisky from the landing late at night.

When the boys come back the next day, his mother makes him go, pushing him gently from the house. "What are you going to do, boys?" she asks.

"We're going to the ruined chapel," the younger one says. "We're going to watch for pirates. I'm going to be the captain." He says it funny, like it was spelled 'captchan'.

His brother shoves him. "We are not. There's no pirates in the Sound of Harris. We're just going to see the chapel and the graveyard. We might find some bones."

"Is it far?" she asks.

The boys shrug. "Quite far."

Another push from his mother. "Enjoy yourselves."

And the door is closed.

Chapter 14

Although the directions to Harris House had seemed straightforward, Joe found himself driving round Tarbert's narrow one-way system twice, before he found the complex of care home and sheltered housing where Morag MacDonald lived. The detour gave Lucy a chance to check out the shops, the pubs, the bus stop and the cash machine, twice. Not that she expected she'd need much cash. Although she was sure that the Tarbert shops could provide everything one needed to survive, she was unlikely to be tempted to make any further dents in her overdraft.

In the car outside Harris House, Lucy pressed the lever to recline the seat. Joe had said he might be a while. He wasn't. No sooner had she closed her eyes than he was back. Morag MacDonald was not up to having a visitor this afternoon. Best to come back in the morning, the staff had told him.

"Great," Lucy said. "Do you think we can find a beach?"

"I think we'd have some difficulty not finding one."

Back round the one-way system, then a left turn at the junction, up a steep hill and they were on their way to South Harris. They didn't get far before Joe's phone rang. He pulled into a passing place and answered. "Roberts," he said. "You missing me already?"

Lucy stopped listening. Beyond a row of weather-beaten pine trees, she saw the ferry gliding back out towards the Minch, a tiny boat on a still sea. In front of the car, behind the car, on the other side of the road, she saw rocks and boulders covering heathery slopes. There were large rocks and small ones, scattered ones and embedded ones, moving ones – moving rocks? No, those were sheep. She watched one of the sheep scratching itself on an ugly telegraph pole. Ugly telegraph poles, ugly sheep, ugly landscape. Dark sky, gloomy thoughts, Sebastian Moore straying into her head.

"You are kidding me!" Joe sat up straighter. He was smiling, for the first time since they'd left Inverness. "When?" Lucy could hear Roberts babbling, though she couldn't make out his words. "Kirkcaldy?" Joe said. "Any photos left at the scene?" Roberts was off again. "Great," Joe said, when Roberts stopped. "Keep me informed."

"Good news?" Lucy asked, when Joe ended the call.

"Not for one Jean Henderson in Kirkcaldy. Looks like our killer has struck again."

As Joe drove south, he thought about Roberts' news. Jean Henderson, a seventy-five-year old widow, had been found strangled in her chair in a house in Kirkcaldy on Friday morning. A reclusive woman, no one had seen anything untoward and no one had missed her. If it wasn't for the window cleaner, she might have been there for weeks. Prints from two door handles matched prints on the photo left at Moira Jacobs' flat. And Jean Henderson was grasping a handful of dark hair when she died.

There was no further news on Moira Jacobs. Roberts had been to the surgical ward in the hospital and visited the women who had shared a room with her. Neither of them could identify Mac from his description; no one like that had visited her in hospital. Joe would ask Roberts to . . .

A suicidal sheep and a shrieking Lucy brought Joe back to Harris. The sheep had been grazing on one side of the narrow road, when it suddenly leapt in front of the car. Joe's tyres stuttered on the loose gravel as he slid to a stop an inch or so from the unperturbed sheep. He beeped his horn and the sheep sauntered off to the other side of the road.

"Are you all right?" Joe asked. He'd almost forgotten that Lucy was there. She looked tired and sad.

"Are we definitely on the right island?" she asked.

"Why?"

"The rocks, the boulders, the general lack of beaches. I know everyone said the beaches are in the south, but, Joe, are we nearly there yet?"

They both laughed as they remembered how often Lucy had asked that question as a child, usually within a mile or so of leaving home. She'd repeat it every few minutes until they reached their destination. And all the way back.

"Lucy, we're nearly there." He nodded into the distance. "Look." There was sand. It was far away, and not quite a beach with rolling waves, but definitely a start. "That's Luskentyre. Taransay's in the distance."

Lucy was smiling. "Taransay, as in the Castaway programme, when I was a teenager? Mum hated it. She said being stuck on a Hebridean island was a form of torture, not entertainment."

"No surprise there, then."

"Why does she hate Harris? Why will no one ever talk about what it was like living here?"

Joe shrugged. "Dunno. It's a long time ago. You know Mum. The past is the past, I guess."

"So there's no dark family secret buried here?"

Another suicidal sheep with a tiny lamb saved Joe from answering. As the mother sauntered across the road, the lamb dancing around it in frantic steps, Lucy shouted at the sheep, while Joe silently thanked it.

The sun came out and Lucy smiled. All thoughts of dark secrets and Sebastian Moore were banished. Her smile broadened as the rocks and boulders gradually diminished to be replaced by lush green slopes and pretty spring flowers, and that golden sand getting ever closer.

And then it was just stunning beach after stunning beach. No sooner had Lucy exclaimed about one, than they were upon another. The sea was turquoise and emerald, gentle waves rolling onto golden sands. It was paradise, a magical paradise.

"Do you want me to stop or will we carry on to the B&B?" Joe asked as they passed Horgabost.

"Better carry on. I'm overwhelmed."

"But happy?"

"Ecstatic."

***

Leaving Inverness had felt so good. Stephen could breathe again, and the great weight that had enfolded him for weeks was gone. When he met the eyes of others, he even found himself smiling. The only niggling doubt he had was his mother. She blamed everyone for taking her thoughts, but she was doing a pretty good job of stealing into his head; she hadn't been far from him all day.

He knew she would be fine. He'd gone away before and she'd scarcely noticed. She didn't seem to live in the same time-frame as everyone else. He'd go up two days in a row and she'd say she hadn't seen him for ages, then he'd be gone for a couple of weeks and she'd act as if he'd only just left. Should he be worrying about her now? He didn't want to worry, not about Betty, or anyone else. He just wanted to be free.

***

The top of the hill was gone, sliced off by a band of low-lying mist. What was left of Ceapabhal was black and gloomy and Joe could hardly bear to look at it. If the DI's secretary had consulted Joe before she booked his accommodation, he would have asked for a room in Tarbert. He wouldn't have got it though, for there wasn't a room to be had in Tarbert that week. That shouldn't have been a problem either; there were other hotels and guest-houses all over the island. But out of all those other guest-houses, June had gone and picked one in Northton, the very village that Joe had lived in as a child.

"This looks nice," Lucy said, as Joe turned off the main road. Nice? Surely she was taking the mickey? The village was surrounded by dark hills, constantly in their shadow. There was a cluster of council houses on the left, followed by a string of disparate dwellings on each side of a narrow road that stretched towards Ceapabhal. Joe glanced at Lucy; she was smiling. How he wished he could see the place through her eyes.

They checked in to the guest-house, dropped off their bags and left the village half an hour later. As they approached the road-end, Lucy looked around and said: "The hills are quite imposing. I bet it could be grim on a bad day."

And then Joe wished that such a thought had never crossed his sister's mind. He needed her to like the place. He needed her cheerfulness to balance his gloom. He needed her more than he had ever needed her before. Great big Jessie.

They ate at the Anchorage in Leverburgh and watched the inter-island ferry, MV *Loch Portain*, wind her way around the rocks and skerries in the Sound of Harris as she approached the harbour, her arrival awaited by queues of vans and cars. She had come from Berneray, North Uist, and the return journey would be her last trip of the day.

"Carla's grandparents came from North Uist," Joe said.

"You should take her there."

"No chance. One Hebridean island is one more than I had hoped to visit this century."

After eating they headed for the beach at Scarista, where they discovered a multitude of tiny wading birds playing in the water as the swirling waves chased them up the churning sands. When the sea retreated the roles reversed, the birds racing after the backwash on clockwork legs, their long bills pecking up delicacies as they went.

Lucy took to the water too, her jeans turned up above her knees, and the waders fled in a shimmering cloud. As she screeched at the cold, Joe watched the birds flitting and swooping along the coastline until they found a quieter patch. He laughed as Lucy jumped the waves, soaking her jeans and splashing her face. He shook his head when she beckoned him in; he was staying firmly on dry land.

They walked along the sand as dusk started to fall, bird song echoing all around them. The scent of sea and sand and flowers was strong and sweet.

"It's heaven," Lucy said. "Absolute heaven." She spread her arms and turned and laughed. Joe smiled. It was beautiful; he couldn't deny it. Maybe it was time to let . . .

"It's so beautiful, I want to be buried here."

Nausea crushed Joe's fickle hope for healing. "No," he whispered. "Don't say that. Lucy, don't ever say that."

A dark shape tumbled from the sky, twisting and turning in front of them as it fell. Surely the bird must hit the ground, but no. At the last moment, it swooped upwards and was gone, a plaintive cry left echoing in the still night.

***

He doesn't even know what to say to the brothers. What if it's all a trick? What if they're going to get him to the chapel and . . . and kill him? He wants to go home. He turns and his mother is at the window. She's waving and smiling and he can't go back.

At the Galbraiths' gate, the perfect father is waving to his perfect wife and kids as they make their way to the bus stop. In the distance, the sun shines on the hill.

The brothers start arguing. The little one's going to tell on the big one for being bossy. The big one doesn't care; he's in charge 'cos he's the oldest.

"You don't say much," the big one says to the boy.

"And he doesn't even smell bad," the wee brother says. "Not half as bad as Kenny Scrog said."

"Duin' do bheul, amadan," his brother snaps.

"Do you know what that means?" the wee brother asks. "You must have Gaelic. Your father . . . "

His older brother shoves him. "He doesn't!"

"Oh. Anyway, it's Gaelic for 'shut up, you fool'," the wee one says. "But I'm not an amadan. I'm very clever for my age; my granny says I took it from my Great-uncle Tormod."

The boy says nothing. He's glad that his mother has started to hang their clothes out on the washing line, instead of leaving them for days on a clotheshorse until they smell damp and fusty.

They take the track that leads towards the sand dunes and soon they're standing above a beach. It's called Tràigh na Cleabhaig, and the brothers try and get him to say the name. He could say it; he could say it perfectly, but he shakes his head, making them laugh. It's not the beach where he skims stones. This one is further round the coast, and he hasn't been here before, didn't even know it existed. He thought the track only led to the hill and he never wanted to go there.

With a yell, the wee brother launches himself down the sloping sand dune, slipping and sliding, laughing as he goes. His brother follows him. The boy smiles. This might be fun. He's about to follow when he feels a tug on his jersey.

He turns and the wee Galbraith girl is there. How did she come this far without being seen? She's wearing a red dress and white sandals. She smiles at the boy, her little perfect teeth sparkling in the sun. "I know you," she lisps. "I've seen you."

He looks at the others. They're running down to the water. He wants to be with them, away from this girl. "Why are you not with your mother and brother?"

"I didn't want to go to Tarbety on the bus with them, so I ran home to Daddy, but he's not in."

"It's Tarbert," the boy says. "And your dad's in the garden. He's always in the garden. Go home."

She shakes her head again. "Why do you watch us?"

"I do not! Go away!"

"No. I want to come with you. Why do you watch us? Why do you go to bed so early?"

The boy jumps from the grass, slides down the dune, runs to the water.

157

Chapter 15

Joe smiled until his teeth dried and his lips hurt. He smiled at the girl behind the counter when he paid for the flowers. He smiled at the lady in the queue behind him, the one that had told him to take the red carnations and the pink roses; that way he couldn't go wrong. He smiled at the man who held the door open for him, at the boy whose bike he nearly fell over outside the shop. He smiled until he was back in the car, where he laid his head down on the steering wheel and let the smile slip from his mouth.

He drove to Scarista and parked below the church. In the cemetery, the gravestones were laid out in careful rows, the grass short and neat around them. The order was in contrast to the old cemetery, perched on a hill beside the church, a scattering of ancient gravestones leaning this way and that. Beyond the cemetery wall, across the sand, there was no mist on Ceapabhal. The hill was low and gentle, and a mocking voice inside Joe's head taunted him. How could he have let it become so huge in his memory? It was nothing; an insignificant hill. It even looked attractive today. But then, everything looked better in good weather; everything but the small grave in the corner.

There were fresh flowers on the grave and Joe wondered who would do that after all this time. On his knees on the lush green grass, Joe closed his eyes and remembered.

***

Lucy laughed at the tumbling flight of the lapwings as they hurtled down at incredible speed, their floppy wings twisting and turning. Inches from the ground, they recovered themselves, sweeping round in a great circle, before soaring upwards and plummeting again, their shrill call echoing around them. Last night their aerial display and plaintive call had been eerie and chilling; today it was comical.

It was another beautiful day, only a slight breeze stirring the grass by the road. Across from the bus stop, two lambs played on a grassy outcrop. They chased each other, bouncing and jumping as if their legs were springs.

Joe had left early. He hadn't slept well, blaming the strange bed. He wasn't the only one. Lucy had lain awake too, despite a comfortable bed and a wonderful silence, but she didn't tell Joe. He hadn't been himself since they left Inverness. She felt a little guilty. It couldn't be easy trying to investigate a murder with her tagging along, acting as if it was nothing more than a holiday. He had offered to take her to Tarbert. She could have a look round the village, or get the bus from there to Stornoway, the main town on Lewis. She told him not to wait for her. There was a bus at 10 o'clock that would give her three quarters of an hour in Tarbert, and she'd be in Stornoway before lunchtime.

She was looking forward to getting the bus, to sitting back and admiring all those beautiful beaches again, without having to speak to anyone. That was the plan, until John MacKay showed up, in a red Micra. "Size isn't everything," he told her, as she hesitated by the road side. The bus was coming. The bus was slowing. John's eyes were pleading.

Scarista, Borve, Horgabost. Nisabost, Seilebost, Luskentyre; John named all the beaches as they passed. They looked even more stunning than they had the previous day. "Joe's going to take me to Luskentyre tomorrow, if he gets time," Lucy said. "We were on Scarista beach last night, and I've been to the wee beach at the end of the village this morning. It's gorgeous. Could have stayed there all day, but I thought I better see some more of the islands while I'm here. There's a medieval chapel near the village, at the back of the hill. I'm going to ask Joe if we can go there tonight."

"If Joe's not free, I'd be up for that. It's a lovely walk."

Lucy didn't answer. She should have taken the bus.

Though they passed few cars on the winding single-track road through South Harris, and though they only saw two men and a three-legged dog, it transpired that it was all happening in Harris, and had been for many years. From the doomed 1990s superquarry proposal that led to the longest-running public local inquiry in Scotland, to the success of Harris tweed at the London Fashion Week, it seemed that Harris was where it was at. "Lewis is nice enough," John said. "But Harris is something else. Even their accents are completely different, which always amazes me, given the geography. Mind you, in bygone days they would have been like two separate islands. They didn't always have these good roads."

Lucy wasn't so sure about the roads. Just because they were on a stretch of double-track, there was no knowing when it would suddenly narrow to single-track, and they'd find a lorry bearing down on them. John was a good driver. Even when he was talking, he was ready for the sudden stops and the suicidal sheep. How the lambs survived their mothers' recklessness, Lucy would never know. She wondered why the crofters didn't fence their sheep in to keep them from wandering the verges and straying onto the road. Mind you, even where there were fences, the sheep were on the wrong side.

At Ardhasaig, on the far side of Tarbert, the landscape changed again as they drove into the looming mountains of North Harris. As they climbed and dipped on twisting roads, in the shelter of the rugged peaks, they both fell quiet.

Then the towering mountains were behind them, and

they were in Lewis. John pulled in to show Lucy the stunning view down Loch Seaforth, before they carried on northwards, passing peat bogs, lochs and open moor-land that stretched on either side until it met gentle distant hills. They sped passed scattered townships and sign-posts to a myriad of other places, until at last, they approached the outskirts of Stornoway.

***

Morag MacDonald was like a tiny fragile bird. Her room smelled of talc, and reminded Joe of Granny Galbraith in the Melrose nursing home. Raymond's mother had forgotten Joe towards the end. She always remembered Lucy though, pulling her closer, insisting she sat on her knee, even when Lucy cried and reached for her mother. But the old woman would scowl at Joe, asking him who he was and why he was there.

Joe shoved the memory from his mind and focussed on Morag. She smiled at him and held out her hand. It felt as fragile as paper and straw, like it might just crumble if he applied the slightest pressure. He didn't. He held her gaze and saw in her eyes the pale blue of an early morning sky over Ceapabhal.

"You're tired," she said. "Your work, it must take it out of you." Her island voice was strong and in such contrast to her frame.

Joe was tired. He nodded. "It can be hard, but I enjoy it."

"And you're good at it."

He grinned. "I hope so. Do you know why I'm here?"

"Donald told me you wanted to ask about Moira Jacobs. I hadn't heard that name for a long time, then I saw it in the papers last week. A sad way to go."

Joe was relieved that she already knew of Moira's fate. "There are no records of her time here. I was hoping you might help."

161

Morag gave a gentle laugh. "Nothing on paper; plenty in here." She tapped her head. "And it's not just me. Many others will never forget Moira Jacobs."

Why? Joe wanted to ask. What did she do to gain such infamy? But he didn't ask, not yet. "Do you know when she came here?"

Morag looked beyond Joe, beyond the room. "Let me see." She was quiet for a time, so Joe looked out the window. He watched a starling on a bush, its plumage glinting purple and green in the morning sun. When the bird took off, Joe looked at Morag. She was still searching for a link within her memory. He saw her find something. A little smile, a nod. "Our Mary's youngest, Gordon, was born in 1986." She shook her head and closed her eyes. "Not that year. Was it Johnny Strond? No. He was 1989. Moira came before that. Ach." She tapped her fingers on her knee. "Annie – her Margaret was born the year Moira came. Margaret married last year; a boy from Berneray – strange boy he is too. Margaret – she was born in . . . " Morag tapped her fingers on the wooden arm of the chair. Another little smile; another nod; she had it. "February; thirteenth of February, 19 . . . 1988. Moira Jacobs came the next month."

"Twenty six years ago," Joe said. The year he left Harris.

Morag nodded. "Sorry, I knew it was there somewhere, but the wheels turn so slowly these days."

"Don't apologise. I'm grateful you've taken the time to speak to me. Anything you can tell me is a bonus."

"The dates might not come easily, but I can picture her like she was sitting where you are, her nose upturned as if someone had dumped a pile of manure in front of her. It didn't matter who she was speaking to, that nose was the same. Strange, strange woman. A sad air about her. Not that she seemed sad; I don't know that she was capable of such an ordinary emotion. Her life, her outlook – that was sad. Nothing was right, as far as she was concerned. I

162

thought maybe it was just that the island wasn't good enough for her, that the island ways bothered her. People either love it or loathe it here; there doesn't seem to be an in-between."

Joe understood. His mother had hated Harris, hated every day she spent on the island, while his father had loved it and would have stayed if things hadn't gone the way they had. Joe wasn't about to mention his own connection with the island.

"And bad-tempered – oh, boy, was she bad-tempered!" Morag laughed, a deep laugh. Again, it contrasted with the fragility of her body. "She terrified grown men with her tantrums. I can't say she frightened me, but she troubled me. The things she said and did troubled me. This was a quiet place, a good place, yet she couldn't see the goodness. I remember a meeting, not long after she came. She said something like, 'I'm going to instil some mainland values into this place'. She shocked me, shocked us all. We were used to people coming to the islands for the values, for the low crime rate, the sense of community." She shook her head. "I couldn't fathom her out, couldn't understand what it was that she saw in the place, in the people, that disgusted her. I can't deny that drink is a problem in the islands; it causes such misery to families, but it was more than that. I think she mistook gentle manners for weakness. I think she despised us."

"Can you remember how long she was here?"

"Just over two years. I remember she left around the time that Duncan Robertson married Floraidh Bheag – that's Wee Flora – in 1990; it was a happy time for everyone."

"Because of the wedding or Moira Jacobs' departure?"

"Both. No one ever thought Flora would get a husband, so that union caused some excitement, but Moira Jacobs leaving – well, that was something else!" Her laughter made Joe smile.

"I'm trying to establish if there was anyone with a

grudge against her from her time here that might want to harm her. There may have been a link between Harris and her murderer."

Morag frowned. "She caused a lot of trouble, right enough. She seemed to think that her profession gave her the right to intrude, the right to judge. The families and individuals we worked with were in the most dreadful of situations, and it wasn't always their own fault. Most of us thought, there but for the grace of God go I. Not Moira. She hadn't a shred of empathy or sympathy. She had the ability and the power to wreak havoc in people's lives."

Joe nodded. He had come across a few like that in child protection. It wasn't limited to social workers; there were some within the force that let their considerable powers go to their head. It frustrated him at times. Ach, maybe Roberts was right; maybe he was too soft for this job.

"Having said that," Morag continued, "I don't know that anyone she was involved with here would have hated her enough to want to murder her so many years later." Her hands clasped on her lap, Morag went quiet. "There was something," she said at last. "Something that led to her leaving. What was it?"

She was getting tired; Joe could see that. Please, he begged silently; please. Just a little longer.

"A boy," she said. "I can't for the life of me remember the name or where he lived, but his mother was a drinker, and the boy . . . the boy." She shook her head again. "I can see him, a poor wee soul holding his mother up as they walked along the road. What was their name again?"

He watched as Morag stared out the window. He saw the ghost of a smile on her lips and he wondered if a name had come to her. She turned something over in her head, then she frowned. "No, it can't be that. Dash it," she said. "I can't remember." Her hands were shaky and Joe knew that it was time to leave.

"Morag," he said, "you've been a great help."

164

"Ach, I haven't. If only I could remember who they were or where they lived, and what happened to them. It'll come to me, you know. It'll likely come to me in the middle of the night."

Joe smiled and took a card from his pocket. "Middle of the night or not, please call me. Anything else that you remember would be very welcome."

"Well, I don't have one of those new-fangled mobile telephones, but I'll ask the staff to contact you if there's anything."

At the door, Joe turned and looked back. Morag was staring out the window, and he knew she wasn't seeing the birds or the sun. She was searching her mind for further clues.

***

A seventeenth century clairvoyant had foreseen the sinking of the Isle of Lewis. No one was too bothered. Although many of the Brahan Seer's predictions had come true, there was no way an island was going to sink. And then, in 1995, a new ferry was introduced to the Stornoway/Ullapool run. It was named *The Isle of Lewis*. Cue some worried people. They had cause to worry again more recently, when Sunday sailings were introduced in July 2009. All sorts of terrible ills had been predicted, including the evils of Sunday shopping. Almost four years on, and little about the island Sunday had changed, but islanders and visitors could now come and go, just as they could in every other part of the country.

Lucy watched the MV *Isle of Lewis* arrive at Stornoway as she walked along the shore road in Lews Castle Grounds. The large ferry docked without incident, and Lucy decided to make her way back towards the town. John had recommended the castle and grounds, situated across the harbour from the town. The nineteenth century castle and the massive forested grounds had been gifted to the people of Stornoway in 1923. Over the years, the turreted building had been a naval hospital, a college and a school, but now it was boarded up and inaccessible. There were proposals to turn it into a museum and hotel. The locals weren't so sure the plans would come to anything, a dog walker told Lucy. It was all very well talking, but the talking had gone on forever, while the building crumbled away.

It had been obvious that John would have welcomed an invitation to join Lucy on her walk; she hadn't complied. Didn't stop him asking to meet her for lunch, though, and how could she refuse without sounding rude? She was paying, she had told him, though she guessed lunch would cost more than the bus fare she had saved. He was certainly persistent, not to mention good looking, pleasant, polite, interesting, and, wonder of wonders, a great listener. That had not been one of Sebastian's skills. The Banishment, she reminded herself.

As she headed for the town centre, she wondered if she could get out of lunch. She had John's phone number; she could call and say she wasn't feeling well, was already on the bus back to Harris. He had things to do in the town; articles to email to a magazine, some library research, a bit of shopping. He might not be ready for hours. She could be safely back in Harris before he'd even left Stornoway. Wouldn't have to see him again. Wouldn't have to look into those eyes. Wouldn't get that feeling in the pit of her stomach, the one she hadn't really had with Sebastian until it was too late.

***

Joe ate a miserable lunch in the car park in Tarbert, surrounded by happy people. Three cheerful tourists queued at the cash machine, while a crowd of laughing teenagers hung around the waiting room and toilets. Smiling bus drivers in shirt-sleeves were chatting, their engines idling in the warm sun. Everyone was happy; everyone but Joe. He should have gone somewhere for a proper lunch, instead of sitting in his car forcing cold sausage rolls down with warm Coke. He sent Lucy a text and waited. He smiled when she answered, his loneliness subsiding a little, then growing when he read that John MacKay had given her a lift to Stornoway. What was going on? Ach, it was a small island – they were bound to meet somewhere.

He phoned Roberts, and immediately wished he hadn't. Hearing the buzz of the canteen in the background, he closed his eyes and wished he was in Inverness. He opened them and he was still in Tarbert.

"Sarge, how's it going?" Roberts asked. "When are you coming back to civilisation?" And before Joe could answer, "Bugger off, Aird. Go and buy your own."

Joe forced a smile, in the hope that it would make him sound brighter. "It's going fine, Roberts. Hopefully back tomorrow."

"You got anything for us?"

"I'm working on it. Met Morag MacDonald this morning – she thinks Moira Jacobs left because of something that happened with a boy whose mother drank, but she couldn't remember the details. She'll get in touch if she remembers anything else. What's going on there?"

"Just got some news. I was about to call you. Jury returned a guilty verdict on your pervert. Guilty on all charges."

"Brilliant. Anything else?"

"Jackson's still off sick."

"Even better. Anything else?"

"Aye." Roberts paused, irritating Joe. Either it was nothing of any worth, or Roberts was at it – savouring the fact that he knew something that Joe didn't, that he was at the centre of the investigation while Joe was banished to the edge of the world.

"And?" Joe said, trying not to sound too desperate.

"We've got a hair match."

"Inverness and Kirkcaldy?"

"Aye, and more. Sharon MacRae's flat – hairs found on the back of the chair."

Suddenly Joe felt the warmth of the sun. "Result. What's the DI saying?"

"Singing your praises – always knew you had a good lead there."

Joe laughed. "What's his position on Clancy now?"

"Saying little; there could still be a link, but he's not going on about it."

"Anything more on Jean Henderson?"

"Waiting for Fife Constabulary to get back to us. DI said I might get a trip down there. Oh, Sarge, I almost forgot; I went to see the dog today. She's getting on so well."

"What a relief; I could hardly sleep last night for worrying about her."

"You know what they say about sarcasm." Roberts sounded hurt.

"Sorry; I am pleased."

"That's not all; I'm taking the vet nurse out tonight."

"I'm very very pleased. Hope you have a lovely evening."

"Any advice?"

"Don't agree to meet her mother."

Was Mac the boy that Morag had mentioned? Did he leave the photo of Ceapabhal at the scene? What was the connection between him, Moira Jacobs and Jean Henderson? While Joe was pondering, his phone rang. It was Carol at the care home; Morag was asking to see him.

He started the engine and pulled out of the parking space. Most of the buses and the youngsters had gone. Slowing down at the exit from the car park, he saw a man making his way down the hill from the shop, with the unmistakable swagger of a drunk. A couple of steps, then he stopped and swayed, moved forward and stopped again. A wee laugh to himself, his eyes closed and his head thrown back. A wagging finger and another laugh. A look around that nearly toppled him, then a hand into the inside pocket of his threadbare jacket and a quick slug from a half-bottle. He saw Joe watching and he raised the half-bottle in mock salute. Joe nodded and drove away.

"Morag's very tired," Carol told Joe when he arrived at Harris House. "She usually sleeps for much of the afternoon, but today she's been agitated and she hasn't rested."

"I won't stay long," he replied.

"She really only speaks Gaelic these days. I think that's why she's so tired – thinking in Gaelic and having to translate for you. I suggested an interpreter – myself, or one of the other members of staff, but she was having none of it. She can be very stubborn, our Morag."

The old lady looked exhausted. She smiled at Joe and held out her hand. "I'm sorry, Detective Sergeant," she said, her voice hoarse. "I wasn't much help to you earlier. Have a seat; you better pull the chair closer; my voice gets weak when I'm tired."

"Call me Joe," he replied, taking her hand gently. "And please don't apologise; you were a great help." He pulled the chair closer. "You know, we could do this tomorrow. I'm getting the afternoon ferry, so there's plenty of time."

She shook her head. "I remembered something; I don't want to forget it again. I . . . I should have remembered before. Do you think people block things out if they don't want to remember? If it's too harsh?"

"Undoubtedly." Joe hesitated, remembering, wanting to forget.

Morag nodded. "It's that boy I mentioned, that boy and Moira Jacobs. I still can't remember his name." She stopped, her brow furrowed. "Sometimes I think it's about to come to me, but then I get confused and it's gone. Anyway, there was a crofter over Amhuinnsuidhe way, in North Harris. James MacLeod – Seumas Mòr, we called him – Big James. He had a wife – a poor wee thing with terrible eye-sight and rotten teeth. She wasn't very old, but she looked so ancient and care-worn. And he, Seumas Mòr, well, he was that full of himself. Always acquiring land and crofts; he was good at that. Clerk of the grazings committee and an elder in the church – always so well-dressed and pious, but there was something creepy about him.

"They didn't have any children, Seumas and Janet. People said that Janet couldn't have children and that Seumas was hard on her because of it. Anyway, as well as acquiring crofts, Seumas got another house when an old neighbour died. And that was where Moira Jacobs lived – she rented the house from Seumas Mòr.

"Well, the boy's mother's drinking became so heavy that she just couldn't look after him. She wasn't feeding him properly and he was so scared of leaving her alone that he wasn't going to school. The mother agreed to a voluntary placement of the boy, and we were looking for a suitable foster home, close enough to his mother so they could still see each other. It wasn't easy to get foster parents. Our own ones often had their hands full with children from the mainland. We were looking for a match, and thinking we might have to send him to Uist or Skye. The next thing we knew, Moira Jacobs was saying that the mother wanted the boy to go and live with Seumas Mòr and Janet, rather than leave the island. It wasn't the way it was usually done. Seumas hadn't been approved as a foster carer, or anything formal like that. I think Moira must have talked the mother into it in one of her sober moments. The mother was adamant then, sober or drunk; that was where she wanted her boy to go."

Morag reached for a glass of water on the small table beside her chair. Her hand was shaking as she raised the glass to her lips. Joe thought the water might slosh over the side of the glass.

She put the glass down and looked at Joe. He saw the shadow of tears in her eyes. "I remember it was just a couple of weeks before Christmas when the boy went to Seumas Mòr. His mother was supposed to have him back on Christmas Day, then she drank herself senseless and ended up in hospital in Stornoway. It was the first Christmas they'd ever been apart.

"That poor boy. He stopped speaking. Stopped eating. Went to school regularly; Seumas Mòr saw to that, but he was worse off than he was with his mother. Ach, I think he was only with Seumas Mòr a few weeks when he was back home, but it was a few weeks too long.

"His mother came to me. I can see her now. She'd been a lovely looking woman, but she was a poor soul by then. She said that Seumas Mòr had . . . had been, well, touching her boy, and maybe more. The great church elder, pious Seumas Mòr, whose prayers were as long and as complicated as Dante's Inferno, he was interfering with the boy." Her shaking hands wiped at her eyes. "I went to Moira Jacobs, but she said the boy was bad through and through. He'd been stealing from Seumas Mòr, according to her, and he would say anything to get back with his mother. I didn't leave it there. I went to our boss and he said he would sort it out. And soon, Moira Jacobs was leaving and the boss was saying there had been an investigation and there was no substance to the allegations."

Morag thought the mother had improved after that, and she was certain that she and her son left the island a year or two later.

"I often wondered if there really was an investigation," she said. "After my boss had retired, I thought of going to the police, but the boy and his mother were gone, and Seumas's wife was ill. Poor Janet; she died not long after that."

"What about Seumas? Is he still alive?"

Morag shook her head. "He died last summer. Fell down his stairs. He was in no state to be living in that house and sleeping upstairs, but he wouldn't hear of moving. He became very isolated as he grew old."

Joe leaned forward. "Fell down the stairs?"

"Aye, he was found by the postie the next day."

The stairs and the postie? That was some coincidence.

"Ach, his carpet was so ragged, it's no wonder he tripped and fell. At least he died instantly, they said. Broke his neck."

As the door closed gently behind Joe, Morag stared at it. She thought again of a name that had come to her so many times since the detective's first visit. But it didn't make any sense. She was just getting mixed up. Shaking her head, she closed her eyes.

Chapter 16

There was a robber on the ward. A sneaky, low-down thief, creeping into Betty's room and stealing things. She refused to leave her room. Wouldn't even close the toilet door. Might be nothing left when she came out. And why would she tell Janey what was missing? For all she knew, Janey might be the robber.

"I'm not a robber," Janey tried to assure her. "I'm worried about you. Are you missing Stephen? I'm sure he'll be back soon."

Betty frowned. "We're not joined at the hip, you know. I think I can manage a few days without him. He has important work to do."

"Is it your thoughts again? Is someone stealing them?"

Betty looked at Janey as if she was quite mad. "My thoughts? Don't be so stupid. How could anyone steal my thoughts? They're mine, inside my own head. No one else can get near them, and I'm certainly not sharing them with anyone."

Whatever it was that was bothering her, it seemed to have done Betty's mental health a power of good; she hadn't been this rational for weeks. "I don't know what else to suggest, Betty. We can bring your food on a tray today, but you're going to have to come out tomorrow. It's not good for you to stay in your room alone."

"Not good for me? It's a damn sight better than mixing with those lunatics, and that's just the staff. I want to see my solicitor; you're not keeping me in this nut-house." A fly buzzed around Betty's head. She swatted at it with an impatient hand. "Bugger off," she said, swatting again.

"We're not keeping you in, Betty. You're a voluntary patient."

"So I can leave any time?"

Janey hesitated. "In theory."

"What's that supposed to mean?"

"You're still not well, Betty. If you tried to leave, the doctors might detain you formally."

The fly landed on the sill, and it was gone, dispatched with a vicious slam of Betty's hand. "Then get me my solicitor," she said, wiping her hand on her trousers. "I want to speak to him now."

"Do you have a solicitor, Betty?"

Betty shrugged. "How should I know? Stephen deals with things like that."

"I'll check your file. Can I do anything else for you?"

"Just close the bloody door and leave me alone."

By the time Janey returned to tell Betty that there was no note of a solicitor on file, Betty had forgotten that she'd ever asked.

***

Watching a policeman almost set himself on fire would be great entertainment for some. It certainly made Joe laugh. PC Derek Russell chucked the extinguished cigarette end over the fence at the back of the car park, then he brushed the embers off his singed trousers.

"Thought you were my colleague," he said. "We've got a bet on; see who can stop first. He's winning. Bugger keeps creeping up on me. It's costing me a fortune. You must be Detective Sergeant Galbraith. I was told to expect you."

Derek Russell was around Joe's age, tall and well-built, with a broad Glaswegian accent and a shaved head. Joe had found him in the car park of the offices the police shared with the local authority. Not someone to be messed with, Joe decided, as they shook hands.

"Found your murderer yet?" Derek asked.

"No. Something has come up, though; I was hoping you could help."

"Anything to tear me away from investigating the heinous theft of heating oil from domestic tanks. Little wonder people are resorting to theft. If the oil producers can get away with daylight robbery, why shouldn't the ordinary people? I'm tempted myself." His grey eyes sparkled as he laughed. "Knowing my luck, I'd get savaged by a demented collie."

"You've certainly got your fair share of demented collies here. Come from nowhere; just a black flash in the wing mirror. Could put you over the edge on these roads."

"That and the sheep – it's a dangerous place."

"How do you like it here?"

"Not bad; my wife's from Harris. She was delighted when I got posted here – happier than I was, but it's grown on me. They closed the station earlier this year; moved two of us in here. We've no local sergeant now, and all the back-up comes from Stornoway. Works okay most of the time, but God knows what we'd do if the natives started rioting. Doesn't bear thinking about."

It was good to laugh. Made Joe feel much better. "Speaking of the natives, do you know anything about James MacLeod, a crofter over near Amhuinnsuidhe? Died a year or so ago."

"Aye, Seumas Mòr. Found dead at the bottom of his stairs last July – broken neck. I was on leave at the time. A stubborn old git, awkward as they come. Wouldn't leave his house though he couldn't look after himself. Looked as if he'd tripped on the carpet. What's your interest in him?"

Joe told him Morag's tale. "She was told there had been a police investigation that cleared the old man."

"Leave that with me; I'll see what I can find out. Call by later, but I'm knocking off at five." He rubbed his hands together and smiled. "Fishing tonight."

"Sea or loch?"

"Sea; just me and my wee Orkney 452. Heaven."

"Sounds good."

"You're very welcome to join me if you've nothing better to do. I'll be setting off from Leverburgh around 6."

Joe couldn't think of a better way to spend his last evening on the island than to get off the island. He'd watched a couple of small boats set out from Leverburgh last night on a still sea and he'd envied the fishermen. "I'm very tempted, but I better see what my sister wants to do. I promised her another walk tonight."

"She could come too."

Keen to know as soon as possible, Joe sent Lucy a text. As ever, she responded in seconds. "*Fishing? No ta,*" Joe read out. "*Will do my own thing. See you at Tarbert for food. B4N.*"

"Bye for now?" Derek suggested.

"When it comes to text lingo, your guess is as good as mine. Doing her own thing, my arse. She'll have made plans with that John MacKay."

"Who?"

"Some guy that she got chatting to on the ferry. He gave her a lift up to Stornoway today. Wouldn't go off with some stranger in the middle of the city, but just because it's Harris, it must be safe."

Derek nodded. "See when my daughters get to the dating age, I'm going to lock them up in a tower. Ach, I'm sure she'll be fine. What do you know about him?"

"A writer from the Black Isle, staying in the bunkhouse at Leverburgh. Looks a bit smooth, if you ask me, but she never does."

"The bunkhouse, eh?" Derek tapped the side of his nose. "Leave it with me."

Joe raised his eyebrows and said nothing. He'd been tempted to take advantage of his occupation in similar circumstances, but data protection, and the fate of others who had given in to temptation, was a deterrent. Maybe it was easier to get away with it in the islands.

Derek smiled, as if he had read Joe's mind. "See the PNC, SID, HOLMES? You can keep your fancy databases. They have nothing on the Harris grapevine. The wife's cousin works at the bunkhouse."

***

The bus timetable had foiled Lucy's plan to return to Harris on her own. She'd just missed a bus and the next wasn't for a couple of hours. Stornoway was too small a place to hide; she was hungry; John was waiting.

At lunch, John told Lucy he'd lost both his parents several years ago, and he saw little of his only brother, who lived in Germany. "Are you and Joe close?" he asked

Lucy nodded. "Don't see as much of him as I'd like. It was easier when he was in Perth; I'd go up to see him for the weekend. Thought I was so cool, hanging about with him and his pals. He shared a flat with his best friend, Matt." Lucy smiled. "I loved Matt; he was great."

"Was?"

"Aye, he was murdered, stabbed, and Joe was devastated. We spent a lot of time together after that, until he left Perth for Inverness. Then my parents moved up there too."

"Is Joe close to them?"

"Not to my mum – they argue a lot."

"Your dad?"

"Aye, they're close. Dad gets on with everyone. I don't know how he puts up with my mother. Much as I love her, she puts a damper on things. Always finds something to complain about; she's just that type. Never seems entirely satisfied, though she's never wanted for anything. Dad and I are experts at walking on eggshells. Joe, not so much." Time to stop talking about Joe. She looked at her watch. "You'll be wanting to get on with your work."

"Done it all. Have you seen enough of Stornoway?"

"Eh . . . "

"I don't mind waiting if you want more time here. Or we could take a detour to the Callanish Stones on the way back. Shame to come to Lewis and not see them. They're amazing." He drank the last of his coffee, put the mug down, smiled. "No pressure. Your choice."

It seemed however she decided to spend the afternoon, it was going to involve John. She'd read about the standing stones and they sounded fascinating. Couldn't do any harm, could it?

***

Big Aggie had knickers as large as tents and reinforced tights that could tether a bull. Betty sniggered as she held them up, then tossed them on top of the heap of clothing on Aggie's bed. Where was it? Must be here somewhere. Betty had never trusted that Aggie; they had rooms next door to one another and it would be easy for Betty's neighbour to sneak in and remove things. She had that kind of look about her.

Betty stepped over the upturned drawers on the floor, then she started on the wardrobe. In Aggie's coat pockets she found only soggy hankies and crumbs. There was a shoebox in the corner. Betty tipped it upside down, its contents scattering around her and falling to the floor. Photos and pens, old spectacles and make-up compacts, hairnets and kirby grips. She kicked them around the floor until she was satisfied that her missing item wasn't there.

Betty crouched on the floor of the wardrobe and gagged at the smell of sweaty feet. She shook the wellie boots upside down, dislodging two spiders and an apple core. She inspected the shoes and slippers, shaking her head and throwing them over her shoulder.

There was a chair under the window and Betty dragged it across to the wardrobe. Standing on it, she peered along the shelf, pulling out blankets and fusty woollen cardigans, hats and scarves and two hot water bottles. There was a bit of folded-up newspaper away at the back of the shelf. On her tip-toes, Betty reached for it. It was too far.

"Aaarrrggghhh!"

Before Betty could turn to investigate the source of the gargantuan roar, the chair was tipped over and she was lying on the floor, her hip throbbing and her head spinning. And then Aggie was on top of her and Betty's hair was being pulled out in lumps and three nurses were trying to lift Aggie off.

When the nurses separated the scrapping patients, Betty was on the side of the bed nearest the door with Janey, and Aggie was on the other side, held by two nurses. They weren't going to risk letting her go while Betty was still in the room.

"Crazy old bat!" Aggie cried. "Get her out of here before I bash her senseless."

"She stole my picture," Betty said. "Common thief, that's what she is."

"Thief? I never stole anything in my life, but I'll go down for murder if you don't get out of here."

"I'll go when I get the picture."

"What picture?" Janey asked.

Betty pointed to the wardrobe. "It's in there, on the top shelf."

Janey got up on the chair and reached for the bit of paper. It was a folded column of singles ads from the Press and Journal, with several entries ringed in red pen.

"She planted that," Aggie shouted. "Never seen it before in my life."

Janey held the paper out to Betty. "Is this what you're looking for, Betty?"

Betty looked at it and rolled her eyes. "Hardly," she said. As she was ushered out the door by Janey, Betty gave Aggie a sly smile. Singles ads indeed.

"I don't know why you're smiling," Janey said to Betty when they were back in her own room. "That was a disgraceful invasion of Aggie's privacy. You had no right to trash her room like that. What picture were you looking for?"

Betty sat on the bed and folded her arms. "My picture. Someone has taken it."

Janey sighed. "I've been asking you for days what was 'stolen' from your room and you wouldn't tell me. What picture?"

"Moira Jacobs."

"The woman that was . . . the woman in that picture you had me cut out of the paper? Why would you want that?"

"I need to speak to her. I need to find out why."

"Why what?"

"Just why."

"Betty, did you know Moira Jacobs?"

Betty shrugged. "Might have."

"I think you should lie down now, Betty. You'll feel better after a rest."

"But my picture . . . "

"I'll see if I can find it. You should have told me this before."

***

As Joe stood before the house that had belonged to Seumas Mòr, he thought of the boy. How had he felt the first day that he travelled that narrow winding road to this remote spot? Wherever he had come from, it couldn't have been as bleak as this, and how much worse must it be in the winter? The house faced inland, towards a rocky hill, allowing very little light into the rooms at the front. There was no garden, and never had been. Just a house, perched on a scrap of heather and rock-strewn moor, as if it had grown there in defiance of the winds that must batter it endlessly.

The roof was missing slates, and those that had survived were covered in bright yellow lichen. Joe stared up at the top windows. The glass was still intact, but the wood had decayed into rotten splinters that would soon give up their grasp and let the dirty glass fall wherever it might. Had the boy slept in one of those rooms? How had he passed his time? What had Seumas Mòr done to him?

Although the front door was lying in the heather, adorned with the droppings of sheep and rabbits, Joe decided against going inside. He told himself he wasn't entering the house because it could be a crime scene. Yet he knew, even if there had been no suspicion of a crime, he couldn't have entered. The smell and the darkness would not let him. His own fears and his memories would not let him. The thought of the lonely abused boy would not let him. Was that boy Mac? And had he come back last July and murdered Seumas Mòr?

There was a commotion going on in Tarbert. A police car, a crowd of children, two mothers, a postman and a drunk. As Joe approached, he saw that Derek Russell was on his own, trying to help the drunk off the road, while the onlookers giggled. No one appeared about to offer Derek any help, so Joe pulled in behind the police car.

"Am I glad to see you!" Derek said to Joe. "My colleague's gone to the dentist. You couldn't give me a hand, could you?"

They took an arm each and propelled the drunk to the pavement, where he sat in a heap, muttering and laughing to himself, his shoe laces undone and his fly open. It was the man Joe had seen earlier in Tarbert.

"Right, Calum," Derek said. "We've had to get back-up in from the mainland. This is a detective sergeant from Inverness. If you don't start behaving, he'll take you away. Porterfield or New Craigs? What's your preference?"

"Dectivsarg," the drunk muttered, as he stared up at them. "Po'field? F'ckat."

"Our Calum MacKinnon has spent quite a bit of time courtesy of Her Majesty in Porterfield, haven't you Calum? And the odd month or two in New Craigs. Dries out and comes back squeaky clean. Wouldn't know him when he steps off that ferry. Quite the gentleman, until one of his pals comes round with a carry-out. He's not long back from New Craigs."

"'Snotnewcraigs," Calum said. "'S'Osphouse."

"Osprey House?" Joe said. It was a centre in Inverness for substance misuse services. "That's a good facility."

Calum grunted. "Ach, fuckem all."

"Well, Calum; what are we going to do with you?" Derek asked. "Can't leave you here. What about Maggie? Will we take you to see your big sister?"

Calum shook his head, shook his body, shook himself to his feet. He wasn't quite steady, but he wasn't far off it.

Derek smiled. "Hallelujah. Another miraculous recovery, thanks to the power of Sister Margaret."

"Speaking of Maggie . . . " one of the mothers said.

Joe followed her gaze. An old woman in a long tweed coat was charging towards them. She wore a head square and a stout pair of brogues, and she was raging. Calum didn't see her coming. He was leaning against the wall, busy poking around his fly, one hand trying to stuff a colourless knot of underwear back inside, the other trying to pull up the zip.

As the children giggled and the mothers shook their heads and smiled, Maggie grabbed Calum by the scruff of the neck and hauled him round. The watchers winced as she berated him in Gaelic before hauling him away.

Maggie walked a few steps, Calum stumbling beside her, then she turned. She stared at Joe, her piercing eyes making him feel like a naughty child. What the hell was she staring at him for? Surely she didn't think he was responsible for her brother's condition. He looked away first.

"Cò esan?" she asked, her voice a harsh rasp.

The mothers shrugged and looked at Derek. "Detective Sergeant Galbraith," he said. "From Inverness."

"Dè a' chiad ainm a th' air?"

"Joe," Derek replied. "Joe Galbraith."

Joe looked from Derek to Maggie, where she stood with her head cocked to the side and her mouth muttering. What the hell was going on? Whatever it was, he didn't like it.

"Eòsaph Mac a' Bhreatnnaich," the old woman said. The anger was gone from her old lined face. In its place, Joe saw sadness. Such sadness. But why?

The old woman shook her head and turned away, dragging Calum with her. As they made their way along the road, Maggie kept turning round and looking at Joe, her lips still moving, her face still sad. She was too far away for him to hear what she was saying.

As Joe watched her walking, an unwanted memory came to him. Hints of whispered Gaelic and ancient lullabies; fragmented and delicate, so subtle that it was gone in a moment, but not before it almost overwhelmed him.

"Thanks for that," Derek said. "And praise the Lord for Maggie. I really did not want to have to take Calum anywhere in my car. Last time, he peed himself. Took ages to get rid of the smell. He's such a bright guy, too; it's tragic."

"What was that Maggie on about?" Joe tried to keep his tone light, his voice steady.

"Just asked who you were; wanted to know your first name. My grasp of the language isn't great, but I'm guessing she repeated your name in Gaelic. Sounded like a mouthful. By the way, I checked up on a few things. There was no investigation concerning Seumas Mòr when he was alive – he was squeaky clean, though the locals might not agree. Found dead on the morning of 6th July 2012 – could have died the previous evening. No apparent suspicious circumstances, but the old man and his house were quite isolated, so you never know. Think I'll ask for the ferry and flight passenger lists around that time. See what comes up. Not that we know who we're looking for, but it can't do any harm."

"Cheers. Good idea."

"By the way," Derek said, "I hear there's some trouble with the mobile mast – you might have difficulty getting a signal on your phone. Happens from time to time."

Great. As if he wasn't isolated enough. He took his leave of Derek. As he drove away, Joe couldn't get Maggie's piercing eyes, or her sadness, out of his mind.

***

The standing stones had once been giants. See how each one was shaped differently, just like humans. Tall and smaller, broad and slimmer, crouched and more upright. They were giants, minding their own business in this beautiful landscape, until the arrival of Christianity. They wanted nothing to do with this new religion. Their punishment? Turned to stone by St Kieran.

"Harsh," Lucy said, as she stood in the long shadow of the central monolith, gazing up.

That wasn't all, John told her. Every year at sunrise on the summer solstice, a shimmering figure walked among the stones, heralded by the sound of a cuckoo.

Lucy smiled. Had he seen this for himself? Nah, he said; you couldn't get near the place at summer solstice for Druids, shamans and hippies, with their drums and spells and rituals.

Even without his stories, it was a place steeped in mystery and atmosphere. An inner circle of stones surrounded the centre stone, and there was an avenue of stones to the north and a single row to the south, east and west. The location was stunning, the stones surrounded by lush greens fields, and the deep blue sky reflected in the sparkling waters of Loch Roag. Lucy could have stayed there for hours, had the peace not been shattered by the arrival of a bus load of German tourists.

The mountains of Harris looked different in the late afternoon sun, their edges blurred and their contours less sharp. The colours seemed to have changed too, and the landscape was softer, gentler. Was it really, or had the Callanish Stones placed Lucy in some kind of hippy trance where everything felt gentle and peaceful? Must have. Why else would she have agreed to a walk with John later?

In Tarbert, close to the primary school, Lucy saw Joe's car. She said nothing to John, just hoped that he hadn't seen her brother standing at the side of the road with a group of people and a policeman.

John stopped at the hotel where Lucy was meeting Joe. She bent to get her bag and her jacket from the floor of the car. As she straightened up, she felt his hand on her arm. Her mouth dry, she looked at him.

"Thank you," he said. "That was one of the best days ever."

Before she could answer, a car beeped behind them; John was blocking an entrance.

Lucy smiled. "Thanks for the lift and . . . and everything." She opened the door, got out of the car, turned and waved as John drove away. Then she sank back against the wall. She wanted to cry.

Chapter 17

There was an old man in the queue in front of Stephen. His hands shook as he tried to find the right money. Eventually, he gave up, held his clawed hand out to the girl and let her sort through the small change. As he shuffled away, clutching his plastic bag, Stephen watched him. Couldn't be much of a life when you got to that stage. The slightest shock and he'd be gone. Like Jean.

Stephen had known she was dead when he left the house, but he was certain he hadn't killed her. Not Auntie Jean. No matter how low he'd sunk, he would never have killed his own aunt. It must have been her heart. She hadn't looked well, and her lungs had rattled like peas in a tin can when she breathed. His hands had only been on her throat for a few seconds. He shouldn't have done that, but she shouldn't have said those things about his mother. No, he hadn't killed her. Must have been her heart. It was a blessing. She'd had no life there on her own in that old house, not since his mother told her that dreadful lie. If anything, his mother had killed her years ago.

And he hadn't killed MacLeod either; it was the stairs that did for the old man. Stupid bugger should have replaced the carpet. And he should have locked his door. They all left their doors open on the island, but he really should have known better. Just showed his arrogance; the great MacLeod, with his crofts and his houses, his prayers and his piety. He could get away with anything. Who was going to challenge him after all this time?

Stephen paid for his goods and left the shop, his mind

still on that night; the night Seumas Mòr MacLeod died.

When he'd pushed the old man's door open, the smell of the house had almost turned Stephen away. A stale mix of boiled mutton, sweat and damp. It was repulsive.

He'd expected to find the old man sleeping in the room he'd shared with his wife on the right of the landing, but it was empty. The bed was made up, with ancient threadbare blankets and a pink candlewick bedspread. There was an old leather Bible on the bedside table, and a small vase with dusty artificial flowers, the colour long gone. Stephen had never been in that room. He'd heard the beating, the sobbing, the praying, almost every night for the few weeks he'd been there. And the grand finale: the self-satisfied echo of MacLeod's release into the tin potty that still lurked under the bed.

The door and the floorboards had creaked as Stephen approached the other room, the room he'd slept in as a child. Not that he'd slept much. Even on nights when the house shook with MacLeod's snoring, Stephen had lain awake waiting for the creaking warning that heralded the bastard's approach.

The summer moon was bright, shining through the bare window, illuminating MacLeod as he slept. It had been such a cold dark room that far away winter, with the heaviest, thickest of curtains. He remembered how MacLeod would tug at those curtains, fearful that the slightest of gaps might expose his depravity.

Stephen sat in the chair by the bed, watching, remembering. He held a grubby pillow in his hands, and listened to the laboured breathing, the guttural moans, the occasional snuffle. The old man's loose skin was pale and wrinkled. The hand above the blankets was liver-spotted, the joints deformed with arthritis. Stephen smiled and looked at the pillow. It would be so simple. No one would ever know. But why should he let MacLeod off that easily?

The moon was shining upon Stephen when the old man opened his eyes. Stephen had thought he'd have to remind him, but no; he knew. He whispered Stephen's name, then he closed his eyes and started to pray in Gaelic. Though he didn't understand the words, Stephen knew it was a desperate plea that it was all a dream. A prayer that, when the old man opened his eyes and reached out with his clawed hand, he wouldn't touch living flesh. MacLeod's prayer was not answered.

***

Roberts hated hospitals. They reminded him of his grandfather. Twenty-odd years and he still remembered the smells and the moans and the shrivelled gnome in the bed. The gnome's face had looked a little like Granda, but it couldn't be him. He was a big, strong man; it just couldn't be him. Roberts remembered how his mother had to force him towards the bed, towards the voice that wasn't his grandfather's, and the outstretched claw that reached for him.

Man up, he told himself; New Craigs didn't smell like that, wasn't even that kind of hospital. He pushed the ward door open and walked in. No one about. He put his hand in his pocket for his warrant card and a voice behind him made him jump. "Can I help you?"

He turned. Help? This sour face could never offer help. She'd be good on reception at the station, though. "DC Roberts." He coughed, lowered his voice. "Here to see Nurse Black." He held up his warrant card. "Janey Black."

The woman looked behind her at the sign on the wall. Roberts saw it then. He stared at her, dared her with his fiercest policeman look to challenge him. She didn't. "Wait here," she barked.

Betty was acting all coy and giggly, pushing up her curls, crossing and uncrossing her legs. Janey had never seen her like that before. Even Danny Ross, intermittent patient and regular Lothario, had not been able to charm Betty. She had seen right through him, mocking the other women, especially Aggie, for taking anything to do with him. "A fly-by-night gigolo, that's all he is," she had said.

"Betty," Janey tried again, "Detective Constable Roberts wants to talk to you about Moira Jacobs. Remember, you had her picture and you lost it? He just wants to ask you some questions about how you knew her."

"Detective," Betty said. "You must have to be terribly clever to be a detective."

Roberts smiled and nodded. "Can you tell me how you knew Moira Jacobs?"

Betty shook her head and grinned. "A detective, indeed. Tell me, are you any good at finding thoughts?"

Roberts looked helplessly at Janey.

"Betty sometimes loses her thoughts," Janey said, "but we have ways of helping her deal with that." Janey ignored the 'huh' from Betty. "He's not here to find your thoughts, Betty. He's here to talk about Moira Jacobs. Remember the picture you had? The one you lost?"

Roberts was looking at Janey; Janey was looking at Betty; Betty was looking at them both. She was smiling, and saying nothing.

Roberts was stumped. What would Joe do? His mouth dry, he reached into his pocket. He leaned towards Betty and smiled. "Was it a picture like this?" he asked, bringing out the small passport photo of Moira Jacobs. He was ready for Betty, pulling his hand back when she tried to snatch the picture. "Betty," he said, his voice low, firm, like Joe's, "we really need to find out all we can about Moira Jacobs. Do you know what happened to her?"

Betty shrugged, oblivious to Janey's frantic head-shaking. "I don't know anything. I just want the picture."

"Remember you told me that you needed to ask Moira Jacobs something," Janey said. "You wanted to find out why something had happened."

"Did I?"

Janey nodded. "It would be good if you could tell

Detective Constable Roberts what it was that you wanted to ask Moira Jacobs."

"Mmmm." Betty thought about it. She thought some more. "It's quite private," she said. "It's a delicate matter." She lowered her voice. "She's not a very good person, you know. Are you going to arrest her?"

Roberts was stumped again, but only for a moment. "We hope it won't come to that," he said, his voice serious. "We just need to find out a bit more about her before we make any decisions as to how we proceed."

Betty considered for a while, then she nodded. "It's my Stephen. It's . . . well, that woman, that awful woman, well, she didn't do right by my Stephen."

Roberts' mind was racing. Betty MacLaren. Stephen MacLaren – was he Mac? Was Betty's son the killer? Oh shit. What should he ask? Should he mention Mac? Should he mention Jean Henderson and Kirkcaldy? Oh, why did he come alone?

"You see," Betty continued, "the picture was in my Kirkcaldy book and it just went missing. I don't like people touching my things. I don't know why anyone would just take it."

Kirkcaldy book? Oh shit, shit, shit. "Do you know anyone in Kirkcaldy, Betty?"

Betty frowned. "Aye, I was brought up on a farm outside the town. My sister, Jean, still lives in Kirkcaldy; miserable old bat."

"But you're always talking about Jean and how you're going to go and live with her when you leave here," Janey said. "I thought you had it all planned: the nice flat above her house."

"Pipe dreams, nothing but pipe dreams. Haven't spoken in years. She let my Stephen down too. She could have taken him instead of letting that Moira Jacobs have him. She could have saved him."

"What's your sister's surname," Roberts asked, although he knew very well.

"Henderson. Maybe you should arrest her too for not looking after her nephew."

Roberts nodded. What the hell was he supposed to say? We'll not be arresting anyone but Stephen? "Betty, do you know where Stephen is today?"

"Don't you go bothering my Stephen. He's very busy and I don't want him reminded of those terrible women."

"It might help to speak to him; it'll help things along."

"He said he was going away, didn't he, Betty?" Janey said. "Something to do with his work."

"Is that right?" Roberts said. Mac had also told Sharon he was going away. "And where does he work?"

"I don't think we know, do we Betty?" Janey asked.

Betty shook her head. "It's something high-powered. He's a clever lad, Stephen. A clever, bonny lad, and he's very good to his mother. I don't think you should bother him."

"Does he live in Inverness?" Roberts asked.

Betty nodded. "He has a house somewhere; it's a lovely house, but I've never been there."

Janey smiled at Betty. "You have, Betty; you lived there. It's your house, remember."

"No; it's Stephen's."

When Roberts asked Betty for the address, she shrugged. "Haven't a clue, but the staff can help you. Remember, I don't want you bothering him. Maybe you could tell him you've come about a parking ticket or something like that."

"Maybe," Roberts said. "You've been very helpful, Betty. Thank you very much." He paused. There were other questions he needed to ask; he was certain of it, but he couldn't think of them. Why had he not prepared more thoroughly for coming to see Betty? Because he hadn't taken the call seriously. DI Black hadn't taken it seriously either. A woman in the nut-house had lost a newspaper cutting? Big deal. Why would he bother sending anyone? Ach, the DI had decided, he could do without Roberts

191

hanging around like an eager puppy waiting for his next treat. "Get up and back as quickly as you can," he had barked.

Betty was staring, her fingers tapping her knee. Roberts looked at the back of her liver-spotted hand and he remembered. "Just another couple of questions, Betty, and I'll get out of here, let you get on with . . . " What did people do in here? Betty leaned towards him, her eyebrows raised, as if she hoped that he might just suggest something really interesting. Roberts smiled. "Did Stephen have any recent injuries to his hand?"

Betty looked disappointed. She said nothing.

"Betty," Janey said. "Stephen did have a bandage on his hand last week. Remember?"

Betty shook her head.

"Didn't he say he injured it while he was gardening?"

Betty pursed her lips, shook her head again, crossed her legs.

"Thank you," Roberts said to Janey. He looked at Betty again. "Does Stephen have a nickname?"

Betty looked at Roberts as if he had just passed wind. "A nickname? I should think not! Hasn't he got a good enough name as it is? That was my grandfather's name."

Roberts coloured. He thought of leaving it there, but he knew the DI's wrath would be much worse than Betty's. "I just wondered if anyone ever shortened his surname, maybe to 'Mac'."

"No, he wouldn't hold with that kind of nonsense. Not my Stephen."

"Thank you. I know this isn't easy, so I'll just ask one more question, Betty. Do you or Stephen have any connection with the Outer Hebrides, particularly with the Isle of Harris?"

Though she said nothing, Roberts saw the answer in her eyes. And then he saw tears. They welled up and spilled over, snaking their way down the furrows on her cheeks. "I want to go to bed." She stood up. "I want to go now."

Janey nodded. She opened the door and called a nurse. "Will you help Betty? She wants to lie down. I'll be through in a minute."

Betty shuffled to the door, where a male nurse waited for her. She turned and wiped her tears. "If you come back, bring me a photo. A bigger one. And I'll not let it out of my sight."

Janey closed the door. "The house is Betty's," she said. "I'll get you the address in a minute. She lived there for a while before she was admitted. Stephen lives with her."

"What's he like?" Roberts asked.

"Tall, dark hair – mid-30s. Deep, serious – doesn't give much away. Visits regularly. He last came on Saturday, said he might have to go away for a while – I got the feeling it might be a long time – there was just something about the way he said it."

Going away for a long time, all right, Roberts thought. "I should have asked Betty for a photo of him – do you know if she has one?"

"Several; do you want to ask her or will I?"

"Might be better coming from you. The more recent, the better."

Coward, he told himself, when the nurse had gone. Dealing with a crying woman was worse than a hall full of dancing pensioners, and that was saying something. While he waited, Roberts glanced over his notebook. This was big; it was huge. Should he phone the DI now or see him at the station? All these questions that might seem really minor to an officer of Joe's experience were suddenly huge obstacles to Roberts. How did you know what to do? What if you did it wrong? Scolding himself for his idiocy, Roberts decided to phone DI Black now – the worst that could happen would be a bollocking. As he waited for the receptionist to connect him, he took several deep breaths. There was no need; the DI had nipped out to B&Q and he was not to be disturbed. Roberts told June he'd be back in the station in the next ten minutes; he'd see the DI then.

Janey returned with the address and a photo that Betty had not wanted to part with. Roberts remembered Liam MacRae's description of Mac. Not big like fat, but big like long. Quite old, like about Joe's age. His hair was not long, not short, not straight, but not exactly curly. A bit like Roberts' hair, but shinier. The child's description was perfect. Stephen was smiling in the photo; he looked like a decent guy.

"I'm grateful," Roberts said. "Do you know if there's a Harris connection?"

"Not that she's ever mentioned, but she can be very private. She didn't come to the attention of psychiatric services until a few years ago, when she was living in Glasgow. I've just remembered something else; Stephen said goodbye around lunchtime on Saturday, but I saw him again outside the hospital a couple of hours later. I was going off my shift and he ran past the hospital on the other side of the road. I think he'd come from the direction of Craig Dunain. I thought it was odd that he was still up this way." She shrugged. "He could have friends nearby, I suppose."

"Perhaps," Roberts replied. Craig Dunain? There had been something about Craig Dunain last week, but he couldn't remember what it was. It wasn't this case, he was certain. "Well, thank you very much. You've been great."

"You're welcome." Janey smiled. She held the office door open for him. "Give my love to Uncle Alec."

"Eh?"

"DI Black, aka Uncle Alec. He's my dad's brother."

"Aye?" Roberts said. How could this be? Janey was so nice.

"My dad's nothing like that miserable old bastard, but don't tell him I said so."

Roberts smiled. "I think I'm about to make his day."

How often did he have to repeat it? Roberts leaned forward in his chair until he was almost half way across the DI's desk. "Betty MacLaren said Moira Jacobs didn't do right by her son; nor did her sister, Jean Henderson, who lives in Kirkcaldy."

The DI studied the photo of Stephen. "And this Betty MacLaren, she's not right in the head?"

Roberts shrugged. "She has her moments. She seemed pretty certain she knew Moira Jacobs, and that Jean Henderson was her sister."

"And you say she had a photo of Moira Jacobs?"

"Earlier in the week – the one from the Press and Journal. Went missing the last day her son visited."

"And Janey – why didn't she phone us when she saw this Betty MacLaren with Moira Jacobs' photo?"

Roberts shrugged. "I didn't question her about that."

"You leave that to me, son. I'll be having words. She's a flibbertigibbet, that Janey; always was."

DI Black lifted the telephone receiver. "June, get me the Procurator Fiscal."

Roberts let out his breath, relaxed back in his chair and grinned.

The DI put his hand over the phone and nodded towards the door. "All right son, you can go."

"But – "

"Don't worry; the party won't start without you."

***

Tinned curry. The frozen stuff was bad enough, but at least the manufacturers had the sense to include rice. Could he be bothered going out to get some? No. Stephen gave the pan another stir, hoping the mixture would somehow metamorphose into something vaguely appetising. It didn't.

He didn't bother with a plate – nothing was going to make it taste any better than it looked. When he'd forced a little down, he chucked the rest, washed the pan, then lay on his bed and closed his eyes.

Ach, things weren't going too badly at all. Maybe fate was on his side. It had brought him Moira Jacobs, hadn't it? All stretched out on a hospital trolley. Hadn't even thought of looking for her. He'd probably have been scared to track her down. She had become the devil incarnate in his head, far worse than MacLeod. Those words she had said, the morning she collected him from that house of horrors and drove him home to his mother; he would never forget those words, and that accent that made his skin crawl. 'Mr MacLeod is a good man,' she had said. 'You are nothing. You and your drunken mother, you are scum, an affront to decent people. You will tell your mother nothing, or I'll make sure you're sent back to MacLeod. If he won't have you, I'll see that you leave the island for good and you'll never see your mother again. That's what happens to liars like you.'

Those words had terrified him. He had tried not to tell his mother. He had tried to pretend that his time in that cold, damp croft house had been fine, that Mr MacLeod had been good to him. And then his mother had asked him to tell her about his Christmas, to tell her every detail of their first Christmas apart, so that she could imagine she'd been there with him.

Stephen could still see his mother's face when he blurted out every detail. The endless prayers and Bible reading, the hard, hard work and rationed food, the bullying and the punishment. He told his mother what MacLeod had done to his wife when she tried to protect Stephen, and how he had done the same thing to Stephen, but in the cold dark of the night. That thing. Stephen had known that men and women did it, that animals did it, but a man, doing that to a boy?

The guilt on his mother's face; oh, that guilt. And the shock. It kept her sober, that shock, though her body suffered terribly for the sudden withdrawal. Stephen had begged her not to go to the police. He couldn't tell anyone else; he couldn't go to court and tell strangers. Most of all, he couldn't risk that they wouldn't believe him, that they would send him back to MacLeod, that he would never see his mother again. For that threat hadn't only come from Moira Jacobs; MacLeod had whispered it too, whispered it in his ear as he grunted and moaned into the darkness.

Stephen knew his mother must have talked to someone, for soon Moira Jacobs was gone, and a kind woman with compassion in her eyes and respect in her voice, took her place. And before long, Social Work didn't need to have any more to do with them, because Betty had stayed sober and she was making plans to leave. She didn't stay sober for long in Glasgow, but her drinking habits changed so that she just kept herself topped up, rarely spilling over into open drunkenness or hilarity. Over time, the booze ate away at her brain, until she lost it one day on a train into town, and ended up sectioned. And that was the start of a pattern. Good months and bad months, the odd good year, and several bad ones. The move to Inverness, and more of the same.

And then it turned out Moira Jacobs was in Inverness too. He hadn't known her surname the day he took her to the operating theatre. She was just another patient, and if she hadn't barked at him for jolting the trolley as he pushed her into the lift, he'd have been none the wiser. If she hadn't spoken to him like he was the chattel of one of her colonial ancestors, he wouldn't have given her a second thought. But that accent; how could he ever forget that? Horrible horrible bitch.

It had been so easy to reel her neighbour in, to get closer to Moira Jacobs. When he saw that letter, and found out she'd already been the victim of a violent crime, he was happy, so glad she'd suffered. He'd almost left it at that. The universe had a way of sorting these things out, paying people back. Why bother trying to speak to her? Because the universe couldn't give him the answers he needed from Moira Jacobs. Why had she sent him there? Had MacLeod asked for a boy like him? A sad, lonely boy with no friends and a mother that couldn't protect him? Had she known what MacLeod would do?

197

Grasping, greedy cow. She was delighted to see him when she thought he was there to discuss money. A different person, a nicer person, might even have remembered him from the hospital, but not her. He was just a porter – she might have shouted at him, but she hadn't seen him. But if he was there to give her money, that was a different story. Couldn't have been nicer, until he put the photo on the table and told her who he really was. She went mental. Started shoving him down the corridor towards the door, and that fucking dog yapping at his heels. Even then, he'd have left without harming her, if she hadn't grabbed the hammer and hit him on the hand, and if that mutt hadn't bitten his ankle. Aye, the mental bitch soon changed her tune when the dog got it, and she knew she was next. She was out of there like a shot, squawking like a banshee.

No, he hadn't planned to kill her, but it felt great. The irony in seeing her and MacLeod lying twisted at the bottom of the stairs. Twisted in life and in death.

***

Of course Lucy didn't mind eating fish if someone else killed it, she told Joe, as she finished her halibut steak; she wasn't that principled. She just didn't fancy an evening of slaughter. Didn't fancy any wine, either, which was a first, as far as Joe could remember. She was going to be busy, she told him; she'd a lot of reading to do.

"Just reading? I thought you wanted to go for a walk."

She looked a little uncomfortable. "I am supposed to be going for a walk later."

"Supposed to be? With John MacKay?"

Lucy nodded.

"And you don't want to?"

She shrugged. "Don't know. Can't decide. Do you think I should?"

"Since when did you listen to my advice?"

"I do. Sometimes. Well, not very often. It's just . . .

he's quite persistent. But he's good company; can't deny that. And he's really interesting. He knows so much about the islands." She told Joe all about the Castle Grounds and the stones at Callanish, the North Harris mountains and the view down Loch Seaforth. She hardly paused for breath, and didn't notice her ice cream melting around the sticky toffee pudding until it was a puddle. "And he's a great listener. He's easy to be with. And we're going home tomorrow, and I'll probably never have to see him again. What do you think?"

Joe hesitated. Lucy had changed when she started going out with Sebastian. Even though Joe had never met him, and though Lucy came home regularly, and alone, he always seemed to be in the background somehow, as if he was casting a shadow over Lucy. It had been very subtle, that shadow, but now it was gone. And Joe was glad, even if it meant that some other stranger was in the picture. "I think you don't need me to tell you just how much you want to go for a walk with John MacKay."

"I think I want you to tell me that I shouldn't want it quite as much as I do."

When Joe was paying the bill, his phone vibrated in his pocket. It was a voice-mail. Presumably the mobile phone signal was still affected and Roberts hadn't been able to get through. Joe waited until they were out in the car park, then he phoned his voice-mail.

At last! He wanted to punch the air, but a couple of German tourists were standing beside the next car. He tried to ring Roberts but the transient signal was gone.

"Something important?" Lucy asked Joe when he got in the car.

Joe started the engine. "Aye. They know who the killer is."

"Anyone you know?"

"We just knew him as Mac, but they've got his name and address now – Stephen MacLaren – they're just waiting for a warrant."

Joe stopped in briefly at the bed and breakfast to change into jeans and trainers. Before he left, he knocked on Lucy's door and went in. She was sitting on her bed reading a textbook, a large A4 pad and pen beside her.

"Where are you going for your walk?" he asked.

"To the beaches behind the hill. Apparently there's a ruined medieval chapel too."

Joe nodded, and shivered inside. Supposing someone offered him a king's ransom and a double Glenfiddich, he wouldn't take that walk. But he didn't tell Lucy. "Have a lovely time. And be careful." He kissed her cheek and left.

Outside, in the shadow of the hill, Joe listened to the voice-mail again. He had never heard Roberts like that, tripping over his words. He'd been to visit a woman in New Craigs. She knew Moira Jacobs, said the social worker hadn't done right by her son, Stephen MacLaren. Neither had her sister, Jean Henderson from Kirkcaldy. Stephen MacLaren had a bandage on his hand last week. Roberts had a photo and he fitted the description of Mac given by Sharon and Liam. MacLaren's mother didn't respond to a question about a Harris connection, but she became upset. They were just waiting for a warrant, then they'd go to the house, see if he was there. Probably wouldn't be – he'd told his mother and the staff he was going away, just like Mac had told Sharon. Stephen MacLaren was Mac; they were certain of it. Joe had been right about Mac all along. Just a shame he wasn't there now to help bring Stephen MacLaren in. Shame? Joe was gutted. Nothing to be done, though. He'd just have to switch off, and enjoy the fishing.

He arrived at Leverburgh early. Checking his phone, he found he had a signal. No point in phoning Roberts – they probably hadn't got their warrant yet, and, if they had, he didn't want to interrupt them in the middle of a house search.

At the sound of Carla's voice, Joe felt that familiar knot in his stomach. He'd thought about phoning her on Monday night from Northton, but he feared that his gloom would tarnish the call. So he had written a text and then spent an age trying to decide how many kisses were too many. He decided four would do it – two more than usual, then he found that the bloody thing wouldn't go. As he tossed and turned, he imagined that text, trapped just like him, in the shadow of the hill. It was luckier than he was; it escaped during the dark night.

Now, it was Joe's turn to commiserate with Carla; she was on night shift. Their chat was brief but cheerful. Joe was smiling as he rang off. He looked at the sea and it was calm and sparkling, moored boats shifting lazily in its gentle swell. The sky was blue, with only the slenderest wisps of drifting cloud. For the first time since he set foot on the island, Joe felt the tension slip from him.

Derek Russell had a couple of fishing rods in the boot of his jeep, along with a net, three pairs of wellies, a pile of oilskins, a thermos flask and a large cool-box.

"Is that for the catch?" Joe asked, nodding at the cool-box. Derek smiled and opened the lid. It was half-full of bottles of beer. "Shame we're both driving."

"Ach, we'll manage a couple," said Derek. "We'll wait until we're out a bit. Wouldn't want anyone reporting me for being drunk in charge of a fishing boat. You want to choose a pair of wellies and a jacket?"

Derek manoeuvred the light fishing boat out into the Sound of Harris, where they motored around and between rocks and skerries, lights and buoys, in the shelter of long-deserted islands. The names of the islands in the Sound all ended in 'ay' in English, or 'aigh' in Gaelic. It was something to do with the Vikings, Derek said. Ensay and Killegray were the closest islands to Leverburgh, both low-lying with rich pasture land. Beyond Killegray was Berneray, the destination of the *Loch Portain* on her regular crossings to North Uist. Although it was a short distance, as the crow flies, from Leverburgh to Berneray, the ferry was forced to take a well-marked roundabout route, to avoid the rocks and sand-banks. Derek didn't follow the route of the ferry. Instead, he headed towards Ensay.

On the south-east coast of the island, as the evening sun cast a golden glow across the water, Derek cut the motor. The boat bobbed gently as the men baited their lines. "Look," Derek said. "We're not the only ones fishing tonight."

A flock of terns flitted across the surface of the sea on shining, tapered wings. Their dipping and diving was tentative, as if they feared the gleaming expanse. As Joe watched them, a larger shadow fell across the boat. He looked up to see three gannets on slender black-tipped wings. The gannets plunged together, their bodies as streamlined as rapiers, slicing through the ocean's surface.

"That showed the light-weights," Derek said, laughing as the smaller birds took off, their rasping cries harsh and forlorn in the quiet evening. "Mind you, the terns are fearsome little buggers if you go too near their nests or chicks on land. A friend of mine got quite a cut on the head last summer – a tern dive-bombed him from behind. He didn't know what hit him. Out for a gentle stroll and he comes back pouring blood. Said it reminded him of policing in Govan."

They cast then, and it wasn't long before there was a glittering heap of striped mackerel on the bottom of the boat.

"When are you off?" Derek asked Joe as he passed him a bottle of beer.

Joe wiped his hands on his jeans and took the bottle. "Cheers. Tomorrow afternoon." The beer tasted fantastic as it slid down.

"I'll get a few of these gutted and ready for you to take, if your sister doesn't object."

"That'll be right. She has no qualms about eating them, as long as someone else does the killing."

"By the way," Derek said, "your man, John MacKay, is kosher. Comes over a couple of times a year and stays in the bunkhouse. Writes about nature, environment, stuff like that. Polite, friendly, clean and attractive, according to the womenfolk."

Joe had forgotten about their earlier discussion. His resolution to put all that was worrying him to the back of his mind had clearly worked. "A womaniser?"

"Apparently not. He has his admirers in the village, but he hasn't given in to any of them yet. They wondered if he had someone at home."

Joe's face was serious. "Probably has. Anyone seen anything he's had published?"

Derek laughed. "I don't think the wife's cousin is all that interested in environmental journalism. Google is probably your best bet."

"I'll do that when I get home." For now, Joe was content to keep John, Lucy and Stephen MacLaren at bay. As soon as he got ashore, he'd be calling Roberts.

Chapter 18

Roberts shook almost as much as the house when the battering ram hit the front door. It wasn't fear that affected him; it was excitement. Would Stephen MacLaren try to run out the back way? Would Roberts and Wendy Aird be able to stop him? There could be a bravery award in this . . .

A shape appeared inside the back door and Roberts relaxed. No mistaking MacKay's dark ginger hair and weedy frame. "Welcome, officers," he said, as he stood aside to let them in. "No one home."

In contrast to a very scruffy garden, the kitchen was immaculate. The worktops were bare and shining, the floor spotless. The fridge had little in it – tomato ketchup, a scraping of margarine and a yellow plastic lemon. The living room and front bedroom were also clean and tidy. Although there were ornaments, there was no clutter, nothing lying around, no sign that anyone had lived there recently. It looked like a house ready for sale.

"No one up here, boss," a PC shouted from upstairs.

"Attic?" the DI replied. "Where's the hatch?"

"Top of the stairs; it's padlocked from the outside."

"Not for long," the DI muttered. He opened a cupboard under the stairs and peered into the gloom. Just boxes and suitcases, a vacuum cleaner and a laundry basket; nowhere for a man to hide.

There were two bedrooms and a bathroom upstairs. The front bedroom had a pink carpet, a flowery bedspread and matching curtains. The DI gestured towards the floor. Roberts looked down; he couldn't see anything.

The DI sighed. "Under the bed, Roberts; under the bed."

Nothing but a little dust. The DI gestured towards the sliding doors of the built-in wardrobe. It was half-full of women's clothes that smelled like Roberts' grandmother. On one of the bedside tables there was a photo of a woman and a younger man in a silver frame. "Is that Betty MacLaren?" the DI asked.

Chuffed, Roberts nodded. "Aye, sir; her and Stephen – a few years back, I'd say."

"Sir," MacKay called from the room next door. "You need to see this."

Aird and Roberts followed the DI to the back room, where the walls were white, the carpet navy blue. There was a single bed, stripped bare, and a tall bookcase full of books. Beside the bookcase, open on the floor, was a large book. Roberts peered closer – pictures of planets and stars, the writing large and the text as simple as astronomy for children could be. That wasn't what had alerted MacKay. He was standing beside a door that looked as if it might lead to an en-suite toilet.

The DI went through the door, followed by MacKay. They were silent for a moment. "Oh shit," the DI said at last. "Oh shit."

Roberts looked at Aird. Was it a body? Had Mac killed himself? Had he killed someone else? Aird shrugged, and chewed. The DI appeared at the door. "Any of you met Galbraith's family?"

Roberts and Aird both paled and nodded. Were they about to meet the Galbraiths again? The shower scene from Psycho flashed through Roberts' head.

"Come on, come on," the DI said. "We haven't got all day."

Roberts went first, Aird squeezing in behind him. It wasn't an en-suite toilet, and there were no bodies. It was a box room, large enough for a desk and a filing cabinet. The walls were covered in newspaper cuttings and pictures. The

DI pointed to a cork notice board in front of the desk. Roberts tried to turn his gasp into a cough; he guessed he was fooling no one. The notice board was covered with pictures of Joe, of Lucy, of an older couple that must be Joe's parents; the woman was the image of Joe, Lucy the image of her father. Unaware of the camera, they were going about their daily business. Joe outside his cottage in Nairn; Joe on a small yacht; Joe coming out of the filling station with a sandwich and a can of coke; Joe and Carla MacKenzie at Nairn Harbour in the dusk. Lucy sitting on a wall with two other girls, a large domed building behind them; Lucy working behind a bar, smiling at a customer; Lucy on her mobile phone, walking down the road. The parents in the supermarket; the father in the garden; the mother getting out of the car. And in the centre of the board, there were four individual pictures of the Galbraith family placed close together, each with a dart through the head.

"Those were taken on Saturday at the Bught," Wendy Aird said, pointing to a group of pictures at the bottom of the board. "That's what they were wearing the day the father was run over." It was clear that none of the subjects knew the images were being captured; Joe and his family had been under surveillance.

Roberts looked at the wall behind him, and suddenly Moira Jacobs was more than just a corpse. She was a patient lying asleep on a hospital trolley, a tube sticking out of her mouth; she was a pensioner out shopping; she was a dog walker. It had been so difficult to imagine her alive. And here she was, maybe just a few days ago, going about her business, oblivious to the silent watcher who was stalking her and probably planning to take her life. They had some idea now why MacLaren had targeted Jacobs, if he was the boy Morag MacDonald had known, but why Joe's family?

DI Black pointed to another couple of photos on the table. "Do you know who they are?" he asked Roberts.

"Sharon MacRae and her sons." Walking up Grant Street, they were oblivious to the camera, Liam holding his mother's hand, Ryan dawdling behind.

"Roberts, get Galbraith on the phone. Aird, get round to the parents' house. And lose that damn chewing gum! MacKay, get SOCO here, then get up to Raigmore. It can't be that easy to get photos of patients just before or after surgery. This bugger must be working at the hospital."

***

There was a stranger in the mirror. The sad person, the one that had been hanging around for weeks, with great, dark circles under her eyes, was gone. Lucy smiled at the happy stranger and decided against renewing her make up. They were only going for a walk, besides which there couldn't be more than a couple of hours of daylight left. She put on her jacket and picked up her mobile phone. No signal and the battery was almost flat. She wasn't likely to need it, so she left it charging in the room.

The village was quiet as she walked towards the end of the road. John's car was parked and he was leaning on a gate, watching a bird through binoculars. When she spoke, John lowered the binoculars, turned and smiled. His white teeth stood out against his faint tan, his deep blue eyes sparkling. He was gorgeous, just gorgeous. Why was he single? He'd told Lucy that he was on his own, as they sat beside the stones at Callanish. He'd had a couple of serious relationships, lived with a partner for two years, but it hadn't worked out. He'd looked at Lucy then, as if he expected her to reciprocate. She hadn't.

John opened the gate and stood aside to let her through. There was bird song all around them, and in the background, the faint murmuring of the sea. The air was heavy with the scents that Lucy had noticed last night on the beach, the mix of sea and sand and flowers. "It smells wonderful," she said.

John smiled. "This sandy grass-land is called machair. It's formed by the wind blowing fine sand inland. It's a rare habitat, only found in the west of Scotland and north-west Ireland."

As they walked along the track towards the looming bulk of Ceapabhal, a flock of starlings danced in front of them in ever-changing pulsing formations. Lucy was mesmerised by the shapes and precision of the birds. How could they fly like that without colliding?

"Scientists have studied their flight patterns," John told her, before she could ask. "Apparently they each track the seven closest birds and that's how they manage to avoid colliding with others in the murmuration."

"The what?"

"Murmuration – the collective noun for a flock of starlings."

Lucy laughed.

"I'm not kidding," John said. "In some cities, the murmurations are so large, they almost turn the sky black."

"I believe you. I'm just laughing 'cos you remind me of my dad; he's big on collective nouns. I'll drop that one into the conversation when I get home."

"I learned that from my dad," he said, his voice a little hushed. "That and so much more."

The path split and John gestured to the left. He didn't speak as they walked across the grass towards the sand dunes. Lucy glanced at him; he looked serious. Had she spoiled everything?

Below the dunes, there was a beautiful beach. As the tide ebbed and flowed it etched gentle patterns into the golden sand. It was perfect. John smiled and Lucy's fear was gone.

It's called *Tràigh na Cleabhaig*," he said.

Lucy nodded. "It's – "

A sudden screech split the air and John hit the ground, grabbing Lucy's arm and pulling her down with him. "Shit!" he yelled, as a white bird streaked past. Lucy turned and saw another bird bearing down on her. As they cowered in the grass, the birds hung in the sky, their long pointed tail feathers shimmering as they quivered, their call loud and angry.

"Are they swallows?" Lucy asked.

"Terns. Some call them sea swallows; I call them vicious little bastards."

Lucy laughed. "They're very pretty, but terrifying. How do we escape?"

John looked around. A few feet away, in a dip in the sand dune, a piece of rope lay half-covered by sand. "Stay here," he said, then he crawled towards the rope. As the birds screeched and hovered above, he pulled the rope free from the sand. It was perfect – a long piece of rope with a large tangled knot at the end. "Are you ready?" he asked.

"I think so."

He held the rope in his right hand, then he gave Lucy his left. Together they ran from the dunes, John twirling the tangled rope above their heads, as the angry birds followed them, but not too close.

At the end of the beach, when they were safely back on the grassy track running alongside the coast, the birds fell away. They were protecting their nests, John told Lucy, and if they hadn't ducked, they'd likely have been hit on the back of the head with the terns' sharp beaks. Lucy felt a little disappointed when John let go of her hand and started pulling at the tangle of rope. It wasn't easy, but he undid the knot until he had a long length of rope.

"We might need that on the way back," Lucy said.

"Aye. Probably should have left it tangled. If we skirt round the dunes, keeping away from the beach, we'll be all right." He shoved the rope in his pocket. "Better keep hold of it just in case. Little buggers. Now, where was I?"

***

Why the hell wasn't Joe calling Roberts back? Things had

moved so quickly. There was a suit, a pair of black shoes and a briefcase in MacLaren's wardrobe – they had been sent to the lab. There was a Scotrail receipt for £134.30 in a jacket pocket, dated Sunday past, but there was no telling the date or destination of the train. It seemed a bit steep for a fare to Glasgow or Edinburgh, but it matched a single fare to London.

The tidiness, the bare cupboards and the almost empty fridge had them convinced that MacLaren was long gone. There was fresh food in the wheelie bin at the gate, though bin day was not until Wednesday, according to the neighbours. They rarely saw Stephen, they told Roberts, and when they did, he had little to say. Wherever he was going, MacLaren didn't intend to return soon. Roberts would have to see Betty again, the DI said, find out if she knew of anyone in London that Stephen might visit.

Roberts phoned New Craigs and found that Betty had taken a bad turn after his visit. She'd got upset and angry, Janey said, then very confused. She was sedated now. Roberts wondered how Betty would be when she heard of her sister's fate at the hands of her own son. He really hoped he wouldn't have to tell her. He was told to call again in the morning, see how she was. That seemed fair enough, but the DI was having none of it. There followed a terse phone conversation between DI Black and his niece. Roberts could only hear the DI, and a lot of muttering about obstruction of the course of justice. He got nowhere. The morning it would have to be, he had snarled, and he wasn't taking no for an answer then, confusion or no confusion.

Roberts was dispatched off to the train station with Stephen MacLaren's photo. One of the men on duty remembered him buying a ticket to Kirkcaldy earlier in the week. Wasn't likely to forget the cheeky wee bugger, he told Roberts. Result. No one remembered selling MacLaren the ticket to London. It would take them some time to link the sale to a particular ticket, and identify the relevant member of staff.

Roberts picked up the phone and tried Joe again.

DI Black leaned back in his chair and looked at the ceiling. It could do with a coat of paint. He'd refused to vacate his room the last time the decorators had been in. Too busy, he'd told the boss. Too lazy, he'd admitted to himself, and he wasn't having anyone else clearing out his stuff. Anyway, a lot of answers had come to him staring up at the cracks and stains on that ceiling. He would think of something, a name or a place, and then he'd follow the lines and come to another clue, then another. Couldn't do that on a fresh, clean ceiling.

He'd been counting on Aird getting some clues from Joe Galbraith's parents, but the mother didn't know a Stephen MacLaren. She could think of no reason why he would target the family. Raymond Galbraith had been asleep and his wife hadn't wanted to wake him.

That was a bugger. He'd been convinced the parents would give him something. Aird was looking at Joe's cases now; perhaps it was something to do with an aggrieved con after all. There was a triangular stain in the corner and it made him think of Ceapabhal. The photo of the hill was troubling him. Stephen MacLaren's fingerprints were all over it. Moira Jacobs had worked in Harris. Joe Galbraith had lived there. Betty MacLaren had become upset when asked about the island. MacLaren was targeting the Galbraiths? What was the connection?

His phone rang. And wouldn't you know it, someone from a care home in Harris was looking for Joe Galbraith's boss. "That'll be me, then," he said to the girl on the switchboard. A moment later, a soft island voice told him that they'd been trying to get in touch with Joe Galbraith. "You and me both," he said. "I don't know how someone can just disappear. If he doesn't show his face soon, we'll be calling the local officers."

"Oh, no need," the woman said. "He's out fishing with PC Derek Russell. My husband's brother saw them set

211

out from Leverburgh at the back of six. It's just that there are problems with the mast today and we can't get through to DS Galbraith on his mobile phone."

"You and me both," he said again. "Anyway, what did you want to tell him?"

The woman paused. "Well, I don't really think it's worth bothering you. It's just that Morag – "

"Morag MacDonald?"

"Yes. Do you know her?"

"Of course I don't know her!" DI Black took a deep breath, shook his head. "I mean, no, dear, I don't know her, but I know that DS Galbraith was visiting her. Did she have something else to tell him?"

"Well, I don't think it's much use to him really."

"Why don't you just let me be the . . . why don't you just tell me what it is?"

He listened. He shook his head. He thanked her through gritted teeth, then he hung up. Waste of bloody time that was.

He got a second call. It was about the hit and run on Raymond Galbraith. It cheered him a little to hear the results of the tests carried out on the car. One more piece of the jigsaw, but what was the bloody overall picture? He stared at the ceiling once more, but there were no answers there; none at all.

***

Sunken galleons and haunted rocks; beautiful mermaids and seals that shed their skins and danced with humans; a giant born in Berneray; and a banshee that washed the blood-stained clothes of those about to die. These were the tales that Derek told as they made their slow way towards land, on a still sea as dusk was falling. In the strange half-light, as Joe breathed in the salty air, the rhythmic, hypnotising movement of the boat brought a memory of gentle arms rocking him to sleep, a soft voice telling similar tales; rocks and hills and place-names all whispered in that ancient language that suddenly seemed so familiar to him.

Derek's father-in-law was a *seanchaidh*, a storyteller, and there was a story to go with every island and rock in the Sound. In the past, people came from surrounding villages to hear his tales. Nowadays, they didn't bother. Not much call for a *seanchaidh* when you had satellite television and the internet. He still had visitors that were interested in his stories, but they came from Edinburgh University to record him; he was the last of his kind.

"My kids are still at an age when they love hearing *Seanair* – that's their grandfather – tell stories. Won't be long until they're past it, though."

And you'll miss it as much as they will, Joe thought. "Did you learn Gaelic here?"

"I started when I met the wife nine or ten years ago. Went to a couple of classes on the mainland to impress her. Didn't work. She just laughed. When she took me home to the island, she and her sisters would talk about me in Gaelic. They don't do it now."

Joe smiled at the pride in his voice. He looked towards the blinking lights of Leverburgh, and he felt a pang of jealousy. Derek belonged to a Harris that Joe had never got to know. And it sounded good – just as Morag MacDonald had said. It was good for Derek's children and good for him. Despite the encroachment of television and the internet, there was still a strong sense of community, a sense of culture and heritage. As the boat headed towards the harbour, and the remnants of Derek's tales lingered in his head, Joe wondered. Was there something in the islands for him? If he spent longer here, would he connect with that intangible but insistent thing that had been niggling at him ever since he'd stared into Maggie's sad eyes?

"Though I hate to say it, I can't see me being here much longer," Derek said. "Don't want to be a PC all my life. Just got to persuade the wife it's time to spend winter in civilisation. You wouldn't believe what it can be like here: gales so rough you can hardly stand, ferries stranded for days, shops empty and no electricity."

"I remember the wind and the power-cuts."

Derek stared at Joe. "Remember? You lived here?"

Shit. He shouldn't have let the sea and the night and Derek's stories lull him into such a relaxed state. "Just a few years. We left when I was eight."

"Where did you live?"

"Northton."

"Lovely people in Northton – salt of the earth. Must be strange being back there now. What took your family here?"

What indeed? Joe wasn't certain of the answer. Before he could speak, Derek asked him what his father had done for a living.

"Secondary teacher – history and modern studies."

"He probably taught the wife or her relatives. Must ask them if they remember Mr Galbraith. Was he a good teacher?"

Joe smiled and told himself to relax. "Very good." He was certain there would be no complaints about Raymond's teaching. And if Derek found out anything else about the family, well, Joe would be gone and unlikely to meet him again.

Joe felt his phone vibrate. Another voice-mail. He dialled 121 and listened to Roberts again. When he ended the call, he stared at the phone in his hand, nausea rising in his throat. How was that possible?

"Typical," Derek said, gesturing to the pier, where a young police officer waited. "I can't even get a night off without someone looking for me."

"I think he's probably looking for me," Joe said.

"Have you heard something else? Have they got Stephen MacLaren?"

"No." Joe hesitated, still trying to take in what he'd just heard. "They know a bit more about him. Nothing much."

Nothing much? Stephen MacLaren had been watching Joe and his family for weeks. His hair was in the car that ran Raymond over. Stephen MacLaren had tried to kill Raymond.

There were only two people Joe knew of that might want to harm Raymond. There was a time when they were both constantly in Joe's thoughts, when he'd worried about them and wondered where and how they were. But that was so long ago. Life had moved on, and Joe had grown up, and he'd had no cause to think of them for years. He thought of them now. Particularly of Stephen. The surname might be different, but Joe was certain that Stephen MacLaren was the boy that had lived next door to him in Northton.

Chapter 19

On the dark sloping rocks beyond the medieval chapel, John and Lucy sat watching the waves break on Pabbay. The island had been cleared in the 19th century to make way for sheep, the inhabitants forced to move from the rich pastures to the rocky east coast island of Scalpay. Although it must have been a shock to them at first, the people adapted well to their life on Scalpay, building up a healthy fishing industry.

"Have you been on Pabbay?" Lucy asked.

John shook his head. "Always meant to go but never got round to it. That's Shillay, on the right; the island of the seals, a Scottish Wildlife Trust reserve. I'd love to go there too. Maybe we could go one day."

When she didn't answer him, he turned to look at her. "Sorry; I didn't mean to sound presumptuous."

"You're not. I'm just . . . just not in a good place right now." She lifted a small stone and threw it into the dark water. She watched the circling ripples as they faded away. Life was unfair. Why couldn't she have met him before Sebastian? How long before she found her way back to her old self?

"I wasn't coming on to you," he said. "Honest. I just like your company. It feels right."

Lucy nodded, and tried to stop the tears from coming. She couldn't. John said nothing while she cried; just gave her some hankies from his pocket, and waited. She knew she didn't have to tell him, but she did, when she composed herself. And it felt good, finally, to tell someone.

Sebastian Moore had been Lucy's tutor for commercial law in second year. Although others found him attractive, Lucy hadn't really taken much notice. She was never going to find commercial law interesting, particularly his speciality, competition law. Mergers, acquisitions, monopolies, cartels – they turned her off completely, as did his name. Could anyone really fancy someone called Sebastian? She had gone to the lectures and tutorials, completed her essays and exercises, and got average marks. She wouldn't have given him and his posh English accent another thought if he and his pals hadn't turned up in the bar where she worked part-time.

They were out on a stag night for another lawyer, and the group had looked a little out of place among the young students. Sebastian seemed the most uncomfortable of the group, definitely the oldest, and possibly the most sober. Rather than join in with the loud nonsense of the others, he had stood at the bar and talked to Lucy between customers. Shy of the smooth city lawyer, ten or more years older than her, Lucy found it a little awkward. It was difficult to remember now what they had talked about; the conversation certainly wasn't flowing. She remembered telling him that she'd have to go down to the cellar. She hated going down there, but that night it was a welcome excuse. He had nodded, said it was time the group were moving on. Thanking her, he'd passed her his empty wine glass. Somewhere between their hands, the glass slipped. Lucy reached for it just as it hit the edge of the bar and shattered. She was left with a handful of broken glass and a deep wound between her left thumb and forefinger. She would remember that feeling over a year later – thinking she had a grasp of something solid, something substantial, and finding that all she was left with were broken shards and the deepest, sharpest of aches.

Sebastian told Lucy to elevate her hand (yes, he really did say 'elevate your hand'), then he pressed a cloth firmly on the wound. He stopped a taxi and ushered her in. She started to thank him, told him she'd see him at the next tutorial, but then he was beside her. In Accident & Emergency, the nurses assumed they were a couple. Within a week, they were. Something had clicked as they sat together in the hospital, Sebastian so intensely apologetic, Lucy feeling a little light-headed and fragile, and flattered by his concern.

Their respective commitments limited their time together. He was dual-qualified in Scots and English law, and he often travelled to London, sometimes abroad. That suited Lucy; she had her own friends, her studies and her work. She didn't want anyone on her course to know about the relationship until she'd finished second year. She wasn't sure if the rules were as stringent for tutors as they were for lecturers, but she presumed that he was not supposed to have a relationship with one of his students. Not all the lecturers observed that rule, but Lucy didn't want her name whispered in the refectory on a sleepy Monday morning or shouted around the Union on a drunken Friday night.

She was glad that her flat-mates were not law students. Other than her pal, Millie, she had never really bothered with anyone on her course. Though she was only a few years older than the youngest in her year, those few years sometimes seemed like decades. And so it was easy to keep their relationship quiet. They drove to country pubs in East Lothian; they walked in Fife and Perthshire; they spent nights in at his sparse apartment in Stockbridge. As soon as second year was finished, Lucy invited him to Inverness for a weekend. She asked him to accompany her to parties and film nights, out for a drink with friends. He always had an excuse. When her family came to Edinburgh, he was suddenly so busy he couldn't see her for a week. When she went up to Inverness, he didn't answer his phone for two weeks. When she invited him to Millie's 21st birthday party, he had a meeting that would last well into the night.

There was only one conclusion; he was ashamed of Lucy and her ordinary background. His parents lived in

London; his father was a surgeon, his mother a QC; his grandparents owned an estate in Hampshire. He wasn't particularly close to his family, he told her, hence his decision to work in Scotland, but there was no getting away from the differences between them, or from his reluctance to become too involved in her life.

Often, Lucy was on the verge of ending their relationship. Sometimes she thought he was. And then he would surprise her with a weekend trip to Paris or a stunning piece of jewellery, with beautiful cards and exotic flowers, with the promise of more time together just as soon as the latest deal was concluded.

Sitting by the side of the water, Lucy was aware that John had said nothing while she talked. "You couldn't write this crap, could you?" she said, picking up another stone and chucking it into the sea.

"Easy to give ourselves a hard time for things that weren't really that predictable, that could have turned out so differently."

"You haven't heard the worst of it."

"And I don't have to, unless you really want to tell me."

Lucy shrugged. "It's good to talk about it – I haven't told anyone else."

"Not even Joe?"

She shook her head. "I felt like a fool. Although he never met Sebastian, or maybe because he never met him, Joe was suspicious. I guess I didn't want to admit that Joe was right. I nearly called him when I found out I was . . . " She hesitated. Was there any point?

"You were . . . ?"

"I was pregnant." She stared out to sea. "I was; I'm not now."

***

Playing at the chapel is boring. He would rather be at home with a comic. The headland is exposed and the wind is getting stronger. He's cold and fed up of the brothers bickering. Sometimes they break into Gaelic and he doesn't know what they're on about. Probably talking about him, though it sounds more like they're insulting each other. And he can't even find a decent stone for skimming.

He's had enough, but how is he going to get away? Although he hasn't enjoyed the expedition much, it was fun playing on the beach, and it isn't so bad having boys coming to call for you. He doesn't want to put them off calling again. The next time might be better; he might get invited to their house. The mothers in the village are good at baking; he knows that from school events, so it would be worth keeping in with them. Perhaps he can say he's ill, or his mother needs him home now. But she didn't say that when they left; they'll never believe him.

"Let's go to Toe Head," the older boy shouts.

"We're not allowed," his wee brother replies. "Only with Dad."

"That's rubbish; no one said we weren't allowed. You're just scared."

"I'm not scared, you are."

The boy sees his chance. "I'd . . . I'd love to go to Toe Head, but I'm really not allowed there. I better go." He runs a few steps, then he turns back. What should he say? "Eh . . . thanks for . . . for calling. It would be nice . . . I mean, I would like if you would do it again." You sound like a right twit, he tells himself. Why would anyone want to play with you?

The older brother shouts after him. "Do you not want to come to – ?"

"I can't." And he's off. Behind him, he can hear the boys arguing.

Running along the track with the wind behind him, he feels a sudden surge of happiness. He nearly has friends. "Boo!" he shouts at a group of sheep on the track. They scatter before him, running down to the beach that stretches in the curve of the Chapel's headland. There's another wee beach just along a bit, before Tràigh na Cleabhaig. He can hardly believe there are all these beaches that he didn't even know about. What other secrets are there on Harris? Maybe there's even a . . . a cinema somewhere. Maybe that's where the village boys saw Ghostbusters. Maybe he can go there too. He can do anything now!

He's getting hungry, so he runs faster. Past the next wee beach, where an orange wellie and a blue plastic crate lie in the sand, surrounded by three sets of footprints. The big brother had tried on the wellie, and the wee one had sat in the crate. He wanted the others to push him out to sea so he could sail to Uist to visit his auntie, but his big brother had just laughed at him.

Tràigh na Cleabhaig is in sight now. Not too far after that. He looks down and sees his shoelace is open. He crouches and ties it, tightens the other one, then he stands. About to take off again, he sees something red on the beach. Red like the wee girl's dress. He left her behind when he ran down the sand dune to join the others. Hadn't given her another thought. Why is she still on the beach? And why is she lying down?

***

Constable Hector Wright didn't look much older than the youths that had been hanging about outside the waiting room in the car park earlier. Was that really just today? Joe felt as if he'd been on the island forever. They'd get away tomorrow; he'd decided to try for the earlier ferry; no need to hang about now that they'd identified the murderer. If Morag MacDonald had more to tell him, it could be done by phone. He just wanted to get home, make sure his parents were okay.

"I got a voice-mail," Joe said to the constable. "From DC Roberts in Inverness. Have they been in touch with you?"

PC Wright nodded. "Aye, DI Black called. Quite frustrated that he couldn't get hold of you. They faxed over some papers." He handed a folder to Joe. "There's a photo of Stephen MacLaren too, but the fax ran out of ink just as it started coming through. Sorry about that, Sergeant. They're going to email it to us. DI Black said he'd get Roberts to send it to you on your mobile, for what your mobile's worth. His words, not mine."

Joe tried to smile. "Thanks; I'm grateful." He'd like to see the photo as soon as possible, but he couldn't face a drive up to Tarbert. Hopefully Roberts' text would come through shortly.

Derek passed the catch up to them, before Joe helped him ashore. "I'm sorry," Joe told him. "I did get more information in that last call, but I couldn't quite take it in. Stephen MacLaren's been watching my family and me. They found photos in his house. My father was run over last weekend, and they think MacLaren was driving."

"Aye?" Derek said. "What's the connection with your family?"

Joe hesitated. Ach, there was no point in trying to keep it quiet; it was all going to come out. "I think he lived next door to us in Northton. I think he was the boy Morag MacDonald talked about, the one that was sent to stay with Seumas Mòr."

"Could be my first Harris murder. But why would he have it in for your family?"

Joe shook his head. Well, he didn't know for sure, did he? There was no point speculating. "I don't know. I just want to get back home as soon as possible, make sure the folks are all right. I had a great evening. Thanks."

"We'll do it again," Derek said, shaking Joe's hand.

Not here, we won't, Joe thought. Not here.

As he sat on the bed in the guest-house and read the papers, Joe couldn't believe it. He had been under surveillance for weeks, and he hadn't even noticed. Some detective. And his family – MacLaren had been watching them on Saturday; he'd been stalking them. He could have mown them all down.

His hands shaking, Joe checked his phone and found he had a signal. No text from Roberts, though. He phoned his mother. She'd been told about MacLaren, and she assured Joe that they were fine – the doors were locked and a patrol car kept driving past every few minutes. "We'll be getting a bad name with the neighbours," she said. "I haven't told Dad; I didn't want to worry him. He's asleep.

What's it all about, Joe? Why would this MacLaren want to harm Dad or spy on us?"

She didn't know? The name must have thrown her. Joe hesitated. "It's – "

"Do you think it could be someone you've arrested, or put away?"

"Possibly," Joe lied.

"How has it been over there?"

"Fine. Home tomorrow. How's Dad?"

"Doing well. Getting about on his crutches and getting in my way. Today he knocked a vase of flowers off the hall table – took me ages to clean up the mess. He's so clumsy."

Her callous comments would normally have irritated Joe, but tonight he was relieved. Everything was just as it had always been.

"I'll tell him you called."

"Okay, Mum. We'll see you tomorrow. Look after yourselves."

"Bye, love. Take care." And she was gone.

Joe looked at the phone. "Mum," he said, his voice hushed, "Mum, I love you." The words shocked him. He was quite certain he hadn't said that to her since he was a wee boy. Hadn't said it now either, had he? Not really, not to her. Maybe he should phone her again. Aye, and really worry her. Idiot.

Roberts sounded pleased to hear from Joe. The excitement in Inverness was something else. Everyone praising Joe. It was all down to him. All right, they didn't have Stephen MacLaren yet, but at least they knew it was him, and they knew why Moira Jacobs and Jean Henderson had died. MacLaren worked at Raigmore as a hospital porter. He was on holiday for a couple of weeks now, but he had been on duty the day Moira Jacobs went for surgery. He must have got her address, then targeted Sharon MacRae to get access to the flats. They reckoned MacLaren was in London now; he'd bought a ticket and booked a seat on the

10.47 yesterday morning, arriving in London that evening. The Mets were onto it; they had MacLaren's picture; Roberts might be going down to London tomorrow.

"A bit more exciting than a trip to Kirkcaldy," Joe said.

Roberts agreed. "The DI wants to speak to you. I'll put you through in a minute. Disappointed I had to call off the date with the vet nurse. Do you think she'll agree to another one?"

"How could she resist?"

"Mmm." Roberts was not convinced. "Did you get that text yet with the photo?"

"No."

"Sharon MacRae's identified him too."

"Good. What's he like?"

"Just as Sharon and Liam said – tall, dark hair, mid-30s. Sarge . . . "

"Aye?" Joe knew what was coming.

"Why would he have it in for you and your family? Why would he have followed you around, taken photos of Lucy in Edinburgh?"

Joe felt his stomach lurch. "Edinburgh? How do you know that?"

"Someone recognised the Old College in one of the photos; apparently that's where the Law School is. Sorry, Sarge; I thought that was in the papers we sent you."

It hadn't been. Thank goodness Lucy was here with him in Harris. Only, she wasn't with him, was she? She wasn't back from her walk with John, and when Joe had tried her mobile phone, he had heard it ringing in the room next door.

"Are you at a computer?" Joe asked.

"Aye, I was just checking details of MacLaren's mother's car – we found SORN paperwork in the house, but there was no sign of the car. I thought it had maybe been sold on, but it's never been taxed again. Why do you ask?"

"Can you google 'John MacKay – environmental writer'."

224

Joe heard Roberts tapping away on the keyboard. "Was he an Australian pioneer, died in 1933?"

"No. Try 'nature writer'."

"Okay, Sarge." More tapping, while Joe willed Roberts to hurry up. "No, nothing that stands out – there's a John MacKay writes novels set in the Hebrides. Oh, there's a picture – I know who he is – I've seen him reading the news. Sarge, have we really got time for this?"

"No. You going to put me through to DI Black?"

Roberts tried, but the DI's line was engaged. "He'll be on to the Met. I'll get him to phone you back."

"If he doesn't get me on the mobile, tell him to phone the guest-house – he's got the number." Joe used his shoulder to hold the phone against his ear while he reached down to open his trainers. He needed a bath, some sleep. What he really needed, more than anything, was to get home.

"Will do. Sarge, I really wish you were here. It's all moved so fast today, my head's all over the place. Oh, here's another urgent memo. Might as well keep you on until I read it."

Joe pulled off a trainer and reached for the other.

"Strange," Roberts said. "That's strange. Oh . . . shit."

Joe's heart pounded. "What?" he said. "What is it?" Was it his parents? Was it Carla?

"It's the car, Sarge, Betty MacLaren's car. It's parked at Uig on Skye, and she's fast asleep in New Craigs. Uig – that's where you left from, isn't it? Sarge? Sarge, are you there?"

Chapter 20

The wee girl has her back to him, doesn't move as he approaches. Her dress and her hair are wet. She's only wearing one of her little white sandals; the other is lying a bit away from her, a length of seaweed tangled in the straps.

"Hey," he says. "Why are you lying here? Why did you not go home to your dad, like I told you?"

Stupid girl ignores him.

"I'm going home now. You can walk with me, but I'm in a hurry. Come on, if you're coming."

She doesn't move, so he walks away, his feet sinking into the sand. He wants to run, but he turns back. "Come on," he says. "Please come."

He should just go. He should just run now. Run home and no one would ever know that he saw her. The brothers didn't even see her; she must have hidden in the sand dunes while they were playing.

"Please, please, please." His whispers are lost in the roaring of the sea, the calling of the birds, the hissing of the wind. His feet sink further into the sand, and then he knows. When they find her, they'll find his footprints. They'll know that he was here, that he walked up to her, that he left her. But will they know how often he wished harm upon her and her family?

"Please. I didn't mean it. I didn't mean it." And now he's walking round her, and he's looking into her eyes and they're all dull and glassy. Her mouth is open and her lips are blue. Her cheeks are grey and her hair is flat and straggly.

As he clambers up the sand dune, the sea and the birds and the wind are all taunting him. You did this. You did this. You did this.

When he reaches the track, he falls and cuts his knee on a sharp

226

stone. All the way home, the blood pours down his leg, and the pain throbs, and he's glad.

The village boys are in the middle of the road. They have a go-cart on a rope. Three boys are on the cart, two trying to pull them. They see him coming and they part, the cart going one way, the standing boys the other.

"What's up with him?" one says.

"Aww," the oldest one says, "he's cut his leg and he's running home to his mammy."

As he reaches his gate, he sees the bus on the main road, coming back from Tarbert, slowing down, ready to stop.

His mother's not in the kitchen. She's not in the living room. His feet thump up the stairs, the pain in his chest crushing his ribs and almost choking him.

"Mum, Mum!" he shouts as he pushes her bedroom door open. "Mum!"

His mother raises her sleepy head from the pillows. "Eh?"

"Mum! It's the Galbraith girl – she's lying on the beach. She won't wake up. I think she's – "

Another head rises from behind his mother. Another sleepy tousled head. The boy's confused. A man? During the day? That stuff is for night time, for the dark, when people are drunk and silly. It's not for a bright, summer's day, when his mother is sober and happy.

The man yawns, lifts his arm from around the boy's mother. He rubs his eyes. Lifts his head further. It's Mr Galbraith.

***

Nothing would make Joe look at the house where they had lived. As he ran past, he didn't see that it was half-derelict, the garden overgrown and the windows smashed in. He wouldn't look on the way back either.

Lucy would be fine, he told himself. Just because Roberts couldn't find anything about John MacKay's writing on Google, it didn't mean he wasn't above board, but could he protect Lucy from Stephen MacLaren? What if Stephen had found them? What if he'd been following

Lucy ever since they arrived on Harris? He should never have let her come.

The red Micra was at the end of the road. Running past the car, Joe clambered over the gate. He jumped down onto the gravel track and he kept running. He tried not to think of the last time he ran along the track, he and four others, stumbling along in the great black shadow of the hill. He tried not to hear the voices from that day, but he couldn't keep them out.

You should have taken Amy with you to Tarbert.
She wanted to go home; you were supposed to be there.
You should have come back with her.
We could see you in the garden when she turned back.
I was in the garden.
You were not! You were in her house! You and her? You and that slut!
Don't you call me a slut. Toffee-nosed cow!

The boys had said nothing to each other as they ran, one slightly ahead, leading the way. And behind them, the sound of sirens. But they were too late. Far too late.

***

A bird mocked overhead as Lucy cried, its raucous taunts echoing across the sea. John held her, his arm pulling her close into his side. It felt so good and so right to be held by him. And it felt even better to finally realise that she wasn't crying for Sebastian; she was crying for a little clump of cells and membranes that she'd only carried for a few weeks, but would miss all her life.

When she was done crying, she felt better. The hurt wasn't going to disappear, but it was good to have talked of it at last, and great to realise that Sebastian hadn't meant as much to her as she had thought.

"Did Sebastian know?" John asked. "Did you tell him?"

Lucy nodded. "Aye, a couple of days after I found out. He'd been away, so I'd had time to think about it, to get used to the idea. Even started planning. I could still finish my degree – plenty others coped. I couldn't really see how it could be a negative thing, having a baby. A bit sooner than I'd planned, but . . . "

"I take it he didn't agree?"

Lucy laughed, but there was no humour in it. "He went mental. Absolutely mental. What was I thinking of? Why hadn't I been more careful? Why was I telling him when he was under so much pressure already? He'd thought he could trust me."

"Selfish bastard," John said. And then his arm was no longer around Lucy. When she looked at him, she saw anger in his hunched shoulders, in his clenched hands. "Lucy," he said, his voice anxious. "Did you . . . ?" He didn't look at her; just scratched and scratched at the lichen on the rock. "Did he talk you into getting – ?"

"He tried. Best clinic; money's no object; a friend of his knew a man; no one else would ever know. Shit like that. I told him where to go. And he went." She gazed across the sea, to where the moon shone on Pabbay. "I didn't even miss him at first. I was relieved. We'd never have agreed on how to bring up a child; we were so different. With him gone, it was like it was just my baby, and no one was going to tell me what to do or how to do it.

"I felt sick nearly all the time; had to leave in the middle of lectures and tutorials so often that my class-mates started asking. I told them it was cystitis, and they didn't probe." She smiled. "I loved having that secret. I loved it. When I went home at night, even though I felt crap, I felt so special. I had new life growing in me."

John was smiling; he understood. "It was amazing," she said. "Just amazing." She took a deep breath. "Until the day I woke with cramps and bleeding, and it was gone. Just like that."

That morning. The memory of it was almost too

much to bear. Why? She had cried that word over and over into the empty flat. Why? No one could tell her. The doctor said it was just one of those things; it didn't mean she'd have trouble conceiving again. According to the internet, it was just chance, and nothing to do with anything she'd done or not done. It was so common that women often didn't even know they'd been pregnant before they miscarried. But she had known.

"It was his fault," John said. "Bastard."

"No. I can't blame him. It's just one of these things – doesn't make much sense." And what had made even less sense to Lucy was the sudden desperate longing she had for Sebastian. She'd been glad that he was gone; she'd hardly given him a second thought. And suddenly she needed him so much.

"Did you tell him?" John asked.

"I tried. Felt I had to see him. There was no one else I could speak to. I waited outside his office. Waited for hours. When he came out, he was on the phone to someone and he was laughing and joking. That gutted me – I was empty inside, and he was just as he'd always been – "

"An arrogant, selfish prick," John said.

Lucy frowned. She hadn't been looking for someone else to hate Sebastian; she had just needed to talk.

"I'm sorry," John said. "Did he see you?"

"Aye, he was still talking on the phone when he saw me sitting on the wall."

"What did he do?"

Lucy held her hand to her mouth. She started laughing, the sound echoing in the still air.

"Lucy?"

"He ran," she said, the words spluttering from behind her hand. "He just ran out in front of the traffic. Crossed the road and there was this couple about to get in a taxi. He pushed them out of the way." She giggled. "Just pushed them aside and got in. I couldn't believe my eyes. And he was gone. Just gone. Never had that effect on a guy before.

Far as I know, he still thinks I'm pregnant."

John stood, and Lucy felt tiny, just as she had felt when Sebastian ran from her. Tiny and alone and exposed, her arms wrapped round her knees, the cold starting to seep through her.

"Amy," John said. "I'm so sorry."

"Amy?" Looking up, Lucy saw shock on John's face.

He shook his head. "Sorry, Lucy. The thing is, you shouldn't have had to go through that on your own. I should have been there for you; I should have stopped it from happening."

Amy? Been there? Stopped it from happening? What was he on about? Lucy stood. She shivered and untied her jacket from around her waist.

"It's getting cold," he said. "We should be heading back." He helped her into the jacket, then he kept his hands on her shoulders. Their faces were so close. Lucy felt his breath on her forehead. She stared up into his dark eyes. Their heads moved closer. And suddenly Lucy was terrified that he was going to kiss her.

Laughter bubbled up inside her again as she realised just how mixed up and wrong she'd been all day. She didn't fancy him. It felt right to be with him, to be comforted by him, to be friends, but she didn't want to kiss him. He didn't try. Just pulled her into a tight hug.

"I don't understand," he said, his words tickling her ear. "How could someone do that to you? Why would he react like that?"

Her chin on his shoulder, Lucy took a deep breath. It would be safe to tell him everything. "I guess he was scared of what it would do to his life. He's married. He – "

And then John's arms were gone. He stepped back. "Married?" His eyes were wide, his upper lip curling with disgust. "Married – you are fucking kidding me."

"Eh, no." Not something I'd really joke about, Lucy thought. She took a step towards him. "But I didn't – "

"Get away from me!" John shouted. He pushed her

backwards, and she felt her feet slide from under her. Pain shot through her right hip as she hit the black rock. She opened her mouth to shout. Before she could get a sound out, John was kneeling on the ground beside her, his hand over her mouth. "Fucking shut up! Silly, cheating cow!"

But I didn't know! The words screamed in Lucy's head, as his hand pressed against her mouth. Maybe I should have worked it out, but I didn't.

With his free hand, John pulled the length of rope from his pocket. "I knew I would need this. Knew you were too fucking good to be true. Little Miss Innocent, with your social conscience and your principles. Really had me fooled." He leaned down so his face was right in hers, his breath tickling her cheek. "The apple doesn't fall far from the tree, does it?"

Apple? What was he on about? He had an ugly smile on his face, and insanity in his eyes. Lucy didn't struggle when he pushed her onto her stomach. She didn't struggle when he tied her hands together behind her back. She was too shocked to resist and felt caught in a time lapse – several minutes behind him in understanding. How could Sebastian's deception provoke John like this? And how could she have been so taken in, again?

Lucy felt John's knee on her back, forcing her into the ground. "You could have lived, Lucy," he said. "You could have lived, if only you'd been good. If only you'd been as good as her."

***

Raymond opened his eyes. It was dark outside. He looked at the clock. Just after nine. He hadn't meant to sleep for so long. Probably wouldn't sleep again for hours. His body was aching, his legs stiff and his ribs tender. He tried to stretch his legs and felt his plaster cast catching on the sheets. How long before the leg started itching, driving him mad? He remembered a cousin that got a horrible infection in her

232

broken arm after using a knitting needle to scratch inside her plaster. He shivered and told himself to lighten up. No point in worrying about something that hadn't happened.

There was a small bell on the bedside table. Fiona had left it there, telling him she would prefer a gentle ring to a shout. Aye, and how was she going to hear a gentle ring over the soap operas and games shows? He'd be glad when Joe and Lucy got back. It wouldn't have been easy for Joe, returning to the island after all this time. He'd seen the tension in him, though Joe had tried to hide it. And Lucy – how would Joe cope with any questions she might have about the past? Would he tell her everything? Might be for the best; they should have told her long ago, but Fiona wouldn't hear of it.

At the thought of his wife, the bedroom door opened slowly, silently. Fiona smiled when she saw that he was awake. "Tea?"

Raymond nodded.

***

An oystercatcher screeched overhead as John tied Lucy's feet with the remainder of the rope, pulling her legs towards her arms so he could make a final knot. The pain from Lucy's hip had been bad before. Now, it was excruciating. Lucy considered screaming, but who would hear her? They were miles from the village.

"You're lucky the rope isn't long enough to go round your neck." He turned her onto her side.

"What the fuck, John? What is wrong with you?"

"Shut up – I told you! I need time to think. Let me think." He sat on the ground beside her and started muttering, his body rocking back and fore, back and fore. "Apple never falls far from the tree. No morals. No standards. No respect for marriage. No fucking respect!"

"But I didn't – "

"Shut up! I should have known – throwing yourself at

me as soon as we met. Is that how you were brought up? Just give it to anyone that comes along?"

Lucy shook her head. It was him; he was the one throwing himself at her. She didn't seek him out on the ferry; didn't ask him to take her to Stornoway, to come for a walk tonight.

He leaned over until his face was right beside hers. "Precious little Lucy – daddy's little girl." His spittle sprayed on her lips. "And nothing but a fucking liar." He screwed up his face. "My wonderful brother Joe; he's a health and safety officer," he mimicked. "Lying bitch. Did you think I didn't know all about Detective Sergeant Joseph . . . " He stopped. It was as if the name wouldn't come out, as if he couldn't say it. "Detective Sergeant Joseph Fucking Galbraith?" he said at last. Did you think I was that daft? Everyone has the right to be stupid, Lucy, but you abuse the privilege." He sat back, shoving his hand into his pocket. He pulled out a small digital camera, his hands shaking. "Fucking thing," he said as he fiddled with the camera.

Lucy thought he might smash the camera on the rocks, so great was his temper. How did he know about Joe? And why did he hate him? She heard the camera beep, watched him pressing frantically at the buttons.

"Look," he said, shoving the camera up to her face, so close that she couldn't make out the picture. She shook her head and he pulled the camera back a little. Her eyes took some time to focus. At last, she saw that it was a picture of Joe with a dark-haired woman at a harbour, and another of the couple, then Joe alone at the door of his cottage, Joe on a yacht, Joe at a petrol station. Her parents shopping, her father in the garden, her mother at the front door. And then it was her with her parents last Saturday, the day that her father was run over. Smiling, John pressed a button and the pictures kept coming, a slide-show of the family from the time they left the house until just before her father was hit. Then there were photos of Sunday, some of them taken outside the hospital, and others of Joe helping their father out of the car and into the house.

As she struggled to comprehend, John moved the camera away. "That's the last time you'll see your family." His voice was calm, and cold. "Shame."

***

Crouched above *Tràigh na Cleabhaig*, beneath the wrath of the screaming terns, Joe scanned the beach. The tide was in, rays of moonlight sparkling on the gentle water. This time, the beach was deserted, the sand undisturbed. This time, there was no screaming, no shouting, no one stumbling and scrambling down the sand dune to the water and the little body that waited for them. Relieved, Joe moved on. He stayed low as he ran, his hands above his head, until he was out of the danger zone and the birds fell away.

Back on the track, before the next small beach, Joe heard the sound of a text. He stopped and pulled the phone from his pocket. It was from Roberts. He tapped the message icon, and knew from the pause and the turning of the circle on the screen that it was a photo, and that his phone could take forever to open it. "Come on," he said. "Come on!"

In the second before the picture opened, revealing Stephen MacLaren, Joe glanced ahead, into the dark shadow of the hill, and a sudden memory came to him. John MacKay on the ferry, standing at the top of the stairs down to the car deck. Joe was in front, Lucy behind. They had both turned to look back at John. He had smiled and waved at Lucy. Joe was a second or two later than Lucy in turning away. He'd seen a hostile look come over John's face, a look that he had seen before, a look that he should have recognised. Any other day, and that look would not have slipped past him. Blame the journey, blame the island, blame his infantile childhood fears that would not let him remember. Stupid stupid bastard. How could he not have known? John MacKay was Stephen.

Chapter 21

Stephen smiled at the confusion on Lucy's face, at the fear widening her eyes. He'd seen the same fear in MacLeod's eyes last summer. The visit to the old man's house hadn't been planned. Stephen had been back to the island often before that night. His first trip had been painful, as had the next few. Painful but necessary, if he was ever to make any sense of his childhood. He'd grown to love the peace first, then the island. And he'd learned to listen, really listen to the land, to the sea, to the birds. He spent days watching the soaring flight of a pair of golden eagles at Glen Miavaig. He braved the winter cold to watch the dancing lights of the Aurora Borealis over the Sound of Harris. He stood on top of the Clisham and gasped at the St Kildan archipelago rising out of the ocean like the teeth of a giant sea monster. He thought of moving to Harris, for it was the only place that he was at peace. But he was scared of spoiling what he'd found, of making it ordinary, rather than the sacred other-world that it had become.

His mother showed no interest in returning to the island, and he never told her that he came back regularly as John MacKay. He said he was going away with his work, going on holiday with fictitious friends, going hill-walking. Anything but the truth.

And then one day last summer, he had thought himself calm enough to stand, for the first time since childhood, at the little grave in the corner of the cemetery at Scarista. He had thought himself centred, at rest, at peace. He had thought that nothing could disturb his inner calm. He was wrong.

The rage came and scattered his foolish imaginings. It rose within him, swamping everything good, flooding his spirit. It brought darkness, bitterness and vengeance. Someone had to pay. MacLeod was the nearest.

That was the night the planning started. Back in his room at the hostel, the blood pumping fast through his veins at the memory of the old man lying at the bottom of the stairs, his dead eyes still wide with fear, Stephen had vowed he'd get Raymond; he'd get Joe; he'd get Fiona. He'd track them down and make them pay. He had no idea where they'd gone, couldn't believe it when Nisbet broke it to him just how close they were. And then Nisbet had found Lucy.

Gullible bitch. It had been so simple to reel her in. The initial approach in the ticket office, the mention of a (non-existent) English accent, thanks to Nisbet's flawless research. The mild flirtation, the lift to Stornoway – she had fallen for it all so easily. He deserved an Oscar. And now he had her here, right here. Everything was falling into place. It was all meant to be. It was fate.

He'd wanted to tell his mother about his plans for the Galbraiths, about MacLeod's fate, about Moira Jacobs; he'd wanted her to know that justice was being done. But she wouldn't have understood. At the thought of his mother, Stephen felt some doubt at all that he had done, at what he was about to do. Maybe he should have gone to London. He could have been John MacKay, the writer, there. He could be published. He knew his stuff; he was good. No one could take that from him.

If he hadn't taken Betty's car out on Sunday and watched the Galbraiths bringing Raymond home from hospital. If he hadn't seen the bond that held them together, the smiles and the frowns, the touches and the whispers. How it had goaded him, watching them like that. He hadn't slept all night, torn between rage and grief. When dawn came, he had packed for London, then he'd cleaned and tidied the house, and still he had hours to spare. And suddenly he was in Betty's car again, and, without even thinking about it, without consciously making the decision to go there, he found himself pulling up across from the Galbraith's house.

At last, he had seen Lucy open the curtains. She'd stood at the window, looking up the street, away from his car, waiting for someone. Stephen had watched for five minutes or so, before he noticed the time; he'd have to go. He started the engine. Took one last look. He saw her smile; he saw her wave. For one stupid moment, he thought she was waving at him. He'd smiled, lifted his hand, and then Joe was pulling up, his car so close to Betty's. Joe didn't see Stephen; he was looking at his sister, smiling, as he got out and went to open the boot.

And then Lucy was at the door, Fiona behind her. Lucy was hugging her mother, shouting a last goodbye to her father. She was running towards Joe, towards her brother. He was taking her case from her and putting it in the boot. They were excited, laughing and talking. They were so alive.

And there was nothing Stephen could do but follow them.

***

Fiona put Raymond's mug on a coaster on the bedside table. She pulled a chair up beside the bed and sat down. There had been so many phone calls, she told him; his cousins and his sister, former colleagues and friends from the horticultural society, neighbours and walking buddies. "Who'd have guessed you were so popular?" she teased. "You even made the evening news and the BBC website, apparently."

Raymond groaned. He didn't like that kind of fuss. Still, it was nice of people to care. He started to tell Fiona of the strange dream he'd had, when the doorbell rang.

"Not another neighbour," Fiona said. "Not at this time."

In the hall, she hesitated. Was she supposed to answer the door? The policewoman that had called earlier hadn't really said. Just told her to be careful and to report anything that concerned her. She'd also said they'd be keeping an eye on the house. As the bell rang again, Fiona went into the living room. Through a tiny gap in the curtains, she saw the patrol car in front of the house.

Five minutes later, Fiona came back into the bedroom. She took Raymond's empty mug from his hand, then she sat on the bed and told him.

In all the years they had been together, Fiona had never seen Raymond lose his temper. Now, she was glad he was in plaster, and that she had removed the mug from his hand.

"You stupid, stupid woman!" he yelled as he shoved the quilt away. "Why did you not wake me earlier, as soon as you heard?"

What was he on about? She didn't know a Stephen MacLaren. Why would she have woken him to tell him that? "The name meant nothing to me. It's just someone Joe's had dealings with, isn't it?"

"Joe?" Raymond shouted. He struggled to sit up on the bed. "Aye, Fiona; you blame Joe. Everything is Joe's fault. Always has been. Even as a boy, you blamed him rather that look at your own shortcomings. You are a selfish, stupid woman!"

Fiona hadn't a clue what he was talking about, and she wasn't happy. Raymond tried to stand, then he fell backwards onto the bed. He shouted at her to get his crutches, to get the phone.

"Just sit there," she said. "I'll get it."

The phone shook in Raymond's hands as he tried to find Joe's mobile number. "Is it on here? I can't find it!"

Fiona grabbed the phone from him and found the number, before passing it back to him. He shook his head as it went straight to voice-mail.

"Phone me, Joe," Raymond said, his voice desperate.

"It's Stephen; he's the killer. He's been watching us all, and they think he's in Harris. Phone me as soon as you get this." The next number he dialled was short. "Police," he said.

As Fiona listened to Raymond, she felt her orderly, safe life slipping away from her. Though she might not always have shown it, she had cherished that life, cherished and protected it for years, and now she was going to lose it.

"Raymond," she said, when he put down the phone, "I didn't know. How could I? The name MacLaren meant nothing to me. And the police are onto it – they've been in touch with Joe; they've spoken to him."

Raymond stared at her, his face pale. "If anything has happened to them, I'll never forgive you. Never."

And then Fiona knew. Despite all their years together, despite the seemingly happy life they had built, deep down, Raymond had never forgiven her.

***

Derek Russell was half way home when his radio came to life. He'd forgotten it was on the front seat. Should have switched it off earlier. He reached for it, but all he got was a handful of waterproof jacket. He pulled in to a lay-by, shaking his head as Hector Wright flew past him. Bloody maniac. He'd really wanted to stay in front for as long as possible, keep the younger PC in his place.

Derek spoke to the control room, and the tale from Inverness made the hairs on the back of his neck rise. He got Hector Wright on the radio then and told him to turn around and get his arse back down the road pronto. They were going in search of Stephen MacLaren.

He checked his mobile. A weak signal, so he tried his wife. There was no answer at home. He'd forgotten; the kids were with their cousins and his wife was at work, cleaning the council offices. He tried her mobile. The line was awful. He'd not be home any time soon, he told her, though he wasn't certain that she could hear him. Her voice crackling, he made out something about the fax machine, a new cartridge. And then the line was suddenly very clear, just for a moment. Long enough for her to ask him why on earth the police in Inverness were faxing through a picture of that nice John MacKay.

***

Stephen grabbed Lucy by the hair and the rope that tied her hands and legs. He pulled her to her knees and held her in front of him. "Here comes Joe," he said, his voice high, like a child. "Police Scotland's finest. Taken his time to work things out, hasn't he? And poor little Lucy, in the dark all these years. So cosy with your perfect little family. So secure. Until now."

The pain made Lucy gasp, but she was determined he wouldn't know just how much he was hurting her. "I don't know what you're talking about," she said.

From behind, he caressed her cheek. "Don't worry, I'll let you live long enough to hear the truth. And to hear Joe beg for mercy."

"No!" She started to struggle against the ropes. "No!"

A vicious tug on the rope stopped her struggling, followed by the cold edge of a blade against her throat.

Joe stopped a few metres from Stephen and Lucy, his breath tearing through his chest. Idiot, he told himself. He could have talked Lucy out of the walk with John so easily, and he hadn't even tried. His sister's head was tilted back, a Bowie knife held at her white throat, the blade glinting in the light of the moon. Her eyes were wide and terrified. Though Joe wanted to throw himself at Stephen, he forced himself to stay calm.

Before he could speak, Lucy shouted. "Go away, Joe! Just go!"

Stephen laughed. "What a noble wee soul. Hear that,

241

Joe? Not only is she willing to lie for you, she'd sacrifice herself too. Speaking of lying, she's quite an expert, our wee Lucy. I wonder who she took that from."

"Stephen," Joe said, trying not to gasp as he fought for his breath. "Please let her go. None of this is her fault."

Lucy stared at her brother. "Stephen? The one you mentioned earlier? The one that killed those women?"

Stephen laughed. "Sorry Lucy. I'd reintroduce myself if it wasn't for the fact that you're about to die. Hardly seems worth it now."

"Hasn't there been enough killing?" Joe took a step forward, and stopped when Stephen pressed the knife into Lucy's throat, forcing a strangled cry from her. Joe held his hands up and backed away.

"Enough killing? I haven't even started. Once I've seen you two off, it's back to Inverness for me. Shame I messed up on Saturday, but running him over was always going to be too good for . . . for Raymond Galbraith." He spat the name out. "You want to know what I've got planned for him and Fiona?"

Lucy tried to shake her head. She winced as the point of the knife cut her skin.

"Careful," Stephen said, Lucy's blood trickling down his hand. "Wouldn't want you to die just yet. Speaking of Fiona, I hear you and she don't get on too well, Joseph. The only thorn in the flesh of the perfect Galbraith family. Why is that, I wonder? Why on earth would you dislike your mother so?"

"You seem to have all the answers," Joe replied, anger in his voice. "Your own mother will be very proud when she hears you killed her sister." As soon as the words were out, he knew it was a mistake. Trying to score points against a killer holding a knife to Lucy's throat? Idiot.

"I didn't kill her. She just . . . she just . . . Anyway, keep my mother out of it. She's the only innocent one in all of this."

"And Lucy."

There was the slightest hint of doubt in Stephen's eyes, Joe was certain, and then it was gone. "Innocent?" His laughter was loud. "See that boyfriend of your sister's, the one you never met? I'll give you three guesses why you were kept apart. Here's a clue – the apple doesn't fall far from the tree."

Joe shrugged. "Sebastian was married? I bet Lucy didn't know."

"I didn't," Lucy said. "I didn't know until we were finished that he had a home in the Lake District with his wife; his flat in Edinburgh was just – "

"Aye right," Stephen said. "She didn't bloody care, and why would she? It's standard practice in your family."

"Please let her go," Joe pleaded. "She doesn't deserve this."

"Maybe not. But you deserve it. Raymond and Fiona deserve it."

"Joe," Lucy said, her voice weak. "Why did he try to kill Dad?"

"Well, Joe?" Stephen said. "Gonna tell her?"

Where would he start?

"You going to tell her the truth about the Galbraith family? No? Didn't think so. You've all lived a lie for so long, you don't know what the truth is any more. Well, I'm more than happy to enlighten her, so why don't we all get comfy? You," he pointed the knife at Joe, "sit."

Joe hesitated. His chances of disarming Stephen were so much slimmer if he was sitting on the ground.

"Fucking sit." The knife was back at Lucy's throat. "Now."

Stephen didn't sit. He remained standing over Lucy, his back hunched. He must be uncomfortable, Joe thought, but it didn't seem to bother him.

Stephen's eyes gleamed as he started his story. "Once upon a time, in the lovely village of Northton, two boys lived next door to each other. One came from a fine, upstanding family, his father a teacher, his mother a loving full-time mum. And he had a wee sister, a beautiful wee sister."

Seated on the cold, hard rock, Joe saw the surprise on Lucy's face.

"As for the other boy, well, he was a poor soul, a bit of a runt. Bullied something terrible by the village boys. Drunken mother, absent father. No positive role models to help him grow up. How was he ever going to make anything of himself? Now, the teacher's son, the Galbraith boy, he was a bit full of himself. He had that certainty you get from knowing where you belong, from knowing that you can do anything you want when you grow up. Always top of his class, he might have wanted to be a teacher, like his dad, or an accountant. Maybe a pilot or an engineer. He might even have wanted to be a tradesman. A joiner, perhaps, though his parents wouldn't approve. Nothing wrong with it, though; plenty money to be made. Then again, he might redeem himself later by becoming, say, a policeman.

"And the girl . . . " Joe saw Stephen hesitate. He saw him swallow the emotions that rose in his throat. "Well, the girl, she might have wanted to travel when she grew up. Maybe she would take her time deciding what to do with her life. And maybe, eventually, she would decide to be a lawyer. She might not be sure it was the right thing for her to do, but, hey, at least it would make her parents happy.

"One day, the Galbraith boy took it upon himself to help his neighbour by stopping the bullying. The village boys listened to him because he was a teacher's son. Life was a little easier for the other boy then. But, really, what was he ever going to achieve in life? You must see it all the time, Joe. Wayward mothers and feckless, soon to be absent, fathers, spawning the next generation of our underclass; poor little bastards without a hope in hell. No wonder they go bad. No wonder they end up killing people."

Joe shook his head.

"You don't agree?"

"No. There is no excuse for taking a life."

"And what about letting someone die? Letting a child die? Is that any better? Lucy, I take it your family hasn't told you that your sister, little Amy, drowned on the beach back there, on *Tràigh na Cleabhaig*?"

Joe could hardly bear to see the shock on Lucy's face. They should have told her.

"I didn't think so." Stephen's voice was bitter. "Not too easy to talk about that afternoon, is it, Joe? I bet you haven't forgotten. And Fiona? Do you think she ever gives a thought to Amy? What about Raymond? Has he forgotten what he was doing while his daughter drowned on that beautiful day in July?"

And then Joe realised. "You killed James MacLeod on the anniversary of Amy's death."

"If my hands weren't full, I'd give you a clap, Detective. Only, I didn't kill him; I didn't have to. Stupid old bastard fell down the stairs trying to escape the Ghost of Christmas Past. You know it was Christmas when Moira Jacobs gave me to that . . . that filthy old pervert?"

Joe nodded.

"No prizes for guessing what he gave me that Christmas."

Nausea rose in Joe's throat. And pity. He squashed it.

Stephen smiled, a harsh smile. "MacLeod might have been old and decrepit last July, but he hadn't forgotten. Knew me straight away, which is more than I can say for you, Detective Sergeant. And you know what? I didn't even mean for him to die. I just wanted some answers from him, maybe a bit of remorse. I wanted him to know what his perversion has done to me. But it was taken out of my hands when he tried to run, and fell. I knew then that his kind of wickedness couldn't go unpunished, that it was meant to be."

"And was it the same for Moira Jacobs too? Was she meant to die?"

Stephen shrugged. "Not really. I'd have been satisfied that justice had been done with MacLeod. I didn't go looking for Moira Jacobs. I was minding my own business, just getting on with my work, and there she was, the same disgusting person that she always was. Fate brought her to me."

"And fate put a hammer in your hand and told you to smash her head in?"

"I went there unarmed. Just wanted her to know what she'd done; I wanted some answers."

"And her next door neighbour just happened to be stoned out of her head at the time," Joe said. "That was convenient, and not exactly unplanned."

Stephen shrugged. "Just a precaution – didn't mean I was going to kill the stupid bitch. She hit me first. What was I to do?"

Behind Stephen and Lucy, Joe could see the tide rising. The dark seething mass bore no resemblance to the shimmering gentle blue of the daytime or the benign gold of the evening. Joe could feel its growing power as it rose and crept steadily onto the black rocks. It made him shiver.

"That's the difference between you and me," Stephen said. "You hate being here. I saw the dread in your eyes on the ferry. Even now, you can hardly look at that hill without wondering if the village boys were telling the truth. The spirits of the restless dead – do they really live up there? Do they come to the village and take people in the night? I bet you didn't sleep last night for wondering."

Joe shook his head. It was just tales the boys had told to scare gullible incomers. He knew that. And yet . . .

"Scared me too, as a boy," Stephen said. "But I made my peace with the island long ago. I climbed that hill and discovered nothing but beautiful wildlife and fantastic views. I watched the villagers scurrying like ants below, going about their pathetic business, some of the same boys that lived here when we were small. They don't even see what's around them. But I did. And I grew to love it. Here, I could be the person I should have been, if it wasn't for you and your family. Speaking of your family, remind me how often Raymond and Fiona have come back to Harris. How often have they laid flowers on Amy's grave or stood above the beach and remembered her?"

Joe was silent. He saw the knife shake against Lucy's throat as Stephen's rage rippled through him.

"Fucking never!" Stephen shouted. "That's how often! She was discarded here without a backward glance, as if she never existed. And you – you have the nerve to lay flowers on her grave today, after all this time! Did he fucking ask you to do it? Did he?"

As an oystercatcher screeched overhead, Joe hesitated. Truth or lie, it was going to anger Stephen. "Aye. He asked me."

"Fucking bastard. After all this time. Fucking treacherous, two-timing bastard." Stephen jerked Lucy's rope. "Like father like daughter."

As Lucy groaned, Joe made to get up.

"Don't even think about it," Stephen said. "I wouldn't want Lucy to follow in her sister's footsteps without hearing the end of this sordid tale. Can you swim, Lucy?"

Lucy didn't answer.

"Amy couldn't swim. She was only four. Isn't that right, Joe? A beautiful little girl. Let down by everyone – left to die on her own."

"It was an accident," Joe said, his mouth dry. "A tragic accident."

"An accident? A fucking accident?"

Joe felt his temper rising. "Yes. And it could have been avoided. Your mother – "

"I told you," Stephen yelled. He took a couple of steps backwards, dragging Lucy closer to the water. "I fucking told you. Keep my mother out of this. She did nothing. She couldn't have known what would happen. Raymond Galbraith; he's the cause of all this. And Fiona. And you, you fucking piece of shit!"

The still night air was suddenly split with a tinny version of Queen's Fat-bottomed Girls; Joe's phone was ringing in his pocket. He knew who was calling; he had personalised his ring-tones. Lucy knew too. They'd had such a laugh about it. Although she didn't have one, Fiona's greatest fear was a fat backside. No one was laughing now.

Stephen gestured with his free hand, and Joe threw him the phone.

"That's nice," Stephen said, as he looked at the screen. "Mummy and Daddy." His mouth curving into a parody of a smile, he lifted the phone, clutching the knife in his right hand, pressing it against Lucy's neck. He looked so sure of himself when he said hello. So cocky. So brave.

And then Joe saw him frown and move the phone slightly from his ear. Whoever was on the other end was shouting. Though Joe couldn't make out the words, he could hear the frantic burst of sound.

The false smile slipped from Stephen's mouth. He looked confused, a little overwhelmed, and then sadness flooded his face, such desperate sadness, followed by fear, and longing, and more than a hint of guilt. And then Joe saw the ghost of the boy that stood beside his mother on the beach so many years ago as Raymond lifted Amy's wee body from the wet sand and howled into the sunny day.

That boy and his mother; Stephen and Betty. Joe had told himself they'd be fine. People got over these things. They moved on. Built new lives. Best to forget about them, leave it all behind

Behind? Who was he trying to kid? His childhood, that day, his guilt – he'd never left them behind. They were like old acquaintances, shuffling along beside him. They might fall behind occasionally, but they caught up with him, always caught up. Whenever he dared to think he was all right, had made something of himself, they were there, nudging and poking, reminding him just exactly who he was.

Detective Sergeant Joseph Galbraith? Destined for great heights, according to DI Black? Big fucking deal. He was nothing, a useless piece of shit, just as Stephen had said. A nobody, driven so hard to prove himself in the face of his mother's disappointment and his sister's achievements. Desperate to show Raymond that he was a good son, as good a son as Raymond could ever have hoped for. As good as Raymond's real son.

***

Mr Galbraith? In his mother's bed? He stares at his neighbour, at the teacher, at the perfect father. He can't understand what he's seeing.

His mother groans and shakes her head. Mr Galbraith clutches at his forehead. "Amy?" he says, his voice sleepy. "Has something happened to Amy? But she's with her mother."

The boy backs away from the bed, from his mother and Mr Galbraith. He's out of the bedroom. He's running down the stairs. His mother calls his name and it echoes through the house.

"Joe! Wait, Joe!"

***

There had been a girl? Another girl, and no one had told Lucy. She'd often wondered about her mother's reaction to Harris, the reluctance to talk about it, the derogatory remarks. When she probed, her mother would change the subject. But another daughter? A dead daughter? Why would they keep that secret?

And now Lucy could hear her father, the most calm, steady, dependable person she knew, and he was spewing out hysteria, his voice high-pitched and frantic. The accident. The photos. The murders. The police. The car found at Uig. It was Betty's car and Stephen was on Harris. Stephen was using Betty's maiden name, MacLaren. He was a killer and they were not safe. Joe had to be careful. He had to look after Lucy. Her father's desperate words didn't tell her who Stephen and Betty were, or why Stephen had tried to kill her father, and was now intent on killing her and Joe.

There was a silence, as Lucy's father paused for

breath. Lucy felt Stephen's body shaking. And then he spoke, and what he said made no sense. It was mental. It was all mental.

Stephen spoke again, in temper, and the truth hit Lucy with such force, she felt as if her head would explode. And with the shock came understanding. The way Stephen talked, the way he looked, the way she felt about him. It was suddenly so clear.

***

Joe's out on the road, tears pouring down his cheeks. Betty Galbraith is at her gate. She smiles her perfect smile. "What is it?" she asks him, in her kind, motherly voice. "What's wrong? What happened to your knee?"

Stephen Galbraith is at the front door of his house. "They're not in, Mum," he shouts. "They must have gone out."

Joe shakes his head. "Amy . . . she's . . . " He can't say it, but Mrs Galbraith's not listening anyway. She's watching Raymond coming out of the house next door, his hair all over the place and his shirt open. He has one shoe on and he's hopping as he tries to put on the other one. Joe's mother is behind him, pulling a t-shirt over her head.

"Raymond!" Betty Galbraith shouts. "Raymond, what are you doing in there?"

"Joe," Raymond shouts. "Joe, where's Amy?"

Chapter 22

His father's voice hadn't changed, not one bit; it was exactly as Stephen had remembered. And he had remembered so often, his mind turning words and phrases over until he didn't know whether they were real, or just things that he wished his father had said. It must be the latter, he had persuaded himself, for no one could really have said those things, and then just walked away. That would be crueller than Stephen, the boy or the adult, could comprehend.

His mouth was so dry, and his heart filled with longing. Maybe it wasn't too late. Maybe everything could be fixed. That's what fathers did; they fixed things. His father had always been good at fixing things.

"Dad," he said. "Dad, it's me."

"Joe?" Raymond replied. "Are you all right, Joe? Is Lucy with you?"

Bastard. Fickle cheating bastard. "Joe? Fucking Joe?" Stephen cried. "I'm not Joe. I'm Stephen. I'm your only son."

Raymond was silent.

"Remember me? The son you turned your back on; the son you deserted for that tart and her brat? Is she there? I hope the phone's on loudspeaker. Wouldn't want her to miss anything. I really wouldn't want her to miss hearing her daughter drown, just like Amy."

"No!" Raymond shouted. "No! Don't hurt Lucy. Please!" In the background, Stephen was certain he heard her, the whore, snivelling over the fate of her daughter.

"Too late. And Joe's next. But guess what? We've had such fun this evening. Lucy's heard all about her dead half-sister, the one that you conveniently forgot to mention. I'm sure she's even worked out the true identity of her little runt of a half-brother. And it's been quite a day for Joe. While running around like a blue-arsed fly, trying to solve the mystery of the murder of Moira Jacobs, he met his real father. Isn't that nice, after all this time?"

Joe shook his head. His father was dead. Fiona had told him when they left the island, after years of asking. Hadn't been worth much in life, she'd said, and now he was gone. And that was that. He had a mother; he had Raymond; he didn't need a name for that space on his birth certificate, that space that had taunted him all his life, just as the whispered jeers of the village boys had taunted him: *Your father's a drunk, your mother's a whore. Your father's in Tarbert; your mother's a liar. Your father's in prison; your mother's a bitch.*

"But Fiona," Stephen said, "did you really have to destroy Calum MacKinnon?"

"No," Joe whispered. Not that old drunk that had peed in Derek Russell's car. Not Calum MacKinnon, the laughing-stock of Tarbert. No. And yet. Maggie had known Joe; she had recognised him. And he had known her too, though he wouldn't let himself remember. The memory of her love was etched deep in his heart, in that hidden place before Northton and the bullies and a mother that he just couldn't reach.

And Calum MacKinnon? Joe had seen nothing but a ragged drunk, an inconvenience to be dragged off the road and dumped on the pavement. If he had looked properly, if he'd seen the man rather than the drunk, would he have recognised the ghost that sometimes lingered in his dreams and always vanished with the light of dawn?

Stephen winked at Joe. "Aye, poor Calum. All it takes is a wee half bottle and a listening ear, and he'll tell anyone his tale. The beautiful woman he met in Aberdeen, his first

252

summer on the rigs. She was so much younger than him; he should have known it couldn't last. But she was the love of his life. And their fine baby boy. How happy Calum was for the first couple of years, his on-shore spells spent in their little flat in the city. Things would have been just fine if he hadn't taken them home to Tarbert. Wasn't long until he discovered the truth. While he was on the rigs, the boy was dumped with Auntie Maggie, and Fiona was whoring her way around the island with anyone who would buy her a drink.

"He had no choice but to throw her out of the house, even if it meant she'd live in a hovel and his son would be kept from him. If Joe really was his son. She hadn't even put his name on the birth certificate, and she'd given the boy a Catholic name. Probably wasn't his.

"But he's done you a disservice there, Fiona. The resemblance between Joe and his father is uncanny. The way they both pull at their left earlobe when they're thinking; the way they hold their cutlery; the way they roll about in the gutter, taking life's blows with the same pathetic acceptance. You didn't know about poor wee Joe's troubles, did you, Fiona? While you were working your way through the island drunks, before you moved on to the married men, the village kids were battering Joe senseless nearly every day. And he hadn't even done anything to deserve it; just had the misfortune of having a whore for a mother. I wonder if that's why he hates you now.

"As for your precious little Lucy – well, she really has taken after both her parents. Fiona, if you weren't so busy trying to protect the life you stole from my mother, you might have noticed poor Lucy's distress since her married lover dumped her, and she lost their child."

Stephen smiled at the shock on Joe's face. "Oh, it's been such a day. Revelations all round, and if I wasn't such a decent person, if my dear father hadn't taught me some values before he fucked off with the village tramp, we might have added incest to the list of family sins and

253

secrets. Your daughter has been offering herself to me on a plate ever since we met. But, hey, we can't stay here talking all night. Here, Lucy, say goodbye for the last time." He held the phone to Lucy's mouth.

Raymond dropped the receiver and slipped from the bed to the floor, his rigid plastered leg stretched out in front of him. Fiona was already on the floor, her back against the wall, her head in her hands. When she heard Lucy's voice from the loudspeaker, she lifted her head and stared at the phone, then she scrambled on her hands and knees towards it.

"Dad, Mum," Lucy said, her voice husky. "Don't worry; we'll be fine. Joe's here. He'll – "

They heard a laugh, then Stephen was back on the line. "DS Galbraith will save the day? Aye, that'll be right. I'd let you speak to him, but he's in a state of shock; I think it must be the news of his father. So, Dad, I'd like to say it's been nice speaking –

"Don't you call me 'Dad'!" Raymond shouted. "I'm not your father. Your mother was the whore, sleeping with her sister's husband just after we married. If you want to point the finger, it's your mother you should criticise. Not us."

"Mum just said that to get back at you for shagging the tart next door while your daughter drowned. It wasn't true, but it didn't take much to persuade you. Didn't matter that you had brought me up for ten years, that we had a bond I thought was unbreakable! All you had to do was look at a photo of us together and see that she was lying. But it suited you better to bugger off with your new family. Well, you know what? Soon you will have no family but that slut."

"No!" Raymond shouted. "Please, don't hurt them!"

"Not very nice when your family's torn apart, is it? And all because you couldn't keep your trousers on. All right, it must have been tempting, Fiona out in the garden

254

in next to nothing, asking for your gardening tips. A good-looking bit of stuff, right enough. But you knew, like everyone on the island, that she'd been putting it about for years. How could you leave my mother for that? How could you just abandon me?"

"Betty wouldn't let me near you," Raymond said, his voice desperate. "She said I wasn't your father, that she didn't want me to have anything to do with you. I tried. She wouldn't answer my letters; she changed the phone number; she moved away. I didn't know where you'd gone. Nor did Jean. I tried, Stephen, I tried."

"Not hard enough. You left me; you left me and Mum with the life that should have been theirs – that slut and her wee shite of a son. You left me to be tormented by gossip, by the village boys, by my mother's growing insanity."

"Insanity? Betty?"

"Aye, Dad; that's what you did to her. And it's Joe that should have no real family, no prospects, no future. He's the one that should have been . . . " Stephen stopped. He couldn't say it; he couldn't tell his father what MacLeod had done, how that depraved old bastard had stopped him from ever being able to love or be loved. "Joe's the one who should be looking after a deranged alcoholic."

"But Betty didn't drink."

"Until you destroyed her! And me. You chose Joe. You gave him my name. You gave him my life. Now I'm going to take his!"

Fiona covered her ears as the line went dead.

How could that bastard still sound the same? Stephen knew from his watching and his photographs, from all that Lucy had told him, that the father he had loved so much, then hated so unrelentingly, was still the same cheerful, steady man. How could that be? Why had he not suffered as Stephen had? Why was he not a shrunken, wizened wreck, crushed by the weight of his guilt and betrayal? Why the fuck not?

Stephen's face was distorted with hatred. He hadn't noticed that his hand with the knife had moved away from Lucy's throat. He hadn't noticed that Joe was crouching now, that Lucy was waiting for Joe to move.

"Fucking bastard!" Stephen shouted, as he raised his left hand high in the air and threw the phone. While Stephen's eyes followed the phone into the dark water, Joe sprang.

Joe and Stephen had fought once before. Perhaps 'fight' was not the right word, for Stephen had beaten Joe so badly, he'd needed stitches in a head wound and two days in his bed. He'd fallen on a stone, he told his mother. He'd slipped while climbing a fence and hit his head. He shouldn't have been out, his mother said; he should have done what he was told and stayed in.

The village was deserted that day, everyone but Joe and his mother at Amy's funeral. Fiona was in bed. She'd been there almost constantly since the day Amy drowned. Joe wanted to believe that it was Amy's death that had incapacitated her, but even at eight years old he knew her well enough to suspect that her grief had more to do with the likely end of her relationship with Mr Galbraith, and the loss of the chance of a better life.

Joe couldn't stay inside. Though he had opened all the windows, the air in the house was so heavy with guilt and fear that he couldn't breathe. It was his fault. He'd wished harm upon the Galbraiths so often, and he hadn't taken Amy back to the village when he'd had the chance. It was all his fault. And if they were outcasts before, what now?

From the field behind the house, Joe had watched the return of the slow, mourning convoy. The villagers first, in their dark Sunday clothes, then the Galbraiths. Raymond was scarcely recognisable. The cheerful man that had whistled while he sculpted his garden in the face of the incessant winds, smiled as he polished his car, waved as he left the house for work each day, was gone. In his place was a shuffling, grey-skinned spectre. His wife came from the car. Betty was shrunken and pale, her eyes glinting with anger and unshed tears. When Raymond reached for her arm, her push sent him stumbling backwards against the fence that separated their garden from Fiona's. That was the first push. In the days to come, she would push and push, until there was nowhere for Raymond to go but over the fence, where Fiona waited, their child already growing inside her.

And when Stephen found Joe in the long grass behind the house, the smaller, weaker boy knew that behind each blow and each kick and each curse was Stephen's grief for Amy, his love for Betty, and his hatred of Raymond. Perhaps Stephen knew then that there could be no reconciliation, that Fiona and Joe would take his and Betty's place, that Fiona and Joe would take their lives. While Stephen laughed, Joe took every blow without a sound. He deserved it. He deserved it all.

And now, in the shadow of the hill, beneath the golden light of the moon, though Joe's guilt troubled him still, though he knew that he and his mother had left Stephen and Betty with a life more terrible than he had ever imagined, there was no way he was going to let Stephen even the score now. Lucy was not going to have the same fate as Amy.

His blow landed on Stephen's right shoulder and the knife fell, clattering to the rock below. Stephen's left arm was wrenched from Lucy, and she was pulled away. His sister behind him, Joe pushed Stephen backwards. If he could get to the knife, he would free Lucy. If he could get to the knife, he would . . . he would . . . he'd do whatever he had to.

Stephen leapt forward, kicking the knife across the rocks, then driving a knee into Joe's belly. As Joe doubled over, he took Stephen with him, grabbing at his jacket and hauling him downwards. They fell to the ground together, and Joe twisted his body round, pinning Stephen to the rock. His fist raised, he looked at Stephen and he saw Lucy, he saw Raymond. How had he not recognised Stephen immediately? And how could he smash his fist into that face?

Stephen made it easy. His face twisted into a mask of cunning and malice, a look that had never crossed the gentle faces of Raymond or Lucy. He smiled and then he spat, his warm spittle stinging Joe's eye and dribbling down his cheek. Joe drove his fist into Stephen's face, again and again. Behind each blow was a hatred of every village boy, every island teacher, anyone that had ever crossed or rejected him. His mother. His real father. And, most of all, himself. For though he had despised the Galbraiths, though he had watched them and hated them, the young Joe had wanted everything they had. And he had almost got it all. A step-father that gave him unconditional love from the start, though Joe never felt worthy of it; a sister that idolised him, though he could never understand why; a proper home; a decent life. Nearly everything. But he didn't get the one thing that mattered most to him: he never saw his mother look at him the way Betty Galbraith had looked at Stephen and Amy. His mother could hardly look him in the eye. All those years of cooking and cleaning for him, they were a poor substitute for the love that he needed. He knew why she couldn't give it to him: she was ashamed of herself. She was embarrassed that Joe knew exactly what she had done, before and after she set her sights on Raymond. Stephen was right; she was a tramp. She would always be a tramp.

The screeching of a bird startled Joe back to the present, and his aching hand, and the sticky warmth of Stephen's blood. His face was a mess, his nose broken and his lips split. And still Stephen smiled. Joe shook his head. "Fucking psycho," he said.

Taking advantage of Joe's distraction, Stephen shoved Joe off and started to rise. Joe grabbed his legs and brought him back down on the rock. Beyond Stephen, Joe saw the knife. It was close. He rolled over, pushed himself to his feet. A couple of steps, that's all it would take. One step, and then he felt a hand on the back of his sweatshirt, grabbing and pulling him back. He turned and saw that Stephen was still smiling. Then he lunged at Joe.

Their heads collided, and Joe's nose exploded. As the blood pumped from him, he staggered backwards and fell. Through a painful haze, he saw a shadowy Stephen walk towards the knife, bend down and pick it up. "Don't go anywhere, Lucy," he heard Stephen say.

Joe tried to get to his feet, but his left leg had twisted as he fell, and it wouldn't take his weight. He was on his knees, Stephen looming over him, his arm raised. "Ready to die, Joe Smith?"

As Joe looked up and saw the rage in Stephen's eyes and the knife that was surely coming, he knew that he was ready. Nothing came free in life. There was always a price, a day of reckoning. And it was fitting that he should take his real name back now. The name that he and his mother had ditched half way across the Minch the day they left Harris, the day they took the lives that were meant for Stephen and Betty. It was time. He felt nothing as Stephen's hand plunged downwards.

Stephen walked slowly towards Lucy, the blood-stained knife still in his hand. Despite his aching face, and the blood that dribbled down his chin, he could hardly believe that fate was still on his side. Even when he had followed Lucy and Joe onto the ferry, he hadn't thought that he would get them both, that they would die here, that Lucy would drown so close to where Amy had lost her life. All his boasting of killing them both, of getting back to Inverness to do away with Raymond and Fiona, it was just bluff. Killing Lucy had been the only realistic goal, after which he was certain he would be caught. Now, they were both his. Double the suffering for Fiona and Raymond. Result.

He knelt in front of Lucy, and he could feel her breath on his face. How could her breathing be so steady now? Why wasn't she crying? Why wasn't she screaming? Her face was calm. She knew. She was ready. But was he?

What the fuck? Of course he was ready. This was what he had wanted ever since Nisbet gave him those photos. This was the goal. To get that self-satisfied bitch that was masquerading in Amy's place. This was the goal.

But it wasn't that simple. She was just as Stephen had always imagined a grown-up Amy would look. So like her that he'd even used the wrong name earlier. Getting close to Lucy had not been part of the plan, but, despite himself, he had found that they were at ease together, that it felt right, that he actually liked her very much. When he'd told her that it was one of the best days, he'd meant it. Couldn't remember a better day, not since he was a child and the whole family was together. He might even have considered telling her the truth, in the hope that they could be a family, that he could have someone. If he hadn't discovered that she was a tramp just like her mother and her father, they would be on their way back to Northton now, and he would have no thought of killing her.

But was she really a tramp, or was she just the innocent victim of someone like their father? And did it really matter? Did anything really matter now?

Behind Stephen, Joe was still, a dark stain spreading across the rocks. Lucy's eyes met Stephen's and she saw the indecision in him; the sad emptiness, the weight of his past, and the void that was his future. She looked down at his hand, at Joe's blood on the knife. Smiling, she threw herself backwards from the rocks.

The water rushed into her mouth and nose, colder than she could ever have imagined. Struggling against the ropes that bound her, she held her breath. As the pain rose in her chest, scattered thoughts raced through her head. Her mother, the village tramp. Her mother, with her airs and graces and her condescending looks. Nothing but a whore. Two half-brothers. Joe Smith and Stephen Galbraith – did two halves equal the whole brother that she'd thought she had? Joe's father, a ragged drunk rolling on the road. Lucy's father, a cheat, an adulterer. Amy, a half-sister that they had all forgotten to mention. Had she looked like Lucy? Had she felt this pain?

Lucy held her breath until the ache in her chest forced her mouth open. Her cry was silenced by an influx of water that tore and burned her nose and throat. She felt her throat closing, stopping the water, stopping her breath. The pain was like a vice, squeezing until her bones must break. Rising, like nothing Lucy had ever known. Crushing and stabbing. Pressing and tearing. Rising and rising.

And then it burst. The pain burst and floated from her. Floated away, on a sea of gold.

Stephen was sitting on the rocks. He shook his head, but it wouldn't clear. Everything was so mixed up. There were sounds that wouldn't go away. MacLeod's fearful prayer. The hammer on Moira Jacobs' head. The clattering and grunting of a body, of two bodies, falling down the stairs. Auntie Jean's last choking breath. The crunch as the car hit Raymond. The water swallowing Lucy.

There were feelings. The feeling of the knife in Joe. You would think a knife would just slide into soft tissue, but it didn't. There were things in the way, and the knife jarred and scraped on those things, reluctantly squeezing between them, searching for something soft to rupture.

He looked up and Lucy was a dark shape, floating face down in the water, her hands and legs still tied together, the moon shining down on her. He had killed her, just as he had killed Amy. Why hadn't he taken his wee sister home that day? Why had he let her go by herself?

Amy had loved the beach. She'd build sandcastles for hours, and Stephen would get so fed up. He'd want to get home, to watch TV or play on his bike, and she'd beg him to stay. Just this much, she would say, holding her tiny hands close together, the sand trickling from them; can we stay just this much? Crouched on her little brown legs on the sand, how could he refuse her?

Had she built a sandcastle that day, so engrossed that she didn't know the sea was creeping up on her? Or had she tried to jump the waves, the way that he had taught her? She was too young to know that it was only safe if your big brother was holding your hands. She hadn't liked the feeling of sand on her feet; she used to complain about it all the way home. Perhaps she'd paddled into the water to wash the sand from her hands and her toes. Was that what had happened? Had she struggled in the breaking waves? Had she cried for her parents, for her brother? Had she known she was abandoned?

Lucy and Amy were together now, and he was alone. His mother was as good as gone; his father had given him up long ago; everyone was gone. He stood and took off his jacket. He stepped forward, and then he saw it. A shimmering red form that danced around Lucy in the grey water, light and effortless. It was Amy. She was waiting for him. They were both waiting for him.

Joe's last coherent thought was of Morag MacDonald searching her memory for the name of the boy, for the name of the place that he had lived. No wonder she was so frustrated and confused at the names that kept coming to her. It wasn't a common name, Galbraith, so she must have convinced herself that she'd got it wrong. And DS Galbraith had told her he was staying in a guesthouse in Northton, so that couldn't be where the boy had come from. But if the boy's name wasn't Galbraith, and he hadn't come from Northton, why was no other name or place coming to her? Little did she know of the tangled web that was woven so long ago. She would soon know. Everyone would know.

Matt knew. One drunken night, Joe had told his first

real friend the truth. He wasn't the person Matt thought he was. He wasn't a Galbraith; he was just a cuckoo in the nest, a usurper. No wonder Raymond's mother hadn't wanted him close to her during her last years in the nursing home. He wasn't Raymond's son; he was nobody. And they would never love him like they loved Lucy. And though he loved Lucy too, he was jealous of her. He was jealous of his little sister, because she belonged.

As consciousness started to slip from Joe, he heard a voice whispering to him. It was Matt, whispering the words he'd said all those years ago, the words that Joe just couldn't accept. Matt whispered that Joe's mother loved him, that anyone could see it. And anyone could see that she was desperate for Joe to forgive her and let her in. If she didn't love him, why would she keep coming back, only to be rejected again and again? She loved him; there was no doubt about it. It was time to forgive her. It was time.

And then, beyond the darkness, there was a light. It shone from afar, and pulled Joe forwards. And Matt kept whispering. And the light was strong. And the love was healing.

Epilogue

On a late autumn day, they stood in the shadow of the hill on the rocks by the medieval chapel. The sea was a little wild as it advanced on the land, the tops of the waves white and restless, the dark head of a seal bobbing in the shifting grey water. Watching the sea, Fiona shivered. It wasn't a cold day; the wind was mild, but she felt chilled inside. Raymond put his arm around her. She leaned her head on his shoulder and listened to the urgent calls of the sea birds as they hurried past.

"Will we go?" Raymond asked.

Fiona nodded.

They stopped at the sand dunes above *Tràigh na Cleabhaig*. Raymond took a deep breath and Fiona looked up at him. He smiled and tightened his grip on her hand. She wondered at his strength, his composure. To lose your children: there was nothing worse. To still be alive when they were dead; it challenged the natural order of life.

Fiona would be glad to leave this place. She understood that they'd had to come. And it had helped, but she hoped she would never have to return. The memory of the last time she had stood here was seared into her brain; it would never leave her, and every beach she ever visited would bring it back with such clarity that it was easier just to avoid the sea, to stay inland.

Before last night, in their hotel room in Tarbert, she had never spoken to Raymond of how that day had affected her, how it felt to watch him cradle his beautiful dead daughter while the first gentle stirrings of new life moved inside her. How it felt to know that, if it wasn't for her and her desperation for a better life, for a better man, Raymond would have been in his garden when Amy left her mother and brother and ran home. How it felt to wait for Lucy's birth, in the dreadful fear that Raymond might never be able to look at their child without being reminded of the terrible sacrifice he'd made. How it felt over the years to wait for him to finally snap and blame her for everything. That was what had kept her quiet – the fear that he would blame her, just as she blamed herself.

No, he had told her, as he held her tight and apologised again. He hadn't meant what he'd said when he found out that Stephen was on Harris, that Lucy and Joe were in danger. He'd been overwhelmed, he'd whispered; overwhelmed by the fear of losing them too. He didn't blame her; he had never blamed her. He and Betty had not been meant for each other. They had met when Raymond first began teaching and Betty was a school secretary. She was several years older than him, and a good woman, a safe choice. That was all he had ever expected, all he thought he needed. And then he had seen Fiona. It was just a few days after the Galbraiths moved to the village, long before Fiona set her sights on him. She had been standing at the bus stop at the end of the Northton road, in a tiny skirt and a pair of long black boots. She was examining her heel, a look of distaste on her face. Raymond had known then that she didn't belong on the island. In his heart, he had known that she belonged with him.

He had tried not to look, a year or so later, when his family were in Fife on holiday, and Fiona took to her garden in shorts and a bikini top, looking for tips. He had tried to be a good neighbour, nothing more than that. He had tried to resist his feelings. Until he couldn't.

He was the one who had cheated, not Fiona. If anyone was to blame for the tragedy, it was him. But there was no sense in blame. No sense in guilt. As the moon shone down upon Tarbert, he held Fiona tight and told her that she was the love of his life. She slept well for the first night in months.

Now, the sound of laughter came from below. Looking down, she saw Joe pulling Lucy by the hand up the cleft between the sand dunes. Joe was much stronger now, ready to go back to work next week. He'd been lucky; the knife had punctured his lung, but the damage was repairable and his progress had been good. Lucy's lungs had suffered too, with severe pneumonia. She owed her life to PC Hector Wright, the doctors said. If he hadn't known exactly what to do after pulling her from the water, she'd have died.

They were quiet as they walked across the machair. Though there had been a great deal of talking, and much still to come, there were some things of which they never spoke. Joe said nothing of Matt guiding him towards the light of Derek Russell's torch. He never spoke of Matt's hand in his as the helicopter lifted him from the shadow of the hill. He said nothing of his friend's words that healed his childhood wounds, so that, when he woke in hospital in Inverness and found his mother beside him, it was the most natural thing in the world to accept her hand and her love.

And Lucy never spoke of the light dancing form that had surrounded her and guided her towards the land. She never spoke of seeing little Amy in her red dress and her white sandals. No one told her what Amy had been wearing that last day, and Lucy did not dare ask. But she knew.

For a time, everyone spoke of Stephen. He was last seen by the Harris policemen as he leapt from the rocks into the dark water. And then he was gone. The lifeboat scoured the sea that night, but they found nothing. Over the next few days, the islands and boats were searched, and the ports monitored. There was a nation-wide appeal, but not a trace of him was found.

As they approached the gate, a massive flock of starlings rose from the fence and danced before them in a dazzling, swirling cloud. Raymond smiled. "Scientists have studied their flight formations," he said. "Apparently they each track the seven closest birds and that's how they manage to avoid colliding with others in the – "

"The murmuration," Lucy whispered.

Raymond nodded and put his arm round her. He looked towards the coast, then he smiled, a sad smile. "Perhaps the sea will never give him up," he said.

Lucy rested her head on her father's shoulder and she wondered. Fiona looked towards the sea and shivered. Joe stared at the hill, and said nothing.

More Books From ThunderPoint Publishing Ltd.

Mule Train
by Huw Francis
ISBN: 978-0-9575689-0-7 (kindle)
ISBN: 978-0-9575689-1-4 (Paperback)

Four lives come together in the remote and spectacular mountains bordering Afghanistan and explode in a deadly cocktail of treachery, betrayal and violence.

Written with a deep love of Pakistan and the Pakistani people, Mule Train will sweep you from Karachi in the south to the Shandur Pass in the north, through the dangerous borderland alongside Afghanistan, in an adventure that will keep you gripped throughout.

The Birds That Never Flew
by Margot McCuaig
Shortlisted for the
Dundee International Book Prize 2012
Longlisted for the Polari First Book Prize 2014

ISBN: 978-0-9575689-3-8 (Kindle)
ISBN: 978-0-9575689-2-1 (Paperback)

Battered and bruised, Elizabeth has taken her daughter and left her abusive husband Patrick. Again. In the bleak and impersonal Glasgow housing office Elizabeth meets the provocatively intriguing drug addict Sadie, who is desperate to get her own life back on track.

The two women forge a fierce and interdependent relationship as they try to rebuild their shattered lives, but despite their bold, and sometimes illegal attempts it seems impossible to escape from the abuse they have always known, and tragedy strikes.

More than a decade later Elizabeth has started to implement her perfect revenge - until a surreal Glaswegian Virgin Mary steps in with imperfect timing and a less than divine attitude to stick a spoke in the wheel of retribution.

Tragic, darkly funny and irreverent, The Birds That Never Flew ushers in a new and vibrant voice in Scottish literature.

A Good Death
by Helen Davis

ISBN: 978-0-9575689-7-6 (eBook)
ISBN: 978-0-9575689-6-9 (Paperback)

'*A good death is better than a bad conscience,*' said Sophie.

1983 - Georgie, Theo, Sophie and Helena, four disparate young Cambridge undergraduates, set out to scale Ausangate, one of the highest and most sacred peaks in the Andes.

Seduced into employing the handsome and enigmatic Wamani as a guide, the four women are initiated into the mystically dangerous side of Peru, Wamani and themselves as they travel from Cuzco to the mountain, a journey that will shape their lives forever.

2013 - though the women are still close, the secrets and betrayals of Ausangate chafe at the friendship.

A girls' weekend at a lonely Fenland farmhouse descends into conflict with the insensitive inclusion of an overbearing young academic toyboy brought along by Theo. Sparked by his unexpected presence, pent up petty jealousies, recriminations and bitterness finally explode the truth of Ausangate, setting the women on a new and dangerous path.

Sharply observant and darkly comic, Helen Davis's début novel is an elegant tale of murder, seduction, vengeance, and the value of a good friendship.

Toxic
by Jackie McLean
Shortlisted for the Yeovil Book Prize 2011
ISBN: 978-0-9575689-8-3 (eBook)
ISBN: 978-0-9575689-9-0 (Paperback)

The recklessly brilliant DI Donna Davenport, struggling to hide a secret from police colleagues and get over the break-up with her partner, has been suspended from duty for a fiery and inappropriate outburst to the press.

DI Evanton, an old-fashioned, hard-living misogynistic copper has been newly demoted for thumping a suspect, and transferred to Dundee with a final warning ringing in his ears and a reputation that precedes him.

And in the peaceful, rolling Tayside farmland a deadly store of MIC, the toxin that devastated Bhopal, is being illegally stored by a criminal gang smuggling the valuable substance necessary for making cheap pesticides.

An anonymous tip-off starts a desperate search for the MIC that is complicated by the uneasy partnership between Davenport and Evanton and their growing mistrust of each others actions.

Compelling and authentic, Toxic is a tense and fast paced crime thriller.

Lightning Source UK Ltd.
Milton Keynes UK
UKHW02f2042020418
320406UK00007B/877/P